Crowfield House

Crowfield House

Monica McGuinness

POOLBEG
CRIMSON

Published 2025 by Poolbeg Crimson, an imprint of Poolbeg Press Ltd.

123 Grange Hill, Baldoyle, Dublin 13, Ireland

Email: poolbeg@poolbeg.com

A catalogue record for this book is available from the British Library.

ISBN 978-1-78199-660-7

www.poolbeg.com

ABOUT THE AUTHOR

Monica McGuinness is an Irish writer and caffeine addict. She began composing intriguing poems about fat cats on mats as a child and has never stopped creating since. She's a writer with a love of surprise twists and unexpected endings which her writing reflects.

Winner of the Maria Edgeworth Short Story Competition in 2024, she also hosts a podcast of original fiction, FearFold. She is a co-host on another podcast, aSpired Writers, which aims to inspire and encourage writers to take up their pen and create.

She lives with her partner and sons in Cavan, the heart of Ireland, surrounded by lakes and forests.

ACKNOWLEDGEMENTS

I'm so grateful to my friends and family who read early drafts of this book. Your feedback and encouragement gave me the confidence to keep going. I would also like to thank all the writers at the aSpired Writers Group in Kells, Co Meath, especially Caroline Mellor and Amanda Gilsenan for their vital insights and love of noodles. I want to say the biggest thank you to Siobhán O'Sullivan, my long-standing cheerleader and greatest supporter on this very epic journey.

My thanks must go to Paula Campbell and all at Poolbeg Press for giving me the opportunity to share my words with you. Special thanks to my eagle-eyed editor, Gaye Shortland. You are an inspiration, Gaye, thank you so much for your patience and insightful comments.

To my family, thank you all for your support and words of wisdom. You are appreciated more than you'll ever know.

And finally, to Pádraig, Fechin and Odhran, the lads who make it all worthwhile, thank you.

Dedication

For Catherine McGuinness
and in memory of Tommie McGuinness

Prologue

It was raining. Water falling in explosive drops, soaking her hair, her clothes and she was running, trying to keep her balance, slipping, almost falling. Pine needles, sharp beneath her feet and cobwebs brushing her face. Thunder erupted, one flash – blinding her momentarily and brightening the dark wood.

In that instant, she could see her surroundings clearly. The tree branches reaching skyward to leaden-grey clouds above and then, in the deafening silence that followed the thunder, she could hear Eric. He was somewhere behind her on the twisting path, out of breath, trying to keep up.

She heard a voice, a disembodied sound, almost lost in the noise of the storm.

"Come on!"

And she knew it was her voice, calling Eric – leading him onwards. She could hear his footsteps now and the pattering of heavy rain falling against broad leaves. Then another sound, low, a background noise at first but growing stronger, louder, beginning to roar in her ears. It was water, rushing, flowing.

Then silence, as she passed into darkness.

Chapter 1

August 2014

Elspeth had the appointment letter in her bag but she didn't take it out – she didn't need to, she had already memorised the contents. Deep in the labyrinth of St Martin's hospital, a psychiatrist named Dr Claire Stanley was expecting her. The coffee in her hand was cold and sour and it hadn't worked as intended – she was only half-awake after yet another sleepless night. She'd debated coming at all. Elspeth didn't trust psychiatrists or therapists or counsellors, anyone who thought problems could be fixed by talking. They were wrong, all of them. Whether or not she was even fixable was also a question – but here she was, she had no choice.

She glanced around the waiting-room and realised with surprise that there was another person there. She looked closer. It was a girl, a teenager perched on a plastic chair with her knees pulled up and her head bent to one side. It was as though she were trying to burrow into herself and, even though she was tiny, she was trying to become smaller still.

Elspeth looked away. She recognised that feeling.

She tried to read, to focus on the "self-help" posters that were displayed everywhere, but her gaze was drawn again and again to the girl in the corner. She didn't seem to notice or care that Elspeth was staring – she was lost in her own thoughts. Her thick blonde hair hung in long unbrushed tangles, completely covering her face. Her hands were also hidden, tucked deep within the ragged sleeves of her jumper. Elspeth could see a single loose thread dangling and now there was movement, one pale finger and a bitten nail worrying at the hole, twirling the strand of wool, over and over.

It could be me, Elspeth thought. She vaguely remembered a similar habit at that age and she found her own fingers searching for stray threads. She hoped the girl would look up, she wanted to see her face. She needed to know what colour her eyes were. The similarity was unnerving, like stepping back in time to meet her teenage self.

Then a door opened with a low creak and a small, dark-haired woman carrying a clipboard stepped silently into the corridor. Without even looking up, she called Elspeth's name.

Elspeth stood, slowly gathering her bag, her coat, even the cold coffee. She was reluctant now to leave the girl behind. She shouldn't be there on her own – she looked far too young to be left alone. Where were her parents?

The woman with the clipboard smiled automatically, a pen in her hand poised, ready to check her off the list.

"Dr Stanley is room five, on the right. You can't miss it."

⁕⁕⁕⁕ ⁕⁕⁕⁕

Room 5 was only a short distance down the hall. Elspeth stopped at the door for a moment. She could see her reflection in the glass door panel and she quickly tucked an errant strand of hair behind her ear. She was nervous, thinking of the girl in the waiting room. That had been her at one stage. And now here she was, unchanged, no taller than when she was fourteen, still little, still anxious, still unsure of her place in the world.

She knocked before she could change her mind and walk away. The room was more homely than she expected, almost cosy in comparison to the dingy waiting-room.

Dr Claire Stanley was busy writing on a thick pad. She gestured, wordlessly, towards a seat in front of her desk.

Elspeth sat, her mind wandering, thinking again about the girl in the waiting-room, her bitten nails and ravelled sleeves. Why was she here? What blackness had come into her life?

Finally, the doctor stopped writing and looked up.

"Elspeth, thank you for waiting. Sorry. I was just going through your file. You were with Dr Moyes ... twenty years ago, is that correct?"

Elspeth nodded. "Yes. I was fourteen."

She could still remember Dr Moyes, a small round man with tortoiseshell glasses, a textbook psychiatrist kicking out his last few years till retirement. He had a strange way of coughing, almost apologetic – as though he knew he shouldn't be coughing on her time, but did so anyway.

It was her father who'd suggested the idea of seeing someone. He had already gone back to Australia for work but he was concerned about her. Her mother must have told him that she wasn't sleeping or even talking about what had happened and he thought maybe a doctor and some pills would help. She'd agreed to go. What else could she do? She was only a young teenager at the time, just a child really. A child who still believed that adults knew best. She also knew that her father was in pain as well and quite possibly pills were the only thing getting him through the day.

Her mother – now that was a different matter entirely. She was barely speaking to Elspeth as it was. She'd refused all offers of help for herself and expected Elspeth to take the same high-minded approach. Eventually, after some persuading, she agreed to take her to Dr Moyes and then waited diligently outside his office every Thursday to take her home again. The appointments only lasted six weeks and Elspeth couldn't even remember what they had talked about. She could recall his face and hear his polite little cough but that was all. She still had no idea who stopped the sessions – her mother, her father, Dr Moyes perhaps?

"Well, we can run through the current issues," Dr Stanley was saying, "and if there are any unresolved matters from Dr Moyes' time, we can revisit them. So, if you'd like to start?"

Elspeth sat up a little straighter on her seat. "Well, I'm struggling to sleep," she said. "I had insomnia when I was a teenager. That was why I came to see Dr Moyes. He prescribed sleeping tablets, and my late GP has been renewing the prescription since then, but now I have a new GP and he referred me to you."

"So up to now you've been still on the same prescription – the one from Dr Moyes?"

"Yes, but my new GP feels you should be the one to prescribe."

"I see." Dr Stanley nodded. She pursed her lips, then looked down at her notes and began writing again.

"So, I just need you to renew this prescription. Rubber-stamp it, I guess – please." Elspeth had added on the "please" a little too late. It sounded awkward and strange, as though she were pleading her case. Nothing was going to plan. She'd simply intended coming in and telling the doctor she needed to be able to sleep. Then she would get the prescription renewed. There was no need to revisit past issues, unresolved or not.

Dr Stanley continued to write – filling another page with her looping script, before finally glancing up at Elspeth again.

"So, can you tell me how the insomnia was triggered to begin with?"

Elspeth nodded. This wasn't going to be easy. This woman was definitely not like Dr Moyes. She wasn't going to rubber-stamp anything. But there might be a way. She sighed, screwing up her face, pretending to remember.

"Well, I had pneumonia and I was in hospital for a while. I've never really put it together, but that could be it. That's when it started."

Dr Stanley nodded. "And what about your brother?" She flicked through her notepad, as though searching for his name.

But it was all for show, Elspeth realised. She had done her homework. She knew.

"Eric." The doctor was watching her again, those grey eyes calm, steady, like rainclouds reflected on a still lake. "Eric disappeared that summer, didn't he?"

Elspeth said nothing. She nodded – she didn't trust herself to speak.

"I went back through Dr Moyes' notes. You were fourteen when you first attended his clinic, you said?"

Elspeth nodded again.

"But you never really talked about your brother or his disappearance, did you?"

Elspeth looked down at her clasped hands.

Dr Stanley opened a green folder on her desk. Then she brought out a small sheaf of yellowing papers. They looked as though mice had been nesting in them at some stage. One corner seemed to have been nibbled away completely.

"Dr Moyes thought you might be suffering from mood disorder. Did he ever discuss this with you or your parents?"

"No."

"*Hmm ...* " Dr Stanley went back to her own notes and picked up her pen.

"So, about the prescription?" Elspeth asked, her voice small in the room.

"I don't think that's a good idea, Elspeth. Those tablets were only ever a short-term measure. In fact, I have no idea why your GP continued to prescribe them all these years. Treatment has moved on a lot and I believe in a more holistic approach. Now, I don't advise stopping these tablets immediately, but we do need to wean you off them and address the root cause of your insomnia. Would you agree?"

"Do I have a choice?"

Dr Stanley smiled, but it didn't reach her eyes. "Of course you have a choice, Elspeth. A choice to heal."

Elspeth felt something explode in her head and she fought back the overriding urge to tell the doctor where to stick her choices. Instead, she tried to think, one jumbled idea following another in quick succession. *What does she want? Perhaps she just needs to be heard, she needs to know that she's right. Just give her what she wants, which was ...*

"Would you like me to talk about Eric?"

Dr Stanley nodded. "I do think that's where we need to start."

Elspeth tucked her hands into her sleeves and closed her eyes. She thought about pulling her knees up to her chest and turning her head away but she didn't. When she began speaking her voice was low, barely audible.

"So when I was fourteen, we left Australia and moved to Ireland. To Glenfeale village. My mother had inherited this old place, Crowfield House. And then one evening, during a storm, we went into the woods, just me and Eric. He was only eight and he disappeared that night. My mother found me by the river but that's all I know. I can't tell you anything more, because that's all I remember."

"And what about your parents?"

"Well, my father wasn't there when it happened. He was still in Australia."

"And how did he cope with the disappearance?"

Elspeth shrugged. "I don't know. He came to Ireland for a few weeks and then he had to go back to work."

Dr Stanley nodded, her head down, scribbling, filling another page. If she was disappointed with the lack of information, she hid it well.

Elspeth decided to try another tactic. "I don't think my insomnia has anything to do with my brother. I've always had trouble sleeping, even as a baby. Perhaps you should talk to my mother about that sometime."

She tried to smile but her lips caught against her teeth – her mouth was dry, as if full of sawdust.

Dr Stanley nodded. "That's not a bad idea, Elspeth. Would your mother consider having a joint session with you?"

Elspeth glanced at the empty chair beside her. Tried to picture Nora by her side, supportive, holding her hand perhaps, reaching for a tissue to dab her eyes.

"No, this is stupid and it should be very simple," she said. "You're making it about something else entirely."

Dr Stanley nodded slowly. "I understand. This reaction is quite common. It's very hard to face our fears. Perhaps you should talk to your mother. It might help more than you realise. When did you last talk to her?"

"A few weeks ago. I see her every month. We have dinner, we talk. But she prefers her own company."

"No – I meant talk about your brother."

Elspeth shook her head. "No. That doesn't happen."

"Why not?"

Elspeth looked away. She looked at the posters on the walls, then the small rust-coloured stain in one corner of the ceiling. She could hear water, a tank filling, above her head. Water, rushing, flowing, covering her mouth, filling her lungs. She closed her eyes.

"She doesn't like to talk about him," she said eventually.

"I think you need to speak with her. It would help both of you to come to terms with the past."

Elspeth nodded, knowing she wouldn't.

"Did you ever discuss your mother's attitude with Dr Moyes?"

"I don't think so, I can't really remember."

Dr Stanley was flipping through the yellow mouse-eaten papers again, as though checking her answers. She looked up, her gaze sharp and direct.

Elspeth felt as though she were actually trying to see inside her – to see what cogs or gears might be broken, to ascertain if she was fixable or not.

"Elspeth, Dr Moyes was very concerned that you blamed yourself for what happened. Why would you think that?"

Elspeth looked away again and fixed her attention on the water stain.

"I was supposed to be taking care of him," she said quietly. "My mother wasn't there, she'd gone out somewhere, I don't remember where."

"And you went into the woods with your brother?"

Elspeth nodded.

"Had something happened to make you leave the house? Was there another person there, perhaps?"

Elspeth stood up abruptly. "I'm sorry, but I have to go. I'm meeting a friend shortly."

Dr Stanley looked up from her notes, her brows knitted. Clearly, she'd hoped for a breakthrough or some revelation. Instead, she smiled – a small quick movement of her lips.

"Certainly. My secretary will be in contact about your next session."

"I don't need another session, I just need – "

"A prescription, of course. I'll have one sent to your doctor."

"Thank you."

Elspeth closed the door behind her. She wanted to slam it shut but she didn't. Instead, she closed it gently and walked away. Now all she could think about was her mother and Eric. It was bad enough that they haunted her dreams at night without plaguing her in the daytime as well. She checked her watch. She was going to be late for coffee with Róisín but that couldn't be helped, not now. She made her way quickly back up the corridor and passed the waiting-room. It was beginning to fill up with people, older men and women, reading newspapers and crumpled out-of-date magazines.

The teenage girl, her doppelganger, was gone.

Róisín had managed to get a window seat and was waiting for her.

Elspeth pushed in through the mid-morning crush – tripping over bulging shopping-bags and slipping past sharp elbows. The conflicting aroma of melting cheese and burnt bread assaulted her senses. She could feel a headache forming already. She thought about mentioning her visit to Dr Stanley to Róisín but then she looked at her friend, smiling up at her, and she pushed all thoughts of Dr Stanley and her incessant note-taking to the back of her mind. There was no point talking about it, not now.

"Sorry I'm late," she said as she squeezed in beside her friend.

Róisín shook her head and laughed. "It's fine – it's not like I've got a plane to catch! Not yet anyway."

"Oh, God, I almost forgot. The fancy job in New York – when are you flying out?"

"Monday, can't wait. What about you? I thought you'd booked a few days off?"

"Yes, finally, but I have to go to Glenfeale after this."

"How is Nora?" Róisín asked softly, her words almost lost among the coffee-shop noise of cutlery scraping on plates and loud, laughing conversations.

Elspeth was silent for a moment. Róisín was her oldest friend and one of the few people who knew anything about her past.

"She's not good, Róisín. I'm really starting to think that she might have dementia. She's getting more forgetful. You know how much I worry about her, alone, in that bloody house, so isolated."

Róisín nodded. "I know. And she still won't discuss moving out?"

"No. It's getting to the point where I have to do something – past the point really."

"Did you ask her about the home help or a nurse?"

"She won't hear of it." Elspeth shook her head in frustration.

"It's so hard, Elspeth. I remember my grandfather was the very same – wouldn't leave the house. He just wanted to sit in front of the telly, all day every day."

Elspeth tried to picture Nora watching daytime programmes in the shadow-filled morning room. It was not an image she wanted to dwell on. She used to wonder if she was lonely or whether she wanted to get away from the house but she always rebuffed any suggestions of even a short weekend away. Then, after a while, Elspeth had stopped asking.

At one time she'd felt pity for her mother. She guessed she couldn't bear to leave the house because of Eric and what had happened there but now, over twenty years later, her well of sympathy had run dry. If her mother didn't want to leave that wreck of a house then she could stay there. Now it was just a duty visit. The last Friday of the month, the final pretence that they cared.

Róisín picked up the menu and began to scan the lunch options. "I don't know," she said, shaking her head. "They're never going to change, are they? When I think of my grandfather and how he died. It was so sad, dying of a brain aneurysm in front of the TV, just sitting there – it was terrible." She looked at Elspeth. "But it's what he would have wanted. The house always felt different after. My little sister was convinced his spirit was still there."

Elspeth smiled. "Watching the telly, perhaps."

Chapter 2

Even though there was no traffic, Elspeth slowed the car as she drove through Glenfeale, the village where nothing ever seemed to change. She glanced at the familiar shopfronts, some faded, others freshly painted, but all with the same recognisable surnames above the door. No new business ever seemed to open. Glenfeale was a place perpetually frozen in time, practically the same as when she first walked its streets some twenty years before.

Perhaps, if she squinted hard enough, that teenage girl across the road could be her and that boy, walking three steps behind his mother, that could be Eric, paused forever at eight years old.

Elspeth looked away – she knew that was why she only visited her mother once a month. Twelve times a year was more than enough, because the memories were always there, just beneath the surface, bubbling away, waiting to rise as soon as she came home. And now the village was behind her and she was almost there, almost "home".

Crowfield House – the familiar hand-painted sign – hanging lopsided on two rusty chains, partly obscured by the ivy growing through the tree branches. But Elspeth knew it was there. She knew where to look. And even if it rusted away to nothing, the name would be forever burned into her mind.

She turned in and began the slow journey up the neglected, potholed drive to her mother's house. It hadn't seen any improvement in the intervening years, not since the night of their arrival. The taxi driver had feared for his back-axle that night with the car lurching perilously across the gravel, while Eric slept like a baby in the back.

The house came into view. Elspeth steeled herself and began closing off as many emotions as was possible.

She would take her mother out for dinner and then drive back to the city. She never stayed the night. In fact, her mother had stopped offering by now. She'd stopped telling her that the bed was ready for her upstairs if she wanted to stay. Now it was a given that after dinner Elspeth would have to leave. Work, that was the usual excuse, and if Nora thought anything odd about this then she held her tongue.

As Elspeth pulled into the courtyard, she could see the front door was ajar but there was no sign of Nora. She got out. It was quiet, the only sound coming from the soft wind in the beech trees, their leaves heavy and whispery in the evening air.

Then she heard another noise, rustling, not leaves this time but wings. She looked skyward. The crows were on their way home, calling to each other, filling the silence with notes of darkness, black feathers whispering, as they flew overhead. Out of habit, she covered her hair with her hands and ran to the front door.

"*Mum!*" she shouted, pushing the door open but remaining on the threshold. She knocked. Once, twice, three times. No answer. She glanced down the hallway but it was empty and full of shadows, as usual.

The crows had finally settled in the rookery behind the house and the silence was back, like a shroud, hanging heavy over the evening.

"*Mum!*" she called again.

Far off, upstairs, she heard the sound of a door closing and a key being turned in a lock. Then footsteps, soft against the wooden boards.

Nora came into view. She was wearing slippers. Worn red velvet, they barely contained her swollen feet. She made her way carefully down the stairs, leaning heavily on the banister for support.

"Ah, Elspeth," she said quietly, standing on the bottom step, waiting to catch her breath. "I thought I heard a car. Are the crows home for the night?"

Elspeth nodded. She wanted to take her mother to task for leaving the door open, to tell her that it wasn't safe, but she couldn't say anything. The words were caught in her throat, meaningless. She knew she would be ignored, no matter what she said.

"That's good," Nora replied, looking towards the dusty clock in the hallway, as it began to wheeze the hour. "They've been late all week. They could do with an early night." She smiled to herself.

Elspeth said nothing. Knowing her mother, it might be a joke or she might be serious. It was always hard to tell.

"Tea?" Nora called, as made her way slowly down the hall. A slipper-clad ghost, lost in the evening shadows already.

"OK," Elspeth answered. "I'll just close this door first," she muttered under her breath.

She stepped inside and pushed the heavy door to. Now the only light in the hall came from upstairs and the green patch from the open kitchen door at its end. She could hear the ancient electric kettle, whistling and rattling already.

She waited for a moment, giving her eyes a chance to adjust to the dim light, then she set off down the hall, stepping quickly. The strange musty odour that belonged to Crowfield assaulted her senses. She pulled her arms tight to her sides, careful not to touch anything as she walked.

Her mother was already sitting at the table. A scattered collection of cups and plates covered the surface. It was as though there had been a tea party earlier and no one had bothered to clear it away.

"Sorry," Nora sighed, waving her hand absently at the mess. "I've been meaning to tidy this."

"Don't worry," Elspeth replied, shrugging off her jacket. "I'll quickly rinse them out."

Nora nodded in response and sat, staring into the distance, her hands folded neatly in her lap.

Elspeth cleared the table. This was the usual routine, the usual conversation. As she scraped burnt toast-crusts and potato peelings into the bin, she tried to make small talk.

"So, have you been out walking?"

"A bit. It's been warm."

"Yes. In the city too. Nearly too hot to sleep some nights."

"Oh, I keep the windows open at night."

And the door too, Elspeth thought to herself. She glanced at the windowsill, the array of tiny plastic pill-bottles with their sun-faded instructions. She could see Dr Lacy's name on a sheet of paper. It was propped against the teabag box – yet another prescription Nora hadn't seen as worth her while to fill.

She looked closer, wondering if one was for sleeping tablets. That might make life easier for her, but no, only blood pressure and aspirin and something else with a long unpronounceable name.

"Are you getting your groceries delivered from the shop?" she asked, opening a cupboard door.

"Most weeks, yes. He's very good. Carries them all the way down to the kitchen for me."

Elspeth nodded. The presses looked empty. "Are you sure you're happy with that? I can set up a standing order. We can do a list over dinner if you like?"

"No, it's fine. I don't eat very much, you know."

Silence then as the kettle clicked off. Elspeth began to make two mugs of tea. She wanted to ask her mother was she eating enough? Was she taking her tablets? Sleeping properly? Was she lonely? But she couldn't say any of it. It was as hard to ask if she was lonely as to ask if she ate breakfast that morning. Her questions would simply be ignored.

She placed a mug of tea on the table before Nora and her eyes came back into focus.

"Elspeth!" she said warmly. "I thought I heard a car. So it was you!"

❧❧❧❧❧ ❧❧❧❧❧

They were sitting in the hotel lobby, waiting for their table, when she realised Nora was still wearing slippers. A girl in a black apron came to tell them their table was ready and Elspeth took her mother's arm. They walked slowly to the dining room while Elspeth tried not to stare at the worn-out footwear.

"This is nice," Nora said. "Have we been here before?"

"Yes," Elspeth replied, looking around. Though, in fairness, after a while their dinner haunts seemed to merge into one. They all seemed to have similar inoffensive background music and the same sort of people.

She helped Nora into her chair and sat across from her. The memory lapses were nothing new. They had happened before but only with little things, forgotten names and places, dates, but now she seemed to be forgetting entire pieces of the day.

"Have you been in with Dr Lacy lately?" Elspeth asked, hiding behind the leather-bound menu.

Her mother ignored her. She may as well have asked about the soup. She decided to try another approach.

"Do you remember we talked about getting someone in? To help you with the housework, that sort of thing."

Her mother began to search through her handbag. "Before I forget," she said, handing Elspeth an envelope. "For your birthday. I know I'm a bit late but perhaps we're all getting a little old to celebrate birthdays. In fact, I try not to think about mine at all."

"Thank you." Elspeth smiled. "I'll open it later."

Her mother nodded.

The waitress had appeared to take their order so Elspeth quickly slotted the envelope away into her own bag. She already knew what it was without looking. For the last fifteen years her mother had given her the same present. The envelope would contain a birthday card, plain and unsentimental, probably with a drab sea vista and then, inside that, an unsealed blue envelope, simply addressed "Elspeth". This would contain a gift-voucher for the local craft shop.

And then, on her next visit to Glenfeale, Elspeth would make a point of stopping at the craft shop in order to buy a present for her mother with the voucher. It was strange unending circle, but one which made perfect sense.

Nora was squinting at the menu and Elspeth realised that her mother had forgotten her glasses. The waitress looked at her, expectant, waiting.

"Mum, you normally get the chicken, don't you?"

Nora nodded.

"So, the chicken, please, and the beef for me. Oh, and two glasses of red wine."

The waitress nodded and took the menus away.

They sat in silence. There was nothing to say.

The waitress brought the wine and Elspeth immediately took a sip from her glass.

Nora stared into the distance, her eyes unfocused, and Elspeth found herself wondering just how regular these occurrences were.

Then there was a crash, the sound of a plate or bottle breaking, startling them both.

"*The chandelier!*" Nora said, in a panicked voice.

"What?"

"*The night the chandelier broke! I knew it! I knew she was spying on me!*"

"Who was spying?"

"Elspeth, of course. It was all her fault, you know."

Elspeth felt her heart pounding in her chest. Her mother didn't know who she was – she was in the past, talking to a different person.

"Why would Elspeth spy on you?"

"Oh, she was always like that, suspicious. She couldn't help it. Just like her father and look what happened. I should have known." She leaned forward and whispered conspiratorially. "And I knew others would blame her."

The waitress appeared and Nora pulled away sharply as though stung. The girl smiled at them both and began to place cutlery and glasses on the table.

As soon as the waitress left, Elspeth leaned closer to her mother.

"Blame Elspeth for what?" she asked in a low voice.

Nora looked around as though wary of eavesdroppers before replying. "For what happened the night Eric disappeared," she replied urgently. "It was all her fault. She never listened, ever. Dragging him after her, going into those woods. I distinctly told her not to and ..." She shook her head.

Elspeth felt her heart beating faster still. She was fourteen again and she was finally going to hear what her mother really believed – at last – after all these years of suspicion. She swallowed carefully before asking the next question. She had to hear her say the name again.

"Who never listened?"

"*Elspeth*, of course, *Elspeth*. I should have known, always dragging Eric after her. Always doing things she shouldn't do. That nasty suspicious nature she had. Got it from her father, you see. Why, I remember – "

The waitress arrived, smiling at them both before placing the food carefully on the table.

Nora looked around, confusion in her face.

"Sorry for the noise earlier," the waitress said. "Some glasses fell behind the bar."

"Oh, that was all right," Nora said, shaking her head. "The one advantage of getting old, you know."

"Oh, and what's that?" the waitress asked pleasantly.

"Going deaf."

The waitress laughed as she left.

Nora nodded towards her plate. "This looks lovely, doesn't it?"

Elspeth knew the moment was broken. Nora wasn't going to say anymore but perhaps she'd said enough.

Elspeth couldn't eat, she couldn't face it. Her stomach knotted and she felt bile rise in her throat. She stood up from the table and excused herself.

Nora nodded. She had her fork in her hand and was busy pushing food aimlessly around her plate.

In the bathroom Elspeth turned on the taps and listened to the running water, hearing only rainfall and wind in her ears.

When she returned to the table, she noticed that her mother was barely touching her food. She seemed content to move it around the plate and only managed a forkful or two. She was becoming more anxious with every passing minute, her right hand reaching across to check the time on her watch now and then. She always tried to do this in a small secretive way, as though she didn't want to offend Elspeth by clock-watching when they were together.

"Will we go home?" Elspeth said eventually. She knew there was no point in trying to persuade Nora to stay any longer. One hour, that was her limit. She never liked being away from the house for too long.

Nora glanced quickly at her watch and nodded.

❦

As they drove back to Crowfield, Elspeth knew she had to do something. But what? Her mother had always implied she would only leave the house in a wooden box and at one point Elspeth would have been quite happy to let that occur. But now, she knew she had to act.

"Would you like to come on a little holiday? Maybe come and visit me in Dublin?"

"No." Nora shook her head. "I'm much happier at home."

"Then what about someone to call during the week? To help you in the house?"

"Why? I'm fine. I don't need any help."

"Well, I'm worried about you. And it might be nice to have someone helping out. To do some cleaning. Make you a cup of tea. Fix your lunch, maybe?"

Nora said nothing.

Chapter 3

The car's engine made another ominous screeching sound and Heather patted the old cracked steering wheel in a reassuring manner.

"Come on, Elmo, we're nearly there," she said in a low voice.

She didn't want her little brother Adam to hear her talking. He was settled and happy on the back seat, wrapped in his favourite blanket and surrounded by boxes and bags. If he realised that Elmo, the car, was in trouble, she'd never hear the end of it and the morning had been stressful enough as it was. The engine growled again and this time Adam heard it as well.

"Is Elmo all right?" he asked, sticking his head out from beneath the tartan cover.

"Yeah, he's fine, probably just tired. It's been a long old drive."

"Cass always promised him a nice wash after a long journey," Adam said.

"Did she?"

"Yeah, he loves the carwash – the brushes tickle his wheels."

Of course they do, Heather thought. In Cass's world everything had a personality, even her toaster, Burning Bill, so named because of its ability to burn everything that came near it. Even now Adam would only eat cremated toast.

The engine squealed again and this time it sounded as close to a death rattle as Heather had ever heard.

"Come on, Elmo," she whispered, willing the old car onwards. "We're almost there."

And then, like a timely gift from above, the signpost appeared, the one that she needed to see.

Glenfeale 6 km

"Not too long now," she called back to Adam. "I'm sure Elmo will manage the rest of the way."

There was no response so she glanced quickly in the rear-view mirror.

"Did you hear me, Adam?" she asked.

And this time she heard him – he was whispering but not to her. It was a one-way conversation with someone that wasn't there. She felt her hands clench momentarily against the steering wheel. She hated the whispering – it meant he was talking to an imaginary friend, again. And she could guess which one.

"Are we nearly there?" he asked a few minutes later.

Heather glanced round, trying to locate another signpost but there was nothing to see, nothing but trees and overgrown hedges.

"I think so," she said. "I hope we're not lost."

"No, we're not lost," Adam said quietly.

"How do you know? You're hiding under a blanket!"

"I just know."

Heather rolled her eyes but said nothing.

"We're here," she said a few moments later.

They were on the outskirts of the village, with tidy verges and flowers planted in neat rows along the hedgerows.

Welcome to Glenfeale

"See, told you we weren't lost," Adam said.

Heather began to change gears and the engine screamed in response. She kept waiting for an enormous bang meaning Elmo had finally died. She knew when she set off earlier that morning that Elmo probably wasn't going to make it but she had no choice.

She changed gears again, going even slower now. There was a small turnoff to her left just before the main street in the village. She'd been there only once before but she remembered the warped monkey-puzzle tree – hanging like an enormous green claw over the whitewashed cottage, its spiky, vibrant branches leaving the house in darkness.

⁂

One viewing, that was all she'd had. The cottage had been on the market for a while but it ticked as many boxes as she could possibly hope for. Their mother, Cass, hadn't left a huge amount of money after she died – just enough to buy this little place in Glenfeale. A fresh start, a new home for Heather and Adam.

At that stage Heather had been appointed Adam's guardian and she was free to make her own choices. There was no need for them to live beside Aunt Teresa anymore. Initially, she feared telling Teresa they were moving, but Teresa didn't seem to mind. She knew that Heather wanted to try and do what was best for Adam, so she gave them her blessing and said she wouldn't mind if they moved away.

Looking back, Heather wondered why she'd worried at all. Teresa was probably glad to see the back of them. She'd even offered to help her pack up Cass's old house, a place she'd studiously avoided when Cass was alive. She called over on a wet afternoon, a week after the funeral and managed to keep her opinions quiet, for a little while at least.

Heather was preoccupied that wet evening, trying to locate some vital paperwork and she left Teresa packing in the front room. Out of the corner of her eye she could see Teresa pulling faces as she took down dream-catchers and gathered up endless bundles of coloured candles. Then she found Poe. She picked up the silver birdcage and squinted through the bars, wondering what was inside. Perhaps she expected to see a budgie chirping away, but no, there was only Poe, Cass's stuffed jackdaw, permanently perched on the wooden rail.

Heather had to intervene but what could she say?

"That's Poe," she said after a long pause.

"Poo?"

"No, Poe, after Edgar Allen. It's fine, I'll take him."

"Oh, you want to keep it?"

Heather nodded. Even though Cass had been absent for much of her childhood, travelling almost all the time, she wanted to keep it all. The fringed silken shawls, the ceramic Hand of Destiny, the Tarot cards neatly tucked away in their well-worn wrappers, even Burning Bill, the dodgy toaster. They were all part of Cass and that meant they were a part of her and Adam, whether she liked it or not.

***

"And here we are!" Heather announced. She locked the steering wheel and turned in through the open gates onto a moss-covered driveway.

Elmo spluttered and came to an abrupt stop.

"We'll have to take Elmo to the carwash. That'll cheer him up," Adam said.

Heather turned in her seat and smiled at Adam as he emerged from his hiding place, blinking like a small creature waking from a long hibernation.

"So what do you think of the house?" she asked.

"*I love it!*" he shouted and threw off the blanket.

"It is nice, isn't it?" she said, nodding. It was important that Adam liked his new home. It would make life so much easier if he could settle in and sleep properly. One step at a time though, she thought.

Then she saw, with dismay, that she had been right. Poe had been tucked beneath the covers with him. Perhaps she should have just thrown him out, like Teresa wanted.

Heather opened the car door for Adam and stood back. She felt stiff after the long drive and one of her legs was full of pins and needles. She stretched her arms for a moment, feeling her back crack as she reached up toward the sky. At that particular moment she felt more like sixty-one than twenty-one.

Adam brushed past her getting out. Poe sat, regal in his silver cage, black feathers shining gun-barrel-blue in the sunlight. For a brief moment he looked as though he just might stretch his wings too. Then the sun went behind a cloud and the moment passed.

Heather looked around, her eyes bright with enthusiasm.

"Right, so let's see. These are the keys. Now, let me give you the grand tour!"

A great pile of leaves and withered flowers had gathered on the step. Heather brushed them away with her foot. The front door was a little stiff and she had to push it open with her shoulder.

It was dark inside, almost black after the bright sunlight outside.

Adam was behind her, suddenly shy as though a stranger was waiting for them inside, one who wanted to take his hand and say hello.

"So, this room is our sitting room, living room or fancy front room, whatever you want to call it. The kitchen is through that door there at the back. What do you think?"

Adam came out slowly from behind her back and walked a little way into the empty space. Some furniture still remained from the previous owner. An old painted dresser sat to the left of the doorway. You could still see the shadows of plates which had once lined the shelves like circular ghosts of the past. Heather was glad to see they'd also left a small couch behind because otherwise they would have been sitting on cushions for the next few days.

"And this is the corridor!" she announced, waving her arm theatrically to the right. The wooden door was slightly open and beyond that was a green, painted wall.

Adam came nervously back to her side again as she opened the door and Heather could feel her heart sinking. What had happened? He'd seemed so happy when they pulled up. He'd even shouted about how much he loved the house.

She stepped into the narrow corridor and Adam followed.

"So, the corridor is very exciting," she continued, "because –" she paused for dramatic effect and waved her arms over her head, "this is where our bedrooms are!" She gestured to the two doors, one on the right and another just in front of them. "Which one will you pick?"

Adam shook his head. "I don't know." Poe hung limp by his side.

"Are you feeling all right, Adam?"

He nodded.

"Maybe you're hungry? I think I'm hungry. And what about Poe? Would he like a worm or something?"

Adam smiled. Just a tiny one, but a smile at least. The first since he'd set foot inside their new home.

"Right. So the bathroom is here on the right and why don't you have this bedroom at the back. It looks out onto the garden. In fact, I think it's the nicest room in the whole house."

She opened the door with a flourish, revealing a small box room with a window at the end, showing the summer-green garden outside. Adam carefully carried Poe to the bright window and set him on the ledge. Then he screamed and ran back through the open door. Poe fell with a resounding metallic bang to the wooden floor.

Heather stood for a moment, trying to process what had just happened. The room was empty, nothing strange as far as she could see. She bent down to pick up the birdcage. Poe regarded her with a bright eye. He didn't seem to have suffered any injury. His claws were still perfectly positioned along the wooden rail.

"What do you think, Poe?" Heather sighed. This was not going well.

She began to straighten up and then she nearly screamed as well. There was someone in the garden, a woman. She was sitting on an old bench with her back to the window. That must be what scared him.

"*Adam!*" she called as she ran back though the corridor, Poe's cage swinging from her hand.

Adam was hiding in the car, tucked beneath the blanket.

"Did you see her?" he asked.

Heather nodded.

"So, she's real then?"

"Yes. Of course she's real," Heather replied, trying not to grit her teeth at the mention of ghosts.

This was another well-known fact, certified by both Adam and Cass. Heather had no "gift". So, not only was she a non-believer but she also couldn't see the things they could and appeared to be totally unreceptive to all inner and outer vibrations.

Heather decided it was probably because of her uneventful upbringing with Teresa and really didn't mind at all that the "gift" seemed to have passed her by but it bothered Cass.

"Such a pity," she murmured a few times to Heather.

Heather always nodded in agreement, not caring a jot about believing in ghosts or seeing things that others couldn't.

Now, though, she was inwardly cursing her mother, for nothing was ever straightforward with Adam. Instead, there was always an undercurrent of doom and watchfulness running through his little mind.

"OK, Adam," she began slowly, bending down so she could find his hand beneath the blanket. "There's a woman sitting in the garden. Perhaps this used to be her house and she came for a visit?" She nodded, yes – that sounded like a perfectly plausible reason once you said the words out loud. "Why don't you wait here for a moment while I go and talk to her? See where she came from?"

Adam nodded. "Can I have Poe?"

"Of course," Heather said and handed him over before setting off around the back of the house.

There was a crumbling concrete path running the entire length of the cottage and she could see the wooden bench as soon as she came round the back. But it was empty.

"*Hello?*" she said. "*Hello? Is anyone there?*"

She could hear footsteps and, as she began to walk towards the bench, an older woman appeared around the opposite side of the house. Small and stocky, her short grey hair looked as though it hadn't seen a brush in days and she was wearing a bobbled green fleece over sensible blue trousers.

"Oh, sorry," she said, not looking remotely apologetic. "You caught me. I really shouldn't be here. But it was such a lovely evening and the sun stays here for so long. Such a lovely little spot. So warm and the sun is good for the bones, you know. Especially at my age – vitamin D decreases after sixty, you know."

Heather didn't know what to say.

"And speaking of age – you're so young! Look at you!" the woman continued. "Are you moving in here?"

"Yes, I'm Heather. We just arrived."

"Well, I'm Patsy – your neighbour." She held out her hand. "I live over there."

As Heather shook her hand, she found herself hoping that she meant at least half a mile away.

"Just there, across the road," the woman said, smiling.

Adam appeared around the side of the house. He was carrying Poe, holding him carefully above his head as though he were an old-fashioned lantern.

"This is Adam – my brother," Heather said.

Adam stared at the woman, saying nothing.

"Adam, this is –"

But her words were drowned out by the birds.

Heather threw her hands over her ears, blocking out the noise, wondering what was happening. But Patsy and Adam simply looked skyward.

"*They're going home!*" Adam shouted.

Heather watched as the noisy flock of crows streamed overhead, hundreds of them, cawing and calling, their wings rustling, thousands of feathers moving in the quiet evening air.

"Where do they live?" Adam asked Patsy.

31

"At Crowfield House, of course – over there!" Patsy pointed towards the distant woods the birds were flying to.

A thin plume of wood-smoke rose in the blue sky but the house itself was hidden from view, nestled amongst the green of the trees.

"Crowfield?" Heather asked.

"It's called after the crows," Patsy said. "The crows are probably there longer than the house!" She smiled at them, as though this fact should please them greatly.

"Can we go and visit them?" Adam asked. "Poe would love to meet his cousins." He held Poe higher so he could see the mass of birds overhead.

"Is he alive?" Patsy asked, blinking against the sunlight, trying to see into the cage. "He's very quiet, even for a pet."

"No, he's not." Heather shook her head. "He's more …" she searched for the most inoffensive term she could think of, "ornamental."

"*Poe is not an ornament!*" Adam said angrily. "He can see things."

"Oh, aye," Patsy replied, still peering into the cage.

"He's a familiar," Adam said.

"Oh." Patsy nodded slowly. "Like a witch's cat?"

"*Yes!*" Adam was delighted. Usually people had never heard of a familiar before.

Cass had always taken great pains to explain what a familiar was and how they weren't dangerous or evil and had just got a bad reputation because of some fairy tale or other. Familiars were an opening to a different world. They were just another set of eyes, ones that could see beyond the narrow boundaries of our own vision.

Heather felt her heart sinking. This was not the first impression on her new neighbour that she'd been hoping for. "I think we'd better get going," she said. "We have to get this car unpacked and pick up some bits from the shop. It'll be dark soon."

"I'll take Poe inside and then I'll help!" Adam ran along the crumbling path and disappeared into the house.

"Sorry about that," Heather said. "He has a great imagination."

"Nothing wrong with that." Patsy smiled. "Sorry if I gave him a fright earlier."

"He's fine. Probably just tired after the journey."

"Let me make it up to him. I've a little sweetshop in the village. Please, call in whenever you like. I owe you both a treat. No tricks, I promise!"

Patsy laughed at her own joke and they began to walk across the moss-covered lawn.

"Oh, one last thing," Patsy said, reaching out and gripping Heather's arm tightly. "Keep him away from Crowfield. It's not a place for children, or familiars for that matter."

And then she left, making her way through the rusting gates and carefully crossing the road. When she reached her own gate, she turned and waved.

Heather waved back, looking at her neighbour's whitewashed cottage which was surrounded by shrubs and apple trees.

Adam came out of the house.

Heather was glad to see he'd left Poe inside as promised.

"When can we visit the crows?" he asked.

"Someday soon," Heather replied vaguely. She was wondering if she'd misheard their new neighbour. Had she just warned her to keep Adam and Poe away from Crowfield? What did she think was going to happen?

Heather began to pull an overstuffed black bag from the car. The sooner Adam started school the better. "So," she smiled brightly at him. "Does Poe like the house?"

"I think so." Adam shrugged.

"Right, let's get working. We have a lot to do. I think poor Elmo has to go to a garage so I need to find a job straight away and you need to think about starting school."

"Do we have to do it all this evening?

"Well, I'd better put a notice in the shop window tonight, looking for a job, but you have a whole weekend off before school starts!"

It was dark by the time Heather got Adam settled for the night, on the blow-up mattress in his new room. Their beds and the other few bits of furniture weren't arriving until the next day. The movers had got the dates mixed up.

As Heather looked around at the mess of half-empty boxes and bags, she was glad of the mistake. It would be so much easier to sort out all the furniture tomorrow. The house didn't seem so strange anymore, with their familiar belongings lying around. But the windows were curtainless and all she could see was her reflection in the dark glass, a mirror twin with wild black curls. She could also see the lights from Patsy's house across the road. The twinkling glow filtered through the trees and she wondered whether the woman lived alone. Was she also sitting in darkness? Watching her new neighbours through a net curtain?

Chapter 4

The night was closing in and Elspeth could see lights ahead. They were nearly in Glenfeale already but she was reluctant to go back to Crowfield after what her mother had said in the restaurant. She'd always felt that her mother blamed her for Eric's disappearance but she'd never heard her say it out loud before. She slowed down.

"We'll stop at the shop. See if there's anything you need."

"It's fine. I can phone them, you know. I've enough to keep me going now till next week."

Elspeth thought of the empty cupboards. "I'll just run in. You can wait in the car, if you like?"

Nora nodded. She was checking the time again, the streetlight glinting on the gold of her watch.

Inside the shop, there was no-one behind the counter. Elspeth made her way through the narrow, crowded aisles – nearly tripping across a large bag of dog food. She picked up a can of condensed milk and then put it back. She couldn't think. She went to the other side of the shop and looked at the loaves of bread, wondering what Nora ate for breakfast these days – probably nothing. She reached for a wire basket and began to fill it.

When she had finished, she went to the counter and rang the old-fashioned bell there. As she waited, she spotted a cork noticeboard behind the till.

Free kittens to good home.

Cleaner available for light housework, also baby-sitting duties.

Handyman/Painter, call for keen rates.

Each with a telephone number underneath.

❧ ❧

The house was in darkness. Sitting in the car, Elspeth could hear her mother searching through her handbag, looking for the keys. She was making small contented humming noises as she scrabbled through the bag. She always hummed when she was safely back at Crowfield. She found the keys and produced them with a metallic flourish.

She turned awkwardly towards Elspeth. She was ready to say goodbye. They just had to endure the necessary small talk first.

"Are you sure you won't come in? Your bed is there for you."

Elspeth began to answer, to make her usual excuses – work, meeting a friend, how it was easier to drive back to the city – and then she heard herself agreeing to stay.

It was hard to say who was more surprised, herself or Nora.

"Oh, that's nice," Nora replied eventually. "I lit the fire in the morning room earlier. I'll stoke it up."

"Lovely."

Nora slowly got out of the car.

Elspeth wondered what the hell had happened. Why did she agree to stay? Where had that come from? She didn't have to think too hard. It was Dr Stanley's fault – she and her "*holistic*" approach. She'd told her to talk to her mother and at the time she'd nodded in agreement, knowing she had no intention of doing so. But the message must have lodged in her subconscious. And now here she was, about to stay the night, voluntarily, in a place she hated.

As she walked to the door, a solitary crow flew overhead, his raucous cry breaking through the night silence. Would Nora notice if she didn't follow her inside? For a brief moment Elspeth hesitated on the doorstep, then she firmly stepped into the darkness that was Crowfield.

She pulled the front door shut. The kitchen door was open at the end of the gloomy hall, the light on. Her mother must be there. She walked quickly, the heavy bag of groceries weighing her down, keeping her eyes firmly on the ground even though every door was closed. She checked them off mentally as she passed, the library, the front room, the morning room.

Then she turned back slightly to look at the stairs shrouded in darkness and shuddered. She didn't want to think about the rooms upstairs and the shrine her mother had created for Eric in his bedroom.

"*I'm in here!*" Nora called from the front room

Elspeth looked at the kitchen door. It was closed now. She shook her head. She had forgotten about Crowfield and its many eccentricities. The doors that managed to open and close of their own accord. The light switches which only worked sporadically and the creaking floorboards which always sounded like stealthy footsteps in the night. They were all a part of Crowfield, a thousand little oddities that had become normal after a time.

"Didn't you bring an overnight bag?" Nora asked as Elspeth wandered into the room.

Elspeth clutched the groceries to her chest now, holding the bag like a shield. "Oh, must have left it at home, wasn't thinking."

"Don't worry. I'm sure there are some of your old clothes upstairs. Sit – we'll put those bits in the kitchen later." Nora gestured towards the dusty couch. "Now, I usually read the paper in the evenings. Sometimes I manage to find a decent book in the library. I haven't looked for one in a while but maybe we could go through some books tomorrow. If you're not in a rush, of course?"

"Yes, maybe."

Elspeth perched on the edge of the couch. Nothing had changed in the front room since she was a teenager. In fact, nothing had changed from when they'd first moved to Crowfield. She looked around. She could see the moth-eaten curtains which hung limp and dusty as though they had given up on life and the spindly-legged desk which crouched spider-like in the corner. All these things were unchanged, even the singed rug in front of the fire was old and familiar.

"Isn't this nice?" her mother said as she settled into her wing chair. Leaning forward, she held her hands towards the warmth of the fire.

If Elspeth squinted a little it almost looked like Nora hadn't aged in twenty years. Her hair was pulled back from her face and twisted into a bun, her dangling earrings sparkling richly, catching the firelight.

"Would you like a cup of tea, perhaps?"

Elspeth shook her head. What she really wanted was for her mother to slip time again and tell her what happened the night Eric disappeared. There were so many questions that had gone unanswered.

She cleared her throat. "I have a bit of news actually."

"Oh, how lovely! A man, is it?"

"No, no. It's not a man."

"Oh."

"I've started to see a therapist. Well, a psychiatrist actually."

"Why? Whatever for?"

Elspeth sat forward on the couch and looked at her mother. Nora had sat back in her chair, throwing her face into darkness. It was almost like talking to a ghost.

"Is there something the matter with you?" Nora asked.

"Can you not guess why I need to see a psychiatrist?"

"No, I can't. I never see you. You never call."

"It's about Eric."

"Oh."

It was the smallest sound in the world and the most heart-breaking. Elspeth could see her mother's face clearly now as she leaned forward from the shadows, the way her eyes fell as soon as she heard his name.

She stood up. "I'm sorry, Mum. I can't. It was her idea, the therapist's, to talk to you. But it's too hard for both of us. I'll see myself out."

She bent down and brushed her mother's hand as she walked by but Nora wasn't looking at her anymore.

She was staring into the fire, her eyes bright with tears, lost in the past again.

And Elspeth wondered, did it matter? Did any of it really matter?

Chapter 5

Róisín handed her another glass of wine. "You look like you might need this," she said.

Elspeth began to apologise. She knew she'd been distant all evening. She'd tried to busy herself in the kitchen and let Róisín do all the talking. She thought she'd pulled it off but obviously not.

"I'm so sorry. I just –"

"Elspeth, it's fine. I know you're worried about her. It's not easy, I understand."

Elspeth leaned across and put the glass on the coffee table, then clasped her hands together. "I haven't been great company this evening, have I? This was meant to be a celebration for your new job and –"

"It's all right," Róisín said, interrupting her again. "And look, my timing isn't great, is it? You really could do with a friend and I won't be here. I know you don't like talking about it but it might help."

Elspeth smiled a little and shrugged. She was thinking of Dr Stanley and her sanitised office. The scratching sound her pen made as it moved slowly across the paper – trying to condense her life into a neat parcel of notes.

"You're right, Róisín. There's no point in holding it in, keeping secrets. That's what my mother has done all her life. You know how she's always blamed me for what happened."

"Oh, Elspeth! You really can't believe that, can you? You were just a child too."

"But I was older. I was the responsible one. It shouldn't have happened. If I could just remember. I dream about it all the time, that night, Eric and the woods. We're running, to somewhere or away from somewhere, or someone. I don't know. But I'm the one calling him, leading him on, so it is my fault. I brought him with me into those woods and he never came home."

"Maybe you were trying to save him from something?"

Elspeth shook her head. "I don't think so. That's not the feeling I have in the dreams. It's not fear. It's hard to explain but it's more like anger or adrenalin. And then it all goes black and there's nothing there, nothing more to see, just the sound of water."

"Did you try to talk to your mother last night?"

"I did. In fact I was going to stay the night."

"But you hate that house!"

"Well, in the end, I didn't manage it. I couldn't. I have no idea how she lives there. Well, I do in a way. But I could never live there again. It's too strange, always was, even before Eric disappeared. Of course, Eric used to think it was haunted. That was because of my mother, I guess. More secrets and lies. She must have told Eric there was a ghost at some stage." She leaned forward and picked up her wine glass. It was almost empty. She held it in her hand, watching the soft light shining through the remnants, glistening like dark water. "But it is a strange house. I've always hated it, even from the first. I wish she never got that letter, telling her that she'd inherited Crowfield. I had a bad feeling, even then. We should have stayed in Australia."

Chapter 6

July 1994

Nora was sitting at the breakfast table and she was holding an envelope. A large white envelope with small green stamps on it. It had come all the way from Ireland.

Elspeth remembered her opening it and reading the contents before placing it by her untouched breakfast.

Her father was also reading and, although he was hidden behind his newspaper, he'd noticed the unusual correspondence. "Hope someone hasn't died," he muttered, sounding as though as he didn't really care one way or another.

"No, well, yes, Harry Enright – I think he was my granduncle. Actually, I'm not sure of the family connection. But he's left me his house, Crowfield. There are no other relatives. I'm next of kin, and I guess that would make sense because –"

The newspaper was lowered and Frank looked at Nora but said nothing. He extended his hand, wordlessly, and she handed him the letter.

She looked slightly shell-shocked, as she always did whenever she talked about her childhood. She'd never known her father. He was an ambulance driver during the Second World War and never came home. As a result, Nora and her mother spent years moving from one relative's home to another, always reliant on their good will and hospitality, until Nora at sixteen got a job and some independence, before emigrating to Australia.

"You can write back and tell those solicitors to sell it," Frank said, handing the letter back to Nora.

And that was the end of the conversation. As far as Frank was concerned it was over. The old house and lands would be sold and life would continue as normal. There was nothing in Ireland worth returning for, especially not an old money-pit of a house.

But it didn't finish there. For once, Nora didn't compliantly agree.

Elspeth remembered lying awake at night listening to the low-level hum of their arguments, two floors below. Her mother's voice, cricket-like, ceaseless, on and on, chirping, until her father's deeper voice interrupted. Then the sounds would crescendo, until doors slammed and the inevitable silence fell once more.

This wasn't a new scenario, though – in fact, for Elspeth it was a common occurrence. The bickering and arguments had been part of her life for years now. Eric seemed to sleep through the madness and, if he ever heard any of the rows, he never mentioned them. Elspeth also decided to ignore it. The disagreements were a constant in their lives. Just another thing to be accepted, like school or homework.

As the days passed, Elspeth wondered who was winning the battle or the war. She was vaguely interested in how it would end but never guessed what would happen next. Her father was called away to work on a project in Melbourne, a rare occurrence – some emergency involving a rogue builder and an outraged client.

Frank left and Nora got them up early the next morning, announcing that they were going on a surprise holiday to Ireland.

"Does Dad know?" Elspeth asked, thinking of the late-night arguments and slamming doors.

"Of course he does. I have to see about the house as well. Call to the solicitor, that sort of thing."

"But I thought you could just write a letter. Dad said that already. I remember him saying about selling the house. How we don't need to go back to Ireland."

"That's how they get you, Elspeth. Much better to go in person. This way we get to check what's happening. Make sure everything is above board. Your father will try and get a flight later on. We're just going first."

At this stage Eric was already waiting with a rucksack over his shoulder. He was always happy to get out of school.

"Are you ready? Come on!" he said.

"But what about my end-of-term exams?" Elspeth asked.

"Look, you're only going to miss a week or two."

"But these exams are important!"

"Don't worry. I'll explain it to them. I can say we had a family emergency. Like when Granny died."

"But there *is* no emergency!" Elspeth argued.

Her mother didn't reply and Elspeth stopped talking. She recognised the warning signs, the tight compression of her lips, and she knew there was no point in trying to push things any further.

"Here," Nora said, thrusting a green holdall at Elspeth. "Use this to pack and make it quick! The car should be here in about five minutes."

Elspeth went upstairs and began throwing clothes into the bag Nora had given her. She had no idea what to pack. Would it be cold or warm? They'd only gone to Ireland once before when her grandmother died and she barely remembered the trip.

Downstairs, she could hear her mother opening the door. The taxi had arrived.

"*Come on, Elspeth! Let's go!*" Eric shouted.

⚜⚜⚜

Once the initial amusement of the airport and the prospect of a plane journey had worn off, Eric began to whine. He twisted in his seat and complained. He didn't like the food on offer and he'd forgotten to tell his friend Daniel where he'd hidden the "*treasure*" and now Daniel would never find it.

Her mother started drinking as soon as the air hostess came around. Elspeth could smell the alcohol and lemon on her breath but at least she seemed happy. Eric spun awkwardly in his seat again, kicking her ankles. Elspeth looked past him, trying to see out the tiny window, but there was nothing there, nothing but grey.

When they finally arrived in Ireland, it was late at night. They had flown into Knock airport on a tiny rattling plane from Stanstead. It was only when they disembarked for the final time, carrying their rucksacks and hand-luggage, that Elspeth realised her mother had no plan. It was clear from the look on her face that she was just one short step away from a complete meltdown. Whatever force had carried her through all the airports and the transfers, the boarding queues and sitting on hard metal seats, eating dried-out plastic food, had evaporated.

"Where are we going now?" Eric asked. "Do we have to get another plane? I'm sick of airports. I just want normal food."

Elspeth shushed him. "We're getting a taxi now. Aren't we, Mum?" she said firmly, catching her mother by the arm, trying to pull her back to reality.

Her eyes remained glazed and Elspeth wondered just how many Martinis she'd consumed over the last few days.

"To Crowfield House. Harry's old place. Isn't that right, Mum? You remember now?"

Nora nodded, the frozen paralysed look still on her face.

Elspeth steered her and Eric towards the solitary phone box so they could call a taxi. Of course, they didn't have the right change but a man passing by gave them the correct coins and then, as soon as the car arrived, Nora managed to switch back to some form of normality. She was all sunshine and laughter and there was much hair-flicking and talk of holidays and how she'd missed Ireland so much.

Elspeth and Eric sat quietly in the back, watching the dark-green of the hedgerows pass them by. Eric fell asleep, his head pressed against Elspeth's shoulder. She was trying to stay awake, reading the unfamiliar names on the strange white pointed signposts. Then one flashed by, black writing stark against the white background: **Glenfeale**.

She whispered the name to herself, wondering if she was even pronouncing it properly and then she could feel her eyes closing, closing.

She was jolted awake by the swaying movement of the car. She heard the taxi-man swear softly under his breath and her mother chattering away in a senseless reassuring manner.

Although it was dark and night had fallen, she could see the square outline of Crowfield House, its many rows of chimneys reaching upwards like pointing fingers.

As soon as the car stopped, she opened the door slowly and got out, waking Eric as she moved.

"Where are we?" he asked, his voice thick with sleep.

"We're home, darling," Nora answered, her voice high and unnatural.

The taxi-driver was asking if she was sure about staying the night and whether she was expected.

"Yes, it's perfectly fine," Nora repeated, as though she were trying to reassure herself more than anyone. "Perfectly fine." She nodded again, looking around the overgrown courtyard.

Eric was out of the car as well and had gone off adventuring through the courtyard. Elspeth could hear him, swishing his way through waist-high grasses and weeds.

"*Be careful, Eric! There might be bats around!*" Nora called.

Darkness lay heavy in every corner of the courtyard and together they watched as the taxi, their only source of light, turned slowly and awkwardly in the weed-choked yard. Elspeth watched the red lights of the car travel the length of the driveway, jolting up and down over the potholes. Then a brief flare of red from his taillights before darkness covered them like velvet.

Even though they were in the middle of the countryside, it was deathly silent. No animal sounds, no insects, no owls, not even so much as a barking dog. All Elspeth could hear was Nora, unzipping bags as she searched for the keys. She looked skyward. A full moon broke through the cloud cover, illuminating the house momentarily. The blank windows seemed to be watching them.

"Now, I remember packing them away in this bag. Or was it –"

"When is Dad coming?" Eric asked, his voice harmonious and clear, like a bell ringing against the night.

"*Hmmm ...*"

"I said, when is Dad coming on holiday?"

"Well, he's a very busy man. And, yes, here they are."

Nora pulled a set of keys from a folded envelope. "This is it," she murmured, holding up a small set of keys. There was a long luggage-label hanging from them with writing scrawled on both sides of it.

"Now, which one?" Nora paused, looking at the lock on the door and then selecting a likely candidate. The key turned easily in the lock and the door opened with a long creak.

And they were inside.

The smell was the first thing that struck her about Crowfield. It wasn't the long dimly lit passageways or the general shabbiness – no, it was that pervading odour. It was everywhere and in every room. A rich earthy scent but not necessarily a bad one. It was almost like being inside an underground cave, one that was filled with moss and densely packed clay. Crowfield never smelled like a normal house, not even when open fires were blazing in the hearths. Even then, it still managed to feel like they were deep underground – moles, blind creatures, just feeling their way about and hoping not to bump into something that would regard them as food.

"Where are the lights?" Eric asked.

Nora began flicking at the switches inside the doorway to no avail. "Perhaps they turned off the power after Harry died," she muttered to herself. "Never mind. It's perfectly fine. There must be candles somewhere. Elspeth – why don't you go and see if you can find some? I'll wait here with Eric."

Elspeth really didn't want to go deeper into the house. "But I don't know where to look. I've never been here before."

"Don't be silly," her mother replied. "Just follow your nose. Now quick smart, off you go!"

And she even gave Elspeth a little push into the gloomy hall.

"I think the kitchen should be down at the end of the hall," she said from the safety of the front door.

Elspeth began to walk in a straight line with her hands outstretched. There seemed to be no windows throwing any light into the house at all. It just seemed to be one endless stretch of blackness before her. She could hear her mother talking to Eric, her words low and whispery. Elspeth was sure she was just reassuring him about the house and where they were going to sleep that night but it sounded ominous. A mocking voice in the darkness. She felt like a sacrifice to her mother's madness.

As her eyes slowly grew accustomed to the low light around her, she began to see objects. A winding staircase to her right and now an open door on her left. The room was lit from the moonlight outside. She could clearly see an overlarge fireplace and a long high-backed couch and there, sitting on the mantelpiece, were candles in two enormous silver candlesticks.

She walked by the couch, arms still outstretched, feeling her way carefully, her mother's voice just the merest hint of a whisper now, a snake-hiss in the background. The moon had disappeared and the room was a mass of shadows but she was able to reach up and pull the first candlestick to the edge. There was a narrow box beside it – matches.

She shouted back into the darkness towards the open door. "*I've found candles! I'm in a sitting room – it's on the left-hand side!*"

She could hear her mother whispering again but she couldn't make out the words.

Elspeth struck a match and it sparked, then burst into a tiny flame. Carefully she lit the wax candle and shone it around the room. She heard her mother and Eric cheer as they saw the light flare into the corridor.

Then she reached for the other candlestick. She could see the room reflected in the dusty mirror above her and that was when she saw the face, thin and hollow-cheeked, eyes deep-set and glittering, almost hidden in the shadows at the back of the room.

Elspeth screamed and dropped the candlestick. Darkness enveloped the room and she heard quick footsteps. Her mother was by her side.

"What happened?"

"There was a man! There!" Elspeth pointed towards the corner where she'd seen him.

Nora fumbled for the dropped candlestick and Elspeth gave her the matches. Light blazed again, illuminating the space.

"*Who's there?*" Nora demanded. "*Show yourself!*"

Silence. None of them moved. Eric had positioned himself between the fireplace and his mother. Elspeth looked at the space where she had seen the face but it was empty, just a curved alcove, nothing to see but darkness and shadows flickering in the meagre light.

Nora shook her head "I don't see anyone. Are you sure you – ?" she trailed off without finishing the question.

Elspeth nodded frantically. "He was over there."

Nora began to walk towards the place she was pointing at. Elspeth and Eric hurried in her wake, not wanting to be left outside the tiny circlet of light. Nora held the candle higher but there was nothing to see, just a tall dusty bookcase set back into a recess.

"No one there now," Nora announced, in a confident tone.

"Was it a ghost?" Eric asked, staring at Elspeth, his eyes saucer-wide as he firmly held on to the back of Nora's coat.

"No. Probably just a reflection in the mirror," Nora replied, shooting a glance at Elspeth.

Elspeth, catching her mother's eye, began to nod. "Yeah. I must have been imagining it, Eric. Seeing things, after the long journey, you know."

Eric didn't look convinced but Nora was drawing back the curtains as much as possible, so the moonlight filtered in. "Why don't we light a fire?" she said with a smile. "Look! Everything we need is here."

She pushed the heavy couch forward so they would be closer to the fireplace. Eric and Elspeth sat, huddled together, while Nora busied herself, arranging the fire-stuff and then laughing with delight as the fire took hold.

"See, I haven't lost my touch! Auntie Caroline showed me how to set a fire when I was a little girl. Not much bigger than you, Eric."

"Can you show me how to do it?" he asked.

"Of course. But it will have to be tomorrow."

She sat between them on the dusty couch and they quietly watched the flames. There was something friendly and warming about the bright leaping colours and the crackle and spit of the burning logs.

"We'd better settle down – I know you must be tired, Eric," Nora said, breaking the silence eventually. "You too, Elspeth."

"Tell us a story about when you lived here?" Eric said, yawning.

Elspeth could hear the heaviness in his voice. Sleep wasn't far away.

"Well ..." Nora sighed, as she always did before embarking on any sort of trip down Memory Lane. She normally never got far in her reminiscences before Frank stopped her with his usual, "*You're prattling, Nora*" – a phrase guaranteed to stop her immediately. "Well ..." she began again hesitantly, as though waiting to hear his voice bellowing at her all the way from Australia, "We moved around a lot. It was nice, I suppose. We were like nomads in a way."

"What's a nomad?" Eric asked.

"A traveller," Elspeth said quickly. "Someone who can never settle for long. They need to keep moving all the time."

"Oh!" Eric sounded disappointed, as though nomads should be more exciting than that.

"And we stayed here," Nora continued. "In this house, only once though. I don't think my mother liked it but I thought it was lovely. I was always asking her if we could come again. But we never did. I remember the stables were full of horses and –"

"I like horses," Eric interrupted, another big yawn escaping his lips.

"I know."

"Are there any horses now?"

"Maybe. Perhaps they're in the fields. We can find out tomorrow."

Eric yawned again.

"I think we should just try and go to sleep now – we'll manage just fine here on the couch for tonight."

"There's not enough room, Mum!" Elspeth argued.

"Oh, we'll be all right."

"But we can't lie down!"

"Elspeth, it's just for one night. Stop complaining."

They settled down, Elspeth at one end of the couch, Nora at the other with Eric curled up in the middle. Nora had laid her own coat over Elspeth and pulled the heavy throw on the back of the couch over herself and Eric.

We're just like kittens in a basket, Elspeth thought, defenceless.

Eric fell asleep at once and Elspeth could soon hear her mother snoring gently. She tried to stay awake, to keep watch. She couldn't help but think about the face in the corner.

Was she just seeing things after the long journey?

Chapter 7

"So, who was it then?" Róisín asked. "Do you think it was just your reflection?"

Elspeth shrugged her shoulders. "I'm not sure. But it certainly set the tone. When I look back it was always such an odd house. And that was only the start, really."

"Maybe if there *was* a man there ... maybe he had something to do with Eric's disappearance. Maybe he took him?"

Róisín's eyes were wide now but Elspeth just shook her head. "I don't know, Róisín. None of it makes sense. And I've have tried for so long to just put it all behind me. Live my life. But I can't. I don't know how to. It's like a black cloud just hanging over me, all the time."

"Oh, Elspeth! You really need to do something about this. Talk to someone better than me, perhaps."

Elspeth pulled a face, thinking about Dr Stanley and her orderly office. "Well, I didn't mention it yesterday but I've been to see a therapist. Just before we met for lunch."

"Did it help?"

"She only wants to talk about Eric and my mother. And I think it's best to forget about them and move on. I don't want to be the girl with the missing brother. I just want to be me."

Róisín was about to take a sip of wine but she paused, the glass aloft, her eyes shining in her head. "Elspeth, I've got it! Why don't you come over to New York? Change your job. You can stay with me. It could be a fresh start. What do you think?"

Elspeth looked at her friend, at Róisín's bright smile. Could she leave Crowfield and her mother firmly in the past? Or would she still wake at night, caught in the familiar dream, searching for Eric's hand, trying to hold on and not let go?

"I don't know, Róisín. She's really not well. I managed to get a number for a cleaning lady just last night. There was a notice in the shop in Glenfeale. I'll make an arrangement, ask her to call in a few days a week. I know it's not perfect but it's a start. Once I can get my mother to accept it, that is. But moving away? I don't know if I could do that, not yet."

"I understand – but if you change your mind, you know where to find me."

Elspeth nodded. If only it was that simple, if only she could just walk away.

Chapter 8

"So which season do you prefer then?" Heather asked absentmindedly as they made their way through the village. She knew Adam was nervous about starting school that morning and she was doing her best to keep him chatting. The weekend had passed in a blur of packing-boxes and trying to entertain Patsy, who seemed determined to find endless excuses to "pop by".

Adam was walking by her side, his brand-new schoolbag on his back. He kept pulling at the straps as though it were a parachute and he needed to check the ripcord, just in case.

"What's a season?" Adam asked, his fingers still playing with the buckles.

"Well, summer is a season and that would mean – what?"

"Sunshine and buttercups, dragonflies and ice cream. Sand and wait, no, I don't like dragonflies!" Adam laughed.

"Right, no dragonflies then. What about the ice cream?"

"Yeah, ice cream. With sprinkles!"

"And what about winter? What that would mean?"

"Snow!"

Heather laughed. "And now it's autumn. So, that means –?"

"Ghosts!"

Heather tried to keep the same smile on her face as before. She looked at the ground. A discarded plastic bag was twisting and moving along the wall, following them as though being pulled by an invisible string.

"You do know there's no such thing as –"

"*I see the school!*" Adam shouted.

Heather smiled, relieved. The ghost conversation would have to happen another day. She was sure Cass hadn't meant Adam to believe it so wholeheartedly but he did.

Adam let go of her hand and began to walk a little faster.

She really hoped this school enthusiasm would be a lasting thing and not just for the first morning.

At the school gates, other parents had gathered already. They were smiling and nodding in recognition to each other. Heather felt herself reaching for Adam's hand but he was gone, talking to another boy already, comparing schoolbags and the array of keyrings hanging from Adam's bag.

"And this is a lucky cat's paw," he was explaining. "Don't worry, it's not from a real cat – but it is lucky!"

A woman looked at her and nodded towards the laughing children. There was a general air of lightness, people talking and smiling, children jumping up and down, small backpacks rattling with each movement, friends calling to each other.

"It's going to be OK," Heather whispered quietly to herself, as an older man came out of the building.

Glasses perched low on his nose, he made his way towards the parents and children waiting outside the gates. "*Half-day today, for all new pupils!*" he announced. Then he opened the gates.

Another teacher had appeared from the building and began to shepherd the children inside. The noise began to diminish as the children filtered through the school doors.

Heather waited for a moment, not sure what to do. She couldn't see Adam anymore and he'd forgotten to wave.

As she left, she felt the knot in her stomach release. She'd expected battles and refusals and at the very least Poe would have to travel with them for good luck – but, no, everything had gone smoothly.

Patsy had popped by that morning with an apple from her garden and then proceeded to tell Adam about her first day at school and how one boy had tried to run away because he was afraid of the teacher.

Heather had tried to nod and smile at her before saying, "Oh, look at the time! We'd better get going!" No doubt Adam would ask about that story again tonight.

As she made her way back towards the village, she tried to remember her own first day at school but it was an absent memory. There were no photos that she could remember. There was a framed one of Michelle, her cousin, smiling, neat plaits, pressed pinafore. She did recall that Michelle was meant to keep an eye on her but had studiously ignored her instead. Which, in hindsight, was probably the better option. Would Adam remember his first day?

Cass should have been there. Dispensing words of advice and instructions. Heather had thought of mentioning Cass earlier that morning. She wanted to tell Adam that Cass would have been so proud of him. But as she watched him slowly spoon cereal, she decided that maybe it was for the best to say nothing. Let the past sleep, for now.

As she walked by the one-stop shop, she remembered the ad she'd placed on the noticeboard. Working as a cleaner or babysitter was the only part-time job that would fit around Adam and her online college course. Money was in very short supply after buying the house and it seemed a car-wash wasn't going to revive Elmo. There was a large puddle of oil beneath the engine and the car was refusing to start. Every time she turned the key, the engine made a low wheezing sound and then a click. It might be a simple fix or the engine might be completely seized – she had no idea.

The little shop was empty. Just one girl behind the counter, reading a glossy magazine from the shelf. She glanced at Heather and went back to her article.

Elspeth's ad was still on the noticeboard but no one had made contact, not yet. She checked her phone again, hoping a miracle might occur but there were no messages, no missed calls.

She bought a coffee and walked back out into the bright sunshine. Give it time, she thought, and continued on her slow walk back to the house.

⁂

If the air that morning at the school was lightness and laughter, then the after-lunch air was positively charged with energy. The parents of the newest pupils stood in little knots waiting, anxious but hopeful. This was the first test their children had to pass, alone. The school doors opened and they came spilling out, blurs in uniform, ponytails askew and bags dragging on the ground. But they were happy, for the most part. One or two looked as though they might have been crying but the rest were smiling.

Heather stood to the side, trying to catch a glimpse of Adam. There he was – laughing and talking – no, shouting at a girl, but she was also laughing. He'd passed the test. He was still in one piece. As soon as he caught sight of Heather, he smiled and waved.

He started talking as they passed through the school gates. "And the girl sitting beside me is called Alice and she has a cat. A ginger cat. And he's a boy, called Buddy. She wanted a girl-cat but she doesn't mind now. And did I tell you about the fancy-dress party at Hallowe'en? We can come dressed as vampires or witches on broomsticks. And I drew a witch today in school. She had a cat. A ginger cat! "

"That's nice, a party. That'll be fun," Heather said.

"Yeah, with sweets and a movie. A spooky movie. The one about the headless horseman."

"Well, that sounds fantastic," Heather said uneasily.

"I hate this walk," Adam said, his feet already starting to drag. "When are we going to get Elmo fixed?"

"That might be sooner than I expected," Heather said. "In fact, I don't think I got a chance to tell you about my day. Did I?"

"No." Adam shook his head. "Tell me."

"Well, I was out at Crowfield House."

"Where the crows live?"

Heather nodded.

"Did you bring Poe for a visit?"

"No." Heather laughed. "I was working. I got a job there, with Mrs Collins. She's the lady who lives there. It's a crazy place, big, so big in fact that we could play hide-and-seek forever and never run out of hiding spots."

"Were you helping her with the cleaning?"

"I was. Her daughter, Elspeth, phoned me this morning. Just after you went to school. I have to go twice a week, on a Monday and a Saturday."

"*Wow*, her house must be really dirty!"

"Actually, it does need a bit of work. Some of the rooms are just shut up, though, with sheets covering the furniture. I think the house is way too big for one person. And she might just live in the downstairs bit. Well, that's all I have to clean anyway."

"Does she have a dog or a cat?"

"No, no pets. But she does have a knight, in a suit of armour, just standing all dusty in her hall. Oh, and one of those tall clocks – I can't remember what they're called now."

"Is it real?"

"The knight? Yes, real rust and real dust, even cobwebs and spiders on it!"

"Can I come someday? Please! I'll be really quiet and I won't touch anything. I just want to see it."

"We'll see. I have to go again on Saturday, so maybe."

Adam was quiet, thinking. "What about ghosts? Did you see any?"

"No, Adam. I did not see any ghosts and, look, we're back at the house already and you didn't even notice the walk."

"My feet hurt."

Heather smiled at him. "You did very well. You can go inside and take off your shoes."

"Can we can have spaghetti for dinner?"

"Sure."

"*Yay!*" Adam shouted, pulling off his schoolbag and shoes as soon as he was inside.

He disappeared immediately and Heather knew exactly what he was doing: he would be in his bedroom, telling Poe about his day.

Heather lifted his schoolbag from the floor and went into the kitchen. She didn't really want to take Adam with her on Saturday. Patsy telling her that Crowfield wasn't a place for children had stuck in her mind, although she had no idea why she had warned her off.

Nora Collins, who lived at the house, just seemed like a very ordinary, if forgetful, old woman. When her daughter phoned her about the job, it was only at the very end of the conversation that she discovered it was at Crowfield House. In that moment she had to decide what to do. The regular cleaning job won out over her neighbour's words of warning.

Adam came skidding into the kitchen, his socks sliding on the floor. "Someone is knocking," he said breathlessly.

"Never heard a thing. Will we see who it is?" Heather asked, although she had a good idea who was standing at her door.

She was right. "Patsy. How are you?"

"I'm fine. I just wanted to hear about school. Maybe you're already doing homework, are you?"

"*No homework! Not for weeks and weeks!*" Adam shouted, jumping up and down on the spot. "I gave your apple to the teacher."

Patsy smiled and looked over Adam's head to Heather. "That's great, isn't it? So, you like school then, Adam?"

"Yes, I do!" Adam replied, skipping from foot to foot and then he disappeared, brushing past Heather and sliding down the hall.

He was back in no time, Poe swinging wildly from his hand. "We're going to visit Poe's cousins on Saturday," he announced to Patsy.

"His cousins?"

"The crows!"

Patsy looked at Heather, confused. "Are you going to Crowfield House?"

"Yes. I was offered a part-time job there, cleaning. And I have to go on Saturday so ... " Heather left the sentence unfinished.

"Did Nora call you?"

"No. It was her daughter."

"Elspeth?"

Heather noticed the raised eyebrow but said nothing. Instead she nodded briskly. "Yes. They both seem lovely."

Adam had vanished again back down the hall to his room but she could hear him chanting. "*Spaghetti, spaghetti!*"

"Sorry, I'd better get back to the kitchen," she said. "Finish dinner."

"Of course. I'm delighted he enjoyed his first day. Call over any time and if you ever need any apples, just let me know."

"Thanks, Patsy. Bye."

Heather shut the door after she left and turned the key in it for good measure. She had a feeling that Patsy would probably just "pop in" again later if there was no answer to her knock and the door was open. Maybe she was the reason the house was so cheap, she thought, for a fleeting moment, as she piled the spaghetti into a tall saucepan of boiling water.

Small towns, villages, they were all the same. People liked to talk and make guesses at others' lives. Heather was sure that her own family had been a rich vein of conversation back home. She wondered what Patsy would have made of her mother? Would she have raised an eyebrow and warned people away. *That woman. She tells fortunes you know. A charlatan, taking people's money, a mug's game. Just a con-artist really.*

Heather had heard all the names before, the sly accusations and insults. When she first discovered that Cass worked as fortune-teller, with a travelling circus, she was curious. Cass had always been vague about her job and then Teresa let it slip one day.

Heather asked Cass on her next visit. She remembered her mother looking down at her hands, turning them over and over, as though the answer were written there, somewhere – in invisible ink perhaps. Then she'd looked up at Heather and back to her hands again.

"I don't know why I do this, if I'm completely honest," she said. "I know a lot of people don't believe and I know Teresa thinks I'm crazy. But it's something I see in others. I can take their hands in mine. I can feel what they're feeling, their worries, their pain. And sometimes I hear other voices, telling me about the person. I know none of this makes sense, but I've always been like this. Ever since I was a little girl. I used to have dreams where I was playing with other children. Then sometimes I could see them in the daytime as well. Just a little glimpse. Shadows moving in the background. But I knew they were there. And then I discovered that if I sat really, really, still and listened, I could hear them too."

Cass stopped talking then and looked at up Heather, her eyes bright with tears.

Heather didn't know what to say but she did know what to do. She simply took her mother's hands in hers and hoped that Cass could sense what *she* was feeling.

Adam bounced into the kitchen. "Is the spaghetti ready?" he asked.

"Not yet. You have a little while more to play."

As Heather opened the cupboards, searching for the pasta bowls, she heard a noise, a small musical hum. She'd heard it before. She put the bowls down gently and went out into the corridor to check.

Adam was in his room, his toy cars and figures arranged in a circle around him. He sat in the middle of his play-mat, his face bent down. Heather knew without checking that his eyes were closed.

He was humming softly. It was Cass's song. He knew the words but he never sang them, not anymore. Heather felt tears filling her eyes. She blinked them away and went back to the kitchen.

Chapter 9

"Tell me more about the knight!"

"Well …" Heather stopped walking and tried to think. She hadn't really paid much attention to the suit of armour. She'd only noticed it on her way out after finishing work. Mrs Collins had walked her to the door, talking about how nice the weather had been and what a lovely job Heather had done cleaning the kitchen window. The whole morning had been a bit strange. "I didn't notice too much about it, to be honest."

"Oh, that's all right."

Adam was skipping by her side. He was almost fizzing with excitement at the prospect of seeing a real suit of armour. At least Poe hadn't come along for the visit with them.

"Does the knight have an axe or a spear?"

"What?" Heather was miles away again.

"The knight? Does he have an axe or a spear?"

"Sorry, Adam. I didn't see."

"Oh." Adam was thinking again. "Can I draw a picture of it? I brought my pencil case. It's here in my bag. I want to show the teacher at school."

"I'm sure you can."

They were nearly at the house.

Heather had almost missed the sign when she'd walked out earlier that week. ***Crowfield House***. The letters were painted in bold upward-strokes and it might have been pretty once. But now rust bloomed in patches along the metal edges and orange saw-teeth showed against the white enamel.

Adam stopped for a moment, staring at the sign. He was only just starting to recognise some letters but the writing was old-fashioned, difficult even for her to read.

"What does it say?"

"It says: *a dragon lives here*," Heather replied, with a straight face.

They both laughed and started to walk up the long drive to the house. The many puddles were layered with ancient fallen leaves, making their journey difficult.

Heather picked her steps carefully but Adam bounced along, splashing both his wellies and Heather when she got too close.

"Careful, or it's wet socks for the day," she warned.

"I know."

He ran on ahead and Heather found her steps slowing. The air was becoming dense and heavy. A storm was forecast for later and already she could see black clouds gathering on the spine of the horizon.

Adam was singing as he jumped and skipped ahead.

"*Don't go too far!*" she shouted. "*Wait for me!*"

Adam stopped.

He had come to the gates and she knew that was why he'd stopped, not because she'd shouted but because he was staring at the pillars. She could see him standing with his head to one side, trying to imagine the pillars in an upright position.

"What are you doing?" she said, smiling, though she knew the answer. She had done the very same thing herself on her first visit.

The limestone pillars were enormous. Both were in a sorry state, leaning askew, but one was worse than the other. It looked as though someone had driven into it once and now it lay, forlorn, against the trunk of an ivy-covered tree. The rusted bars of the open gates were barely visible amongst the dense foliage.

Heather had almost turned to go home when she reached that point on Monday. It made the house look abandoned, unlived in, but then something had made her go forward and pass through the rusting gates.

"I'm seeing what it used to look like," Adam answered, tilting his head again. "Maybe there really was a dragon?" he whispered, his eyes growing wider.

"No, I was only joking about the sign."

"But maybe the knight was fighting the dragon and ... " Adam stopped talking and looked towards the house.

They continued to walk until they were in the courtyard and Crowfield House stood before them in all its tattered glory. Adam's face was tilting up higher and higher as he tried to see over the chimney-tops, stretching away into the pale-blue sky.

Heather looked harder this time, trying to see past the neglect, the years, but the age of the house showed plain upon its face and it was nearly impossible to see beyond the ravages of time.

The original building was just a square box with peeling plaster and ivy tendrils creeping across its scared and cracked surface. Over time additions and embellishments had been tacked on to the original building so that now it was a monster. A patchwork Frankenstein of a house, with gaping rusty bars at some of the windows, like rotten teeth, and blank watching panes of glass for eyes.

All the paintwork seemed to be peeling and the black cast-iron downpipes were as rusty as the sign at the road. Lace-patterned holes showed through the pipes, so when it rained water spewed in all directions, leaving green blotched faces growing on the walls.

A water-stained pixie face winked at them from behind one of the gutters.

"*Wow!*" Adam said when he spotted it.

"What do you think? It's a crazy place, isn't it? We could definitely play hide-and-seek here forever. Couldn't we?"

Adam nodded slowly, trying to take it all in. He began to turn slowly in a complete circle, first looking at the house and then the high crumbling walls of the courtyard, a few parts of which were collapsed revealing stone outbuildings and empty stables. Weeds grew waist-high, unchecked, everywhere. Fat pink foxgloves and abundant patches of nettles obscured the stone walls.

It was quiet, almost too quiet, just the crows calling to other from the rookery and the low background hum of bees and insects. There were no other sounds. No road noise managed to break through to the courtyard.

It was like stepping back in time to a forgotten land. In the farthest corner of the courtyard, by a giant pair of curved wooden doors, a car sat, rust-red and forgotten, its windows hazed with green, moss slowly creeping over metal and chrome.

"Are your sure someone lives here?" Adam said to Heather, glancing around him with saucer-eyes.

She nodded and put a hand on his shoulder, gently propelling him towards the front door, which was slightly open. Mrs Collins must have heard them already.

"*Hello!*" Heather called, stopping on the step and peering in.

There was no one there. A thin wedge of sunlight lay across the darkened hall, showing a glimpse of the wide curving staircase to the right. The knight stood watch from his shaded corner, barely visible in the shadows.

They heard footsteps. Both of them stepped back quickly from the open door.

A tall frail woman appeared, her fine grey hair swept upwards in an untidy bun, tiny wisps and tendrils hanging about her lined face like ivy strands, her face as much a ruin as the facade of the house. She raised one hand to shut out the morning sun, blinking as she tried to see who was standing there.

"Can I help you?" she asked politely.

"Yes, it's Heather. I'm the new cleaner. I was here earlier in the week and now I've come back for the Saturday visit."

Nora Collins looked puzzled. A cloud of confusion crossed her face, gathering her forehead into a map of wrinkles.

Heather cleared her throat, buying time, hoping Nora would eventually remember her.

She didn't.

"Your daughter, Elspeth. She made the arrangements. Do you remember?"

"Are the crows here?" Adam asked, looking skywards.

"Elspeth?" the old lady repeated, lifting a hand to her cheek, thinking.

She looked from Heather to Adam and then off into the distance. Her gaze fell upon the limestone pillars. "I ran into one of them years ago," she murmured. "Elspeth wanted to learn to drive and ..."

She stopped talking and looked at Heather again, as though only seeing her now for the first time.

"The new cleaning lady," she said eventually. Then she smiled, a real smile. One that reached her faded blue eyes and made all her wrinkles even more pronounced.

"Yes," said Heather. "That's me."

"You were here on Monday. And this is your little boy. Is that right?"

"This is my brother, Adam."

"Hello. Can I see the knight now?" Adam asked politely.

Both women laughed and Mrs Collins pulled the door open, letting the sunlight spill into the darkness.

They stepped inside. It was like walking into a cave after the morning brightness. Heather could feel Adam's hand searching for her own. She found it and held it tight, giving his fingers a quick squeeze before letting go.

Mrs Collins had gone on ahead, her figure disappearing into the shadows, her long green skirt rustling against the stone flags as she walked, the sound both muffled and strange, a whisper, silk-on-stone.

"Let's go," Heather said, but Adam stayed put.

"Adam, I have to get to work now, please."

Adam shook his head. "No, please," he whispered. "Let's go home. This house is sad."

Heather bent and took both his hands in hers. Mrs Collins was gone and it was just the two of them standing together in hallway. The house was silent, expectant, as though it were listening and had heard Adam's whispered words.

"What do you mean?" she asked.

Adam glanced up from the floor. His hands were sweating in hers. She could feel the heat radiating from him. Even his cheeks were glowing, not a good sign.

"What about the knight?" Heather asked. "It's just over there, look!"

The suit of armour stood in the corner, its rusted spear hanging precariously to one side.

Adam turned his head to look and very slowly took one hand away from Heather and then the other. His face began to look a little more normal, the redness beginning to subside.

"It's just hard to see things in here, after all the sun outside," Heather explained.

Adam took a step away from Heather across the stone flags. "I see him now."

"Oh, and how do you know it's a him? It could be a girl knight."

"Because he has a spear. Look!"

"And can girls not carry spears?"

"No, silly!" Adam laughed. "They're much too small to fight dragons."

"Right, let's get going. You can come and help me fight the dust. But you won't need a spear, a duster is fine."

Adam nodded and they made their way down the wide hallway.

Just like on the previous visit, all the doors were closed. Heather wondered what was in the other rooms – were they empty? Or just shut up with dust-cloths draped on the furniture? The house felt as though it had almost given up. It was nearly ready to be sealed shut forever.

Mrs Collins was in the kitchen. She was sitting at the table with her back to them, her hands folded neatly in her lap. The table was a mess, unwashed plates and dirty cups strewn haphazardly across its surface.

"Perhaps you'd like some tea before you start?" she asked, turning her head slightly towards the door as they came in. "I made a pot this morning. Well, I think I did?" The confusion was back. It flitted quickly across her face and then it disappeared. She looked at Adam. "Now, why don't you sit up here beside me, young man. Tell me your life story."

Heather had to gently push Adam towards the table where he reluctantly pulled out a chair and sat next to Mrs Collins.

"I have biscuits, somewhere," she said, her brows knitting together. She looked around as though expecting someone else to come through the door. "Elspeth? Do you know where we put the biscuits?"

Heather made her way to the table and began to collect the unwashed cups and plates. The ancient kettle was beginning to spit as it came slowly to the boil.

"I'm sure we're fine without biscuits," she said with a smile.

"Yes, of course, thank you –" She paused and looked at Heather questioningly.

"Heather."

"Heather," Mrs Collins repeated.

"We're here to clean," Adam explained.

"Of course. I'm sorry. I don't know where my head is these days. Well, I'm getting old, I suppose. Not like this young man. Now, what age are you?"

Adam opened his mouth to answer.

"No, no," Mrs Collins shushed him. "Don't tell me, I like to guess. I like my little games. Now you're quite tall, so I'm going to say six years old."

"I'm only five and a bit," Adam said, laughing.

"Well, that's close enough, isn't it? There was a time I always guessed correctly."

Heather tried to rinse the cups quietly in the enormous ceramic sink but they bumped against other, making a sharp clinking noise. Mrs Collins looked at her for a moment, that flash of uncertainty back in her eyes again.

The kettle had boiled and Heather made a pot of tea for Mrs Collins. She managed to find a clean cup and saucer in the cupboard and left them beside her on the table, with a teaspoon, before fetching a fresh jug of milk.

She could feel Nora Collins watching her the entire time and she was beginning to regret bringing Adam. She poured the tea and smiled.

"We'd better get down to work, Mrs Collins," she said. "Right, come on, Adam. You're my helper today, aren't you?"

Adam pushed the chair out from the table, awkwardly scraping the wooden legs against the stone as it moved.

Mrs Collins winced at the noise, then she reached out and closed her wrinkled hand over his. "No. Please don't go. Stay. Stay and talk to me."

"But I have to help!"

"I'll show you the knight in the hall and tell you all about him. He's had a wonderful life."

"Is he really a boy?"

"Why, of course he is. Didn't you see his sword when you came in?"

"Is that a sword? I thought it was a spear."

"Did you? Well, let's go and check. Maybe you're right."

Adam stood up and waited for the old woman and they set off together down the long dark hall.

Heather shook her head, hoping Adam wouldn't ask Mrs Collins too many questions. The old woman was clearly lonely and showing obvious signs of dementia but she was sure they'd be fine together for a short while.

She only needed a few hours – the list of cleaning wasn't very long. Perhaps Elspeth simply wanted someone to check on her mother in an unobtrusive way. Still, she decided to clean the morning room first instead of sweeping the kitchen. That way she could keep an eye on both Adam and Mrs Collins. She pulled the ancient hoover out through the hall. As she passed, she glanced up towards the entrance. She could see them both, silhouettes in the shadows, deep in conversation, talking about the knight, most likely.

Heather went into the room and plugged in the hoover. Before switching it on, she quickly went back to the open door and glanced up at the hallway again. They were still talking, but Adam had his schoolbag open now. He was kneeling on the floor in front of the suit of armour and Mrs Collins was waving her arms around, probably telling him the life story she'd promised.

The morning room was thick with dust. There was an open fire and a fine coating of ash lay on every surface. She ran a finger across the mantelpiece and sneezed.

She pulled the heavy armchairs to one side and hoovered beneath them but it still felt like a losing battle.

This was the room that Mrs Collins used most apparently. There was a very old television set in one corner with yellowed switches and a tiny screen. A basket of mending lay beneath one of the armchairs and Heather could picture Mrs Collins, sitting before a blazing fire, her hands busy mending, while the ancient television flickered in the corner.

She thought of Cass and wondered what she would have made of the situation? Cass always seemed able to get to the heart of any problem instinctively. Why was Mrs Collins living here alone? Why was Elspeth so far away? Did she not realise how lonely her mother was? It was an odd arrangement all right.

Heather went back to the open doorway to check on Adam and Mrs Collins but they'd disappeared. His pencil case and open copybook still lay on the floor. Where had they gone? The front door was closed. Had they gone into another room or upstairs? She switched off the hoover and listened.

She could hear footsteps. They were upstairs. Now she could hear Adam talking and Mrs Collins answering back. She began to make her way down the hall. She could hear their voices, getting louder. They were coming back down the stairs. Then she heard something that made her stop abruptly.

Mrs Collins was singing.

Now she could see them, outlined in a small puddle of light which had managed to come through the dusty side windows.

Mrs Collins was by the suit of armour, one hand holding on to her long skirt as though she were dancing in a great hall. She spun in a half-circle, her feet moving automatically in some elaborate step while her thin wavering voice echoed up through the stairwell.

"She stepped away from me, and she moved through the fair and fondly I watched her, move here and move there!"

Adam was as still as the suit of armour, his hands across his chest holding tight to the straps of his schoolbag.

"Adam!" Heather called softly as she began to walk up the hall "Adam, can you come and help me, please?"

He turned his face to Heather. His dark eyes were bright with tears. "She knows the song," he whispered.

Heather was beside him now and she realised Mrs Collins had her eyes closed. She probably wasn't even aware of their presence. She could be anywhere. She might be at a Christmas ball or a summer party, completely lost in her own past.

"I think we should go home now," Heather said, bending down to Adam.

"But you didn't get to finish the cleaning."

"Don't you worry about that. But wait here for just one minute – I left my bag on the kitchen table."

Adam nodded.

"She doesn't understand about the song, Adam. You know that, don't you?"

He nodded again. Tears were threatening to spill over his dark eyelashes.

"She can't even see us. I think she's away in the past. I'll get my bag. I'll be really quick. Don't forget your copybook and pencil case."

Heather took one last look at Mrs Collins. She was still singing to herself and swaying lightly with the tune, her eyes closed and one hand holding her skirt, as though she were stepping through the fair herself.

"*Last night she came to me, my dead love came in, so softly she came that her feet made no din ...*"

Heather held up one finger to Adam, turned and ran back down the hall to the kitchen. By the time she'd retrieved her bag and run back, Mrs Collins had stopped singing.

She was standing, still holding her skirt, looking up through the stairwell.

Adam was by the front door.

"We have to go now. Goodbye, Mrs Collins. I'll try and call next week."

"It's getting lonely here, Elspeth." she replied. "I hear the past all the time and I need help. Time is running out."

Heather didn't bother to correct her. Instead, she simply smiled and bundled Adam out the door.

"But you always say that, Elspeth, and then you never come. You never call."

"I'm sorry, Mrs Collins. We really have to go."

"You think I blame you, don't you? You always have, Elspeth. I know you do."

At that point the old lady was getting upset and Heather knew the best thing was to say nothing in response. It was hard though – she was at the door, watching them.

"Next week, I promise," Heather said and turned to leave.

"No!" Mrs Collins reached forward and gripped Heather tightly by the elbow. "No. Please. I need your help. I don't know how to – I need to –" she stopped talking and closed her eyes.

Heather could see the tears forming and, even with her eyes closed, one managed to escape, a tiny crystal caught against her sparse eyelashes.

"I'm sorry," Heather said again, trying to remove her arm, burningly aware that Adam was watching the entire altercation.

Then Mrs Collins let go abruptly. She opened her eyes, her gaze wandering now towards the limestone piers and the overgrown laneway.

Heather seized the opportunity and, taking Adam by the hand, began to walk away. She didn't look back.

Adam was quiet on the walk home. He hoisted his bag ever higher and higher on his shoulders, pulling awkwardly at the straps.

Heather asked him if he'd managed to draw a picture of the knight fighting his battle.

He shook his head and pulled the straps tighter again.

"We'll cook something really special for dinner. What do you think? How about pizza?"

"I'm not hungry."

"Well, not now of course but when we get back home. We can look in the cupboards and –"

"Why was she singing Cass's song?"

"Well …" Heather drew out the word, buying time, thinking. She was glad he was asking the question but she hated going through it all again.

"When you get sick, like Cass, is that the song you'll sing?" Adam asked, keeping his head down, watching his feet shuffle through the loose gravel on the road.

"No, it's just a song. It was Cass's special song because she loved it and she loved singing. But lots of people know it. I'm sure Mrs Collins was just trying to make you smile by singing a song she liked."

Adam sighed.

She could tell he wasn't happy with the explanation. And, to be honest, neither was she. Why was Mrs Collins singing that bloody song? On Monday she'd seemed fine, no memory gaps, no vague staring into the distance. Of course, Heather knew that people with dementia have good and bad periods and they were simply unfortunate to have been with her for a bad day. But she'd made her mind up.

As soon as Adam fell asleep and there was no chance of him overhearing the conversation, she was going to call Elspeth. Then she was going to explain that she couldn't fit the cleaning into her schedule anymore. That was all she was going to say. There was no point mentioning Mrs Collins' obvious health issues. She had a distinct feeling that Elspeth was well aware of the problem and was busy ignoring it.

Adam didn't even think to complain about the walk home. He remained silent for the rest of the journey. Heather sighed with relief when she unlocked the door and turned to help Adam with his coat and bag.

He shook his head, obstinately. "I can do it," he said, a stubborn crease across his forehead.

"Fine." Heather held up her hands.

Then he stomped off and disappeared into his room.

Heather sighed. It was a tinder-box moment, so she walked away.

In the kitchen she could hear him through the closed door. He was hitting his cars against each other. There was the sound of shouting and pretend explosions. War had descended on his green farm-rug. The plastic cows had probably fallen and there might even be a super-hero or a bad-guy locked in battle, creating havoc.

She could hear the furious banging of the metal cars being bashed together. There would probably be nightmares tonight. Why did that have to happen, Heather thought bitterly. Just when things were beginning to settle down.

She knew there would be tears in a while, and Adam would regret breaking the little world he'd spent hours making. But, for now, it was destruction. There was no point in trying to stop the whirlwind of pain.

***

She'd read as many articles and books as she could stomach after Cass died. Some were beyond ridiculous in their well-meaning advice but others were simple and relatable. They'd been offered grief counselling but she never made the appointments. It felt a little like picking at a scab that would never heal.

Instead, she'd taken her own approach and so had Adam. She lost herself in the self-help books and learning how to be a parent overnight. And Adam had taken to whispering to Poe and carrying a small silver locket that once belonged to Cass. If Heather looked under Adam's pillow, she knew it would be there, waiting for him before he went to sleep.

In the weeks and months afterwards, she'd hung on to some of the words and phrases from the self-help books. The ones she'd understood and the feelings she could see in both their faces.

There will be anger.
There will be pain, a sense of loss.
Try not to deny or bury your feelings.
Time heals.

The last one was the one she put most of her hope into. Time heals. On those nights when Adam was crying in his sleep, she thought of that phrase. She crept into his bed and held him. *Time, we just need time – it will get better*, she would say to herself.

And it had. The sleepless nights were becoming less and less. And though Adam still talked about Cass and asked questions, it was no longer very day now. It was becoming every second or third day, or whenever something happened that reminded him of their past, and that other life they used to have.

Adam pushed the pizza slice around the plate. He picked off some of the pineapple and sweetcorn but that was all he ate.

Heather had no appetite either so she let it go.

"I'm not hungry," he said eventually.

"That's fine. Bath and bed, I guess."

Bedtime was usually a battle of wills but he waited patiently while Heather ran the bath and later got into bed with no arguments. Finally, after reading what seemed like ten stories to him, his eyes began to close.

She lit the nightlight on the locker beside his bed and quietly got to her feet.

"Don't leave till I'm asleep," he whispered, so Heather sat back down and waited.

Adam was only just asleep when she heard a noise. It was coming from outside. She stood up and, as quietly as possible, pulled his blinds open a crack and looked out. A loud bang and then a flash illuminated the trees behind the house and the hills above.

"Fireworks," she muttered to herself. But from where?

She hated fireworks. It was something about their unpredictable nature. The way the wind might take them and throw them back to you. The fact they needed darkness to be effective. And those television ads every autumn had terrified her as a child. Missing fingers, house-fires and once a gruesome close-up of a teenager's face, with an empty eye-socket and an angry red ragged scar.

Then she heard another noise, a gentle thump. Something had fallen in the room. The enormous teddy that sat on the end of his bed might have toppled over.

As another firework screamed, she turned away from the window. It took her eyes a moment to adjust. The teddy was still sitting there, his crumpled face with its glass eye winking at her in the dull glow of the nightlight.

She walked around the bed. Adam was just a tiny mound tucked and twisted into his covers, one toe sticking out.

And then she saw it, on the floor.

She jumped back, not realising what it was for a moment. She looked closer. It was a puppet, a wooden marionette. She could see the strings and the worn wooden holders. She bent down and picked it up. It must have been in the bed with Adam, tucked away beneath the covers.

She gathered up the strings and left the room carrying the toy loosely in one hand. She didn't even like the idea of holding it. It was warm, as though it were alive.

Back in the kitchen, she put the marionette on the table and looked at it more closely. It was ancient, a dreadful-looking thing with a carved wooden head and a shock of unruly black hair. Most of the painted features were faded except for the eyes which opened and closed. They were still a vivid shade of blue, vibrant, watching her now as she lifted one limp arm by the yellowing string. The puppet obliged and waved at her. The sleeve of its threadbare grey suit jacket fell back and she could see the woodworm holes along the wooden wrist. The jacket had probably been fashionable once, with its leather elbow patches and silver buttons.

Where had it come from? Maybe a child in school? Maybe from the school itself? And then in a rush of clarity, it came to her. Mrs Collins – this looked just like something that belonged in that ruin of a house. But when had she given it to Adam? When they were in the hall? No, when they went upstairs. Heather thought of their footsteps above her head and she remembered Adam hoisting his backpack tighter and tighter as they walked home and how he didn't want her to help with it when they came in.

Heather paused for a minute. She was thinking about Poe and how firmly Adam latched on to things. Then she gathered up the ratty, wood-wormy puppet and took it over to the kitchen bin. She stood with the lid open, looking at congealed pizza slices and one dry twisted teabag.

She could stuff the puppet in there and perhaps Adam wouldn't mention it. After all, he didn't tell her about it in the first place. But she couldn't. Adam shouldn't have taken it from Mrs Collins – they'd had the chat a long time ago about accepting gifts – but, no, she couldn't throw it out. She'd have to take it back to Crowfield tomorrow. There was only one small problem. Would Mrs Collins even remember?

Heather took a bin bag from the kitchen drawer and dropped the puppet inside, wrapping the black plastic tightly around it. She put it on the kitchen counter beside the sink. She would worry about it in the morning. Another firework went off and this time Heather could see the colours in the night sky through her kitchen window, blues, reds and sparkling yellows. The shape of the explosion blinded her momentarily and, when she finally went to bed, she could still see it when she closed her eyes.

By then it had turned into a heart, exploding, over and over.

Chapter 10

At first, Heather thought the noise was part of her dream. She'd been dreaming about a little boy. A funny boy with dark eyes, not much bigger than Adam, but he was lost, he needed her help. She could hear him following her. Soft footsteps on wooded ground, a *shush-shush* brushing sound. He was asking her to help him. He was trying to find his way home. *But I can't help*, Heather said. *I don't know who you are. I don't know where you live.*

Then she woke, her head groggy, unsure if she was awake or still dreaming. She opened her eyes slowly, blinking against the bright sun. Hearing a noise in the corridor, she got out of bed and picked up her dressing gown from the floor. Pulling it on, she walked unsteadily to the kitchen, half-asleep.

And there was Adam, balancing precariously on a chair, reaching up to the highest cupboard for his breakfast cereal.

"Adam, wait! I'll get that for you!" Why had she put the box up so high?

"I can do it," Adam replied, trying to reach, his fingertips barely grasping the side of the box.

"Adam, get down! This is not a good idea."

She stepped forward, tying the knot on her dressing gown, and the chair began to tip. She barely managed to catch him as the chair fell, the sound echoing like gunshot.

Neither of them said anything for a moment, then Adam began to laugh.

"You nearly fell, Adam. That's not funny. It's dangerous. Don't ever do that again!" But she knew it was her fault, she was to blame. She shouldn't have put the box on the upper shelf.

"OK," Adam replied, still laughing.

Heather reached up for the box of cereal and put it on the table. It was as though yesterday had never happened. She was glad.

She sat down and he sat across from her, pouring milk into the bowl and trying to listen to the rice popping.

"Did you sleep all right?" she asked, yawning, just for something to say.

"*Mmmm-hmmmm,*" he said though a mouthful of cereal.

"I didn't," Heather said, more to herself than Adam.

She'd been dreaming, which was very unusual for her. But the dream was already beginning to lose its urgency. It was starting to drift away like an early mist, cleared by the sun. It would be fully gone in a few moments, if she didn't try to remember.

"Were you dreaming?" he asked, the words muffled by another mouthful of cereal.

"I was. But I don't really remember it now. That's funny, isn't it? In the dream someone needed my help."

"Oh!" Adam was all wide-eyed at this development. "What did they want you to do?" he asked, the spoon abandoned in the bowl.

Heather cursed herself. She'd forgotten how much importance Cass had placed on dreams and now Adam was more than willing to carry on the tradition.

"I don't know, Adam," she said brightly. "I can't remember and it was just a dream anyway. It really doesn't matter."

Adam was shaking his head vigorously in disagreement and then he stopped and stared, looking over Heather's shoulder.

Heather glanced behind her and saw the bin-bag-wrapped package on the counter. She had forgotten about the puppet. She sighed. She really wasn't looking forward to this particular discussion.

She got up and brought the parcel back to the table.

"You know what's more important than my dream? This." She nodded towards the package as she sat down. "We have a job to do. We have to go to back to Mrs Collins today, don't we?"

She gestured towards the parcel.

"Why?" he asked.

Adam's face was a picture of innocence and for a moment Heather doubted her instincts about making him return the puppet. There was a hole in the plastic and one wooden hand seemed to be battling its way out. She reached across and began to unwrap the layers. "I think you know why," she said, as she pulled the puppet from its package. "Why didn't you tell me?"

He blushed and shook his head, barely mumbling. Heather only caught a few words – "present" and "little boy" ...

"Adam. You know we've talked about this. About accepting presents from people we don't really know."

"*But she wanted me to have it!*"

Heather was silent, waiting for the outburst to subside.

She looked at the puppet. It really was an awful thing. If anything, it looked worse in daylight than in the forgiving darkness of the night before. The painted wood was either flaking off or had worn away completely and the marionette strings were yellowed with either age or dirt, it was hard to tell.

Heather lifted the wooden cross, trying to touch it as little as possible. The puppet obliged by lifting its grubby arms. She shuddered involuntarily. There was something obscene about the way its head bobbed awkwardly and the worn, shiny-at-the-edges suit didn't help matters. It made the puppet look like a down-at-heel salesman. All that was missing was a tiny battered briefcase, containing his wares.

Adam was saying nothing, his brows knitted together, watching the puppet intently.

"*Hello, Adam!*" Heather said in a squeaky voice, making the puppet wave one of its jerky wooden arms towards him in a jaunty salute.

"*Stop it!*" Adam yelled.

"*OK, that is enough,*" Heather said, dropping the marionette carelessly, in a clatter of wood and noise. "That is a time-out." She pointed towards the bedroom.

"No. I don't want to go."

"You know the rules."

"*No!*" Adam whined.

"We don't shout, Adam. You know that."

Adam started to cry then, real tears, burying his head in his arms.

Shit, she thought. Why was this so hard? This wouldn't have happened if Cass were here. What would Cass have done? *Think.*

Heather picked up the puppet and put on the squeaky voice, again, trying harder this time. "*Please don't cry, Adam. She doesn't mean it.*"

"*Stop it!*" Adam shouted, standing up from the table and knocking the chair backwards unto the floor. "*He doesn't sound like that!*"

And then he was gone, and she heard him running down the corridor to his room.

"What the hell was that?" she asked the grubby marionette. "Well, I definitely think it's time we took you home." And she shoved the puppet back inside the bin bag.

⊱⊰

She managed to get Adam dressed, teeth brushed and coat on, without any of the usual silliness but Adam still wasn't talking to Heather as they walked to Crowfield House.

The air felt strange and the world was much too quiet, even for a Sunday. Adam was walking two steps behind and Heather kept turning around to check that he was still following. For some reason she kept thinking he might just run off. There had been rows and arguments before but nothing as strange or out of the blue as this one

She kept mulling through the morning's events in her mind. What could she have done differently?

She opened her mouth to ask Adam about the puppet and then she closed it again. She still didn't know what to say. There had been days like this before. Days of outbursts and silence and all the books and articles had said *wait*, wait and do nothing. Grief was a process, a long one, especially with children.

In the early days, after Cass died, Aunt Teresa had tried to help. She'd insisted on telling Heather what to do and what was for the best. How she was simply too young to manage by herself. That was the prevailing truth in every discussion. Heather was too young to care for Adam alone. She would fail.

But she wanted more for him than the bleak upbringing Teresa had given her and there was no reason why she and Adam couldn't get through this together. She would help him and he would help her. They would have each other and surely that was all they needed?

Some days Heather still believed that was true and then, on other days, days like this one, she knew she was failing. She was letting them both down. She could try to be a family to Adam, but was she enough?

Adam was singing. Heather could hear snatches of words, floating by her like falling leaves.

"*Fighting Fred,*
Has lost his head.
Poor old Fred.
Better off dead!"

Probably some rhyme from school, maybe a skipping-song he'd heard from the older children.

They were nearly at the end of the footpath. The rest of the way to Crowfield House was on the road. It wasn't a busy road, but still …

She stopped and waited for Adam to get closer.

"Are we friends again?" she asked, holding out her hand.

Adam smiled and took her hand. "Course we are."

"I heard you singing a song."

"Was I?"

"Yes, about Fred. He lost his head."

"I don't remember." Adam shrugged.

Then he laughed and they talked for the rest of the walk about normal things, like dinosaurs and school and the different types of leaves that would soon fall from the trees around them.

And then they were at the overgrown entrance to Crowfield House.

"Well, here we are already," Heather said lightly.

She was wondering now if she'd done the right thing in bringing Adam with her. Yes, of course, there were lessons to learn and you should never miss an opportunity to teach a life-lesson, but which version of Mrs Collins was going to be waiting?

They walked up the driveway, Adam two steps behind again. The front door was closed and the house looked more abandoned than the day before.

Adam hung back, his hands on the straps of his backpack. The puppet was inside, still wrapped in the plastic bag.

"Right. Let's do this," Heather said briskly, more to reassure herself than Adam.

She was dreading seeing Mrs Collins again and the effect that returning the puppet might have on her. It could set her off down a rabbit-hole of past memories and turn Heather and Adam into different people again. People that she might be angry or upset with.

Heather stepped up and knocked hard, once, against the door. She could feel tiny slivers of peeling paint brush against her knuckles. Then she stood back and waited.

"What will I say?" Adam began.

"*Shh*, listen. Is she coming?" Heather said, holding up her hand to silence him. "No, it's just the wind. I'll knock again. I don't think her hearing is so great anymore."

Adam nodded slowly. "What will I ...?" he began again, but Heather wasn't listening.

She was knocking, harder this time. Actual flakes of paint fell as she knocked, dusting the doorstep. She waited. But no-one was coming, no footsteps on the floor, no soft brushing of skirts against stone. She wasn't there, there was nobody home.

"Maybe she's gone shopping. Or perhaps her daughter called and took her out for lunch," she muttered. Yes, that was probably what had happened.

Heather had already called Elspeth the night before to tell her she couldn't continue with the cleaning, but only got to leave a message. Perhaps she heard the message and came down to check on her mother. Yes, that was the most likely thing. Elspeth had called for her and now they were in a hotel together somewhere, a fancy place, one with cloth napkins and a log fire burning in the background. It sounded like a nice way to spend time on this crisp autumn day.

Heather looked at Adam, his small face closed off and his knuckles white from holding onto his schoolbag straps.

"We can leave the puppet here. On the doorstep," Heather suggested. Adam shook his head.

She bent down to talk to him. "Adam, Mrs Collins isn't here. Now, I've knocked a few times, and there's no one home. What else can we do?"

"We can call another day."

"But you're back at school tomorrow. Maybe it's easier to leave the puppet here. I'm sure it'll be safe, propped against the door. It's not raining and she'll be back soon." Heather smiled and waved her hand towards the doorway. She resisted the urge to bend down and pat the ground – that might just be a step too far.

"Don't be silly," Adam said, his eyebrows creasing.

"Why?"

"Walter doesn't like the cold."

"Oh." Heather straightened up. This wasn't working and now the puppet even had a name. Perhaps Adam was getting too old for this. Maybe she needed a different tactic. "Right, this is what we're going to do, Adam. We're going to leave the puppet here, on the step. I'll phone Mrs Collins later and explain."

Adam shook his head. "*No.*"

"Well, what would you like to do?" Heather asked, regretting the words as soon as they came out of her mouth.

"I want to take him home and we call another day."

Heather shook her head, looking around, thinking, trying to find some inspiration in the desolate overgrown courtyard. She could see that he was on the verge of another meltdown. There had been too many rows lately.

"Fine, let's do that then but only on condition we bring it back as soon as we can."

Adam nodded and loosened his death-grip on the bag straps. "Can we go home now? I'm hungry."

"Sure, let's go."

Heather turned back to have one last look at the house. Earlier, she'd felt as though someone was watching. A hidden pair of eyes, upstairs perhaps. Maybe Mrs Collins was at a window, watching them and wondering who they were. Still, it didn't matter, the decision was made.

Heather followed Adam out through the lopsided pillars.

He was singing again, the rhyme about Fred, who had lost his head and was better off dead.

Chapter 11

Dr Stanley was busy writing in her notepad, but this time Elspeth knew what to expect so she just sat very still and ignored the copious notetaking. What could she have to write about already? It had only been three weeks since the last visit.

She looked up as though she'd only just noticed Elspeth in the room. "Elspeth, I'm so glad you came back. Tell me how you're getting on with the new medication."

Elspeth shifted awkwardly in her chair. "Well, I'm not sleeping anymore."

"And you were able to sleep before I changed the tablets?"

"Yes, no problem. The old ones always worked."

"*Hmmm* ... that's funny," Dr Stanley replied quickly, one eyebrow raised.

"Why?"

"I didn't change anything. They're the very same, just a different brand."

Elspeth was speechless for a moment. She almost didn't trust herself to speak. "Why would you do that?" she asked eventually, her voice unsteady.

"It was a hunch." The doctor shrugged. "I really don't think you need any of those tablets, Elspeth. And you've just proved this."

"But I'm still not sleeping," Elspeth argued, trying to keep her emotions in check. This was not the place to lose your temper.

Dr Stanley nodded somewhat sympathetically. "I see, well, I can change them back to your usual brand if you prefer. But we have to look at the underlying issues involved and then we can wean you off them."

"This all sounds very easy." But Elspeth knew in her heart that it wouldn't work. She'd tried so many times before to cut down on the dosage and it always seemed to end the same way, with long sleepless nights, where the ghosts of Crowfield held court in her mind. No, the deep drugged sleep was what she needed and, even then, the awful nightmare of reliving that night managed to break through.

"Oh, you know better than that, Elspeth – this will be hard."

Elspeth was taken aback. "I know it will be hard. I just meant it sounds like an easy fix. How do you know it'll work?"

"I had a patient with very similar circumstances before, a past trauma, sleeping issues, practically identical."

"And did it work out?"

"Yes, it worked out fine in the end. So, would you like to continue talking to me about your family? Or is there anything else you'd prefer to discuss?"

"Well, I did call to see my mother." She was thinking of the worn red slippers and the quiet dining room, the accusation, knowing for sure that her mother did blame her. She wasn't imagining that. It was a fact.

"Very good. Were you able to ask her about Eric?"

"I tried but I think she may have dementia. She was getting very confused."

"She lives alone?"

"Yes. I need to do something about that."

"Well, the first step is getting a diagnosis. Is she managing on her own?"

"If you call sitting at the fire and staring into space managing, then she's fine."

"Elspeth, I think you may need to deal with this quite urgently. From what you say, it's not safe for her to be alone."

"I've already made some arrangements. There's a local woman calling to check on her regularly and I'll phone her doctor later, get the wheels in motion."

Dr Stanley nodded. That seemed to satisfy her. She went back to her notes.

Elspeth leaned back against the plastic chair. She was thinking about her father now – "getting the wheels in motion" had been a great favourite of his. She was wondering now where he was buried. She knew he'd died some years before. The news had come to her in a strange way, through a chance meeting with an old work colleague. At the time she pretended to know all about his death and the friend just shook his head sadly and mumbled about what a pity it was.

The doctor seemed more concerned about Nora than anything else. It worried Elspeth that the cleaning woman had only managed two days before quitting. God knows what her mother had said or done to scare her off. It was the always the same with any help she tried to organise. Nora took it as a personal slight and sent them packing. She never wanted anyone in the house, not even Elspeth. Despite the fact she asked her to stay, she knew she wasn't really welcome. Nora wanted to be alone, always. That way she could pretend. She could tell herself that Eric was just outside, collecting apples in the orchard perhaps. She wanted her world paused forever so she could keep the house in stasis – a shrine to the past, a past where Eric still played and laughed and roamed around the grounds of Crowfield.

Elspeth looked up. The doctor was speaking to her.

"Sorry, I didn't catch that?"

"Yes, I was just saying that I'll send the new prescription on and if you're still having difficulties sleeping let me know." She looked at her notepad. "So – I'd like to clarify a few things from our last session."

Chapter 12

It was getting close again, the last Friday of the month. The day she must visit her mother. The dread feeling was already building in her stomach. She glanced at the clock. It was nearly lunchtime and she'd spent the morning reading and rereading tenancy contracts. The words kept shifting on the screen before her, blurring into meaningless lines and squiggles. She couldn't concentrate.

Her mother had been on her mind since the night before. She hadn't talked to Nora in almost a month and she knew there was no point in phoning because she never answered. As far as Nora was concerned, if someone really wanted to talk to you, they would call in person, not by phone.

Her desk phone rang and she answered it without thinking, on autopilot, the words automatic.

"Elspeth speaking, how can I help?"

A shadow fell over her. It was Geraldine, her manager. Elspeth hadn't even noticed her coming into the office.

Geraldine remained silent, waiting for Elspeth to finish the call.

Eventually Elspeth put the receiver down and smiled at her.

"Hi, Geraldine, what can I do for you?"

"Sorry, Elspeth, would you mind coming with me please." Geraldine gestured towards the corridor and walked away.

Elspeth followed, feeling the dread return in a stronger wave than before.

"Is everything all right?" she asked.

Geraldine said nothing, just continued walking, making her way towards the big conference room at the end.

Elspeth could see them already through the open door, the ominous blue of their uniforms. One of the gardaí turned to look in her direction. She was young, younger than Elspeth and all of a sudden Elspeth felt very, very, old.

She stepped into the room and Geraldine said she would give them a moment, then left, closing the door softly as she went.

Elspeth knew why they were there. They didn't really have to explain anything, their faces said it all. She sat down heavily as the younger woman began to talk.

"Elspeth. We spoke earlier to Dr Lacy from Glenfeale. We're so sorry for calling to you at work but it's about your mother. I'm afraid it's not good news. I'm afraid she's gone."

Elspeth heard her voice replying as though from another room, trying to finish sentences early, trying to get through the conversation as quickly as possible. She'd thought about this eventuality more and more, especially after her last visit and the increasingly hard to ignore signs of dementia.

What would Dr Stanley say? She'd promised her that she'd phone Dr Lacy and get an assessment for Nora and now it was too late. She'd long known her mother's time was measured and that time was getting shorter but, even still, to hear the words, to hear the garda say that she was gone. It was a shock.

Her mind was racing, thinking of the steps ahead. She listened to her own voice, speaking calmly.

"I understand ... Thank you, no ..."

And then she was walking with them out of the conference room and they were leaving, saying their goodbyes, and she was assuring them that she was all right and that she would make her way home now.

And then she was alone, in the corridor, thinking of the duty visits, the hotels and restaurants they'd visited and Nora, twisting and turning awkwardly in her chair, trying to check the time, worrying, always worrying that she was away from the house too long.

"*It's getting late, Elspeth.*"

"*We should be getting back.*"

"*It's getting dark.*"

Why are you in such a rush, Elspeth always wanted to ask. She wanted to see her mother squirm and turn away from her. It was cruel and yet she couldn't help herself: "*We've plenty of time. There's no rush, is there? What are we rushing back to?*"

And then she'd wait to see if she would say his name, but she never did. So Elspeth sat, tight-faced, hard, holding her nerve while watching her mother flounder and fuss, until eventually she'd give in, smiling and magnanimous.

"*Yes, of course we'll go back. I understand.*"

"*I'm getting old,*" Nora used to say, as though that made any difference.

And Elspeth would harden her heart and think, no, that makes no difference at all. You were never there for me. You always pushed me away. Why should I care? And then eventually, smiling, she'd help her mother into her coat and take her home to Crowfield, that ancient mausoleum she liked to call home.

And now she was free, finally. If she didn't want to, she'd never have to set foot inside Crowfield again. She didn't know whether to laugh or cry.

She walked the short distance to Geraldine's office and began to explain what had happened, how her mother had died suddenly. She started to tell her about the postman and a note about a parcel and how a few days later the note was still there and then he'd tried knocking, before realising the door wasn't locked and then ...

Elspeth stopped at this point. She could see the look of shock register on Geraldine's face and she didn't know if she should continue or not, but she had to. She had to finish the story.

"So he went into the house, the postman, and he found her. She was in the library and ..." What was her mother doing in the library? Was she searching for a book to read or ... She closed her eyes and continued. "So Dr Lacy, my mother's GP, went to the house. There'll be an autopsy. Just as a matter of form, nothing sinister. Heart attack, most likely, she thinks."

Geraldine said nothing for a moment.

Elspeth waited, one hand on the chair in front of her. The large corner office suddenly seemed very small.

Geraldine stood up and went to Elspeth, gently taking her arm. "That must have been such a shock. Are you sure you're all right?"

Elspeth nodded hesitantly.

"Please, let me call you a taxi. Would you like someone to accompany you? Brenda, perhaps?"

"No, no, it's fine. I'm fine. It wasn't unexpected – but, it's just ..."

Geraldine nodded sympathetically. "I understand, Elspeth. But, please, go home. I'll arrange that taxi now."

"Yes, thank you, I will go home. That's a good idea."

"And please take as long as you need."

Elspeth nodded and walked back to her desk. She turned off her computer, collected her bag and left.

⁓⁓⁓

Hours later, flowers arrived at her apartment. Geraldine had wasted no time. She took the bouquet of white roses from the delivery man wordlessly. There was a tiny card attached.

We are all thinking of you at this most difficult time. Please take as long as you need. Geraldine.

Elspeth thought of her colleagues. Were they really thinking of her? Would they even notice her absence? Someone else would answer her emails and deal with the phone queries. There would still be lunches and nights out, life would continue.

She placed the flowers on her coffee table, their heavy scent perfuming the air. It was a funeral smell, one of death. There was no arguing with the facts. Nora was dead and Elspeth would have to return to Crowfield.

She tried to recall her mother's face and the last time they'd been together. They'd gone for dinner to that big hotel, the one with the enormous dining room and Nora had forgotten to change her shoes. Elspeth could still picture the worn velvet slippers and the smallest twinge of guilt entered her heart. She'd known that evening as she was driving away that her mother shouldn't be on her own. She knew deep down anything was possible. Nora could get lost, or set fire to the house, or forget who she was – but that hadn't stopped her driving away.

And why was that? It was because of what she'd said, wasn't it?

Elspeth felt her lips tighten in that same hard line, the very same reaction she'd had that evening. She knew her mother always blamed her in some way for Eric's disappearance but to finally hear her say it out loud, to her face as well, not knowing who she was. That hurt. To have her suspicions confirmed after so many years.

That night, she'd said nothing in response. She just told her mother she needed to go to the bathroom. There, in the safety of that clean, white space, she ran the tap and pressed the dryer button – listening to the vibrating, humming noise it made and instead hearing rain-sounds.

⁂

Rain had fallen continuously that summer. She could remember the squelching feeling of mud as her feet got bogged down on the path. She could hear Eric running behind as best he could – trying to catch up, his feet refusing to cooperate. He was slipping and sliding over to one side and then pulling himself upright. Then he was gone from sight and the memory shut off, as it always did. That was the last time she could remember seeing him.

On that fateful night Nora had managed to pull Elspeth from the rain-swollen river but not him. He was gone and never seen again. But why had her mother thought it was her fault?

Chapter 13

The sound of children playing always made Heather smile. There was something about their high-pitched screams and laughter that managed to block out all her other troubles, for a short while at least. She tried to pick Adam out of a dozen other children, bobbles on hats dancing as they ran, chasing each other through the playground.

A teacher appeared. Not much older than Heather, she had a woollen hat on as well, jammed tight on her head. She carried a heavy brass bell and began to swing it in measured languid movements as she called them in. Slowly they began to file inside and Heather could hear birdsong again. The world was quiet once more.

Heather looked around. She was alone. All the other parents had left. Now she had a job to do. She had to get rid of the puppet.

※

She hated him and hated what he had done to Adam. He was becoming more and more attached to Walter with every passing week. She had noticed that Adam's farm was no longer in action. The toy cars and figures had been pushed under the bed, forgotten. Even Poe sat abandoned in the sitting room, his glossy feathers gathering dust.

Adam seemed to spend all his time curled up with the puppet – giggling and telling stories to it. At least Poe had a gleam of intelligence in his beady eyes, unlike the flat dead countenance of Walter.

At night, Heather consulted her books and articles and, yes, it was very common for children to become overly attached to an object following a loss. But why now? It had been over a year since Cass died and he'd seemed to be doing so much better. But all progress seemed to have gone backwards in the last few weeks. And the nightmares had returned as well. Heather had been pulled from sleep too many nights now. She could hear him crying and begging in his dreams. It sounded as though he were pleading with someone.

She remembered this from the first weeks after Cass died, the tears in his sleep, his arms lifted high, as though trying to hug an invisible being. She'd taken to sleeping in the bed with him as it was then easier to turn and comfort him, while she wondered was it Cass, was she there, had she come to say goodbye?

But these dreams were different than before. They always seemed to start not long after Adam fell asleep. She could hear him, talking, crying, as though he were trying to reason with someone. Sometimes she caught snatches of words in between the gibberish but, when she went to his room to check, he was always fast asleep with the ratty, worn puppet lying beside him on the pillow.

She hated the puppet and some nights her hand hovered above it. She wanted to snatch it away, but also for some bizarre reason she didn't want to touch it. She was on dangerous ground and she knew it. It's just a toy, she told herself, just an old wooden toy. But it sat there, taunting her, Pinocchio-like, just waiting for the magic dust.

The only question now was how to get rid of Walter without upsetting Adam. Heather had been running through possible scenarios in her head. He could get "lost" or Mrs Collins could ask for him back as she missed the puppet. Or she could just try and ride it out, hoping the interest in the puppet would wane and they could just drop the toy back eventually with no rows or fuss.

That had been the first option after the unsuccessful trip to Crowfield. A few days with Walter and then they would call back to Mrs Collins. But Heather hadn't wanted a repeat of the first visit. She wanted to ensure Mrs Collins or Elspeth was there when they called so she could hand over the wretched thing and walk away without a backward glance.

She wished she hadn't deleted Elspeth's number off her phone but she managed to find a phone number for Mrs Collins in the big old phone directory in the library. She tried calling it after Adam went to bed but every night the phone just rang and rang, not even giving her a chance to leave a message. Heather imagined it ringing in the morning room, shrill and relentless. She was certain the phone would be outdated, a heavy old-fashioned thing sitting on a doily-covered table, most likely. She thought of the dusty closed-in room with its old-fashioned wallpaper and groups of paintings, murky watercolours and faded pictures of thin-necked ponies.

Maybe Mrs Collins was gone to stay with her daughter? Maybe she'd gone into a care home?

Nearly three weeks had passed since their last visit and Heather knew that Adam was convinced Walter belonged to him now, forever.

❦

She turned away from the school and began the short walk back to her house. Although it was a perfect day, with bright autumn sunshine and a washed-out blue sky, she felt heavy inside. She knew Walter was sitting on Adam's bed, waiting, just where he'd left him before going to school. She'd eavesdropped on the whispered conversation between them.

"Now, you be a good boy today, and don't miss me too much. I have to go to school because it's really important but we can play later. I promise. Then we'll have a whole weekend together."

Back at the house, she went into the kitchen and got a bin bag and some tape. She felt guilty already, as though she were about to commit a terrible crime. She glanced through the windows, wondering if Patsy was at home or in her shop. She tore a sheet from one of Adam's copybooks and sat at the table. Then after thinking for a minute, she scribbled out a short note.

In Adam's room she bent down and, using the black bag as a glove, she lifted the puppet from the bed. It felt heavier than she remembered, the joints limp and boneless in her arms. Working quickly, she tucked the folded note into the breast pocket of the suit, sticking out on top. Then she took a deep breath and twisted the plastic rapidly around Walter as though fearful he might try to wriggle free. The parcel looked like it contained a badly mangled little corpse, odd angles and strange lumps protruding from the bag, but Heather didn't care. She was starting to feel better now that she couldn't see Walter's painted eyes anymore. Finally, she threw the toy into her college rucksack and left the house.

⚜ ⚜

Heather was nearly through the village. There was only one shop left to pass on the way out to Crowfield, the old-fashioned sweet shop. Patsy's sweet shop.

Sweets and Ices. The writing was dirty-white on a faded brown sign. Heather had only gone to the shop once to visit Patsy, not long after they moved in. Adam asked for an ice cream but it turned out the ice-cream machine was broken and possibly had been since the nineteenth century, Heather guessed. But, otherwise, it was a proper old-style sweet shop, with glass jars behind the counter and a kidney-shaped silver scale, all covered in a fine layer of sugar dust.

Adam hadn't cared about the lack of ice cream on offer and instead spent ages deliberating over which sweets to pick from the coloured jars, before eventually declaring it to be the best shop ever.

Heather had just smiled at both Patsy and Adam and then on the way home she told him that too many sweets were bad for your teeth so they could only have sweets as a special treat and, so far, she'd stuck to her word. Patsy would get just a bit too involved in their life otherwise.

Heather put her head down and started walking faster. She was getting dangerously close to the shop now.

The door opened and Patsy stepped out with a broom and began to sweep the step. Heather didn't slow her pace. She had no intention of stopping.

"Lovely morning, Patsy!" she called.

"Yes, it is, isn't it?" Patsy replied, putting the brush aside, getting ready for a chat. "It's perfect weather for a walk."

"Oh, no walk for me – I have to call and see Mrs Collins about something."

Patsy looked confused. "Mrs Collins?"

"Yes!" Heather gave a little wave as she kept on walking.

"Oh God, haven't you heard?"

There was something in Patsy's voice that made the hairs stand on the back of Heather's neck. She turned around, feeling the weight of Walter shift within the rucksack.

"Heard what?"

"About Mrs Collins?"

"What about her? What's happened? I've not been to the house in a while. "

"You'll have to come into the shop," Patsy said, pursing her lips. "I can't just tell you here on the street. Come on in and I'll get you some sweets for Adam as well."

"But what's happened – just tell me," Heather tried to protest but Patsy already had her by the elbow and was pulling her awkwardly into the dimly lit shop.

"Such a sad thing though, such a shock," Patsy said, shaking her head. "It was the postman."

For a wild moment, Heather thought she meant the postman had done something terrible to Mrs Collins.

Patsy was now pouring apple drops in a noisy waterfall onto the kidney scale. "She never got much post, you know. Maybe once a week or a fortnight." Her voice had become lower and she was clearly determined to spin a good tale. "But anyway, there was a note he'd left, about collecting a package. She'd never answered the door, nothing strange there of course. Think she was quite deaf. But then he called this morning and the note was still there in the letter-box. So he kept on knocking, no answer, but ... " She paused, glancing around the tiny shop. "He tried the door and it was open, so he went in ... "

The last part was almost inaudible and Heather looked around to see if perhaps someone else had come in, but they were still alone.

"And there she was ..." Another dramatic pause. "Dead. In the library, at the front. You know the house, don't you? Apparently it's just inside the door. Never set foot in the place myself."

"Oh, poor Mrs Collins!" Heather said, thinking of her cornflower-blue eyes and the way she'd lifted her skirts so elegantly as she danced in the hallway.

"Massive heart attack apparently, maybe a stroke, not sure yet. But no one knows how long she was there. Elspeth comes and goes." Patsy shook her head, as though it didn't bear thinking about. "Oh, but what about you? When were you last there?"

"Not since that Saturday – after Adam started school – a few weeks ago."

"Did Adam go with you?"

"Yes, and it was fine and Mrs Collins was fine too," Heather lied, thinking of her swaying in the hall, holding on to the hem of her skirt.

"You know what that means though, don't you? That means you're probably the last person to have seen her alive, you and Adam."

"Do you really think so? Surely, in all that time, someone must have called. What about her daughter – or the postman?"

Patsy shook her head before handing the sweets to Heather. "You should go on up to the house. The Guards are there still, I hear. Are you all right, Heather? You look a bit pale."

"Yeah, I'm fine."

"Sorry to be the one to tell you. Terrible old house, though, probably for the best that she's gone."

Heather found herself nodding in agreement, even though she had no idea what Patsy was talking about and why the house was so terrible.

"Thanks for the sweets," she said, backing away towards the door.

Then she was safely on the street again, the ringing bell echoing behind her. She could feel the weight of Walter inside the bag – one tiny wooden hand was poking her in the back, as though he were marching her at gunpoint, back to the scene of the crime. She took off the rucksack and gave it a shake, dislodging the puppet, and then she tucked the sweets inside.

She felt sad about Mrs Collins, dying alone in that strange house, but it didn't change her plans. She thought again about the Sunday morning visit with Adam. Was Mrs Collins alive then? Could things have been different? But how was she to know? No, this changed nothing. In fact, it probably made it easier. Now, she could walk out to Crowfield and leave Walter there with a clear conscience, without upsetting Mrs Collins. She was only taking him home after all.

At Crowfield, the courtyard was deserted, but the front door was ajar. Heather paused for a moment. She didn't really want to have to talk to anyone. Then she heard footsteps and for a moment she imagined it was Nora Collins – swaying her way down the hall, her skirts brushing against the stone. Heather stepped back from the door as it opened wide.

"Can I help you?" A tall garda stood in the doorway.

"Yes, sorry, I-I ..." Heather stammered. "I have this for Mrs Collins. Well, Elspeth, I guess now." She thrust the package at him.

"Certainly, I'll pass it on. If you'd like to leave a name and contact number?"

"They're with the package – I mean, there's a note inside."

"Of course, but I'll just take your details as well."

Heather nodded and the garda took her name and number. He told her they would be touch if they needed any more information and then he walked off down the hall with Walter tucked safely under his arm.

What now, she wondered, as she walked back home. What would happen to Walter and the house? She guessed it all belonged to Elspeth, the mystery daughter. What was it that Mrs Collins had said before, when she was dancing? Something about hearing the past and asking Elspeth for help.

Later that afternoon, as Heather waited outside the school, she ran through the list of excuses in her head. She knew Adam was going to ask where Walter was and she wanted to be ready. Top of the list was that Mrs Collins had asked for him back. She knew, of course, it would result in tears and the fallout would be immense but it was the simplest reason. They couldn't go back and reclaim the toy if Mrs Collins had requested its return.

Heather ran through her story again. She had no intention of telling Adam that Mrs Collins had died, he really didn't need to know yet – losing Walter would be bad enough for the moment. But she was so terrible at lying – it was not something that was hardwired into her brain.

A distant bell rang somewhere, deep within the walls of the school. She glanced around at the other parents, grouped together, smiling, talking. A few others stood apart from the rest.

The children were coming out now, in little knots and clusters, just like the parents. Birds of a feather, Heather thought for a moment, and then she could see Adam. His fringe falling over his eyes, wearing an animated smile as he talked to the boy walking beside him.

He caught her eye and waved.

As they began the walk home, she was happy to let him chatter on. He was busy telling her about his day and the games they'd played at lunch time. How the teacher had left the classroom to take a call and then one of the boys had run around her desk for a dare.

But Heather wasn't really listening, her mind on what would happen when they got to the house. Lately, as soon as they came in, he ran off to his room straight away, not even stopping, just peeling off his coat and discarding it on the floor before skipping down to his room. Once there he would stay hidden, shut in until dinner time and after, if Heather allowed, just talking and whispering to Walter, his wood-wormy friend.

Heather plastered a smile on her face as she turned the key in the door. "*Home sweet home!*" she sang.

Adam laughed, dropped his schoolbag and began to barrel his way across the room, shrugging his shoulders out of his jacket as he ran.

"*Oh, wait, Adam! I have a bit of news!*" Heather shouted at his retreating back. "*Completely forgot till now!*" She quickly followed him.

Adam burst out of his room. "Where's Walter? Is he playing hide and seek?"

"No, he's not. Why don't you come into the kitchen and –"

"*Why? What have you done with Walter?*"

"Me, nothing. He's safe, but he had to go home."

"*Home?*"

"To Crowfield."

"But you said he could stay until –"

"Yes, I know what I said," Heather interrupted. "But Mrs Collins wanted him back."

Adam looked at Heather, his eyes narrowing, as though he knew she was lying but didn't want to call her out on it.

Heather looked away from Adam and concentrated on picking up his abandoned jacket from the floor. "She called earlier when you were at school and asked me to bring him home."

"But she said he was for me!" Adam argued, his voice beginning to rise.

Heather knew the tears weren't far away and she was starting to feel guilt. She had caused this – no, wait, she corrected herself, Mrs Collins and her foolish generosity had caused this. She looked at Adam, waiting for the inevitable explosion but he said nothing and that was worse. His heart was breaking.

He turned away and walked back into his room, shutting the door gently.

And that was it, no tantrums, no tears or shouts, none of what Heather expected to happen occurred.

He didn't mention Walter again that evening.

And later that night she could hear him talking in his sleep. She could make out two words, two names repeated, over and over. *Walter* and *Eric*.

Chapter 14

As the day wore on Elspeth felt as though she'd stepped onto the escalator of a well-oiled machine. Death, like many other things in life, followed a set protocol. Decisions were made for her. She was just a player in a rehearsal, where everyone else knew their lines. No-one noticed that she wasn't really participating. They said their words, nodded in sympathy, then pushed her on to the next stage. It was like a gruesome board game with no winners.

It began with the gardaí informing her of Nora's death at work, followed by a call from Dr Lacey. Then just as she was wondering if it was too early to open a bottle of wine, another call, this time from the local coroner's office telling her that there would be a post mortem, due to the sudden nature of Nora's death.

Elspeth knew this already as Dr Lacy had explained it earlier. Apparently, it was a matter of formality, a suspected heart attack, but it must be confirmed. The doctor had also advised contacting a local undertaker as the body would be released within days.

"Thank you," Elspeth said repeatedly during these calls and others. These seemed to be the only words required in most interactions.

Elspeth looked up a list of undertakers, her actions mechanical, robotic. She needed to keep moving. If she stopped, then she started thinking. She called the first one on the list and the phone was answered within moments. The undertaker was sympathetic, helpful, as he ran through another barrage of questions.

"Her final wishes?" he asked.

Elspeth racked her head. What would her final wishes be? To have more time? To have Eric with her instead of Elspeth.

The undertaker, a soft-spoken man named John Cullen, cleared his throat. "As in, where would she like to be buried?"

"Oh, *em* –"

"Perhaps with your father?" John suggested quietly.

"No, he's not … I mean …"

"I'm so sorry. I didn't realise he was still alive."

"No, sorry, he's not alive. But they were separated and …" She couldn't bring herself to tell this stranger that she'd no idea where her father was. "He's buried with his other family," she said eventually, assuming that much to be true. She knew he'd remarried and there were stepchildren but beyond that her relationship with her father had faded to nothing. After Eric disappeared, he stayed away, permanently. It was as though he couldn't bear to see Nora or Elspeth anymore.

"I understand," the undertaker continued. "We can discuss this tomorrow, if you wish. I can call over to the house. Crowfield House, is that correct?"

Elspeth could hear him rustling through papers as he spoke, ascertaining the correct name before he said it.

"I'm not there," she replied, panic escaping into her voice. "Do I have to be there?"

"No, we can meet here, at our office. Let me give you directions."

Elspeth heard herself thanking him as she scribbled down notes on the back of the condolence card from her workplace.

"Ten o'clock is fine, perfect, of course. Thank you again."

As soon as she got off the phone, she had to restrain herself from calling the quiet-voiced undertaker back and telling him to go ahead with the whole charade without her. Was she really needed? What part did she have to play in any of this? It was all a lie and everyone knew that. All she had to do was pay the bill – that was where her responsibility ended. But she couldn't do it. She knew she would have to see it through, to the bitter, bitter end.

⁂

Dawn was breaking when she left the city early the following morning. She had spent hours on the phone the night before with Róisín. Her friend had done most of the talking. She seemed to know all the right words to say and, for some time after, Elspeth had almost felt at peace with her mother's death. Róisín wasn't able to get time off to come back to Ireland for the funeral but Elspeth understood.

It was all so sudden, so unexpected, she wasn't sure how she was going to manage. She hadn't even got as far as the city outskirts and already she felt weighed down with what she had to do. At least there were no other family relations or long-lost cousins to be informed. They'd always been isolated, hidden away. Even as a young girl, she'd noticed it. She didn't belong, not in the village nor in Crowfield. She definitely didn't belong there, though it was her home as Nora was so fond of reminding her.

And now it belonged to her alone. She didn't want to think about the house but she couldn't help it. She'd hated it and always had. There were so many things to dislike. The perpetually dark corners and heavy moth-eaten brocade curtains. Nothing about the house pleased her, even the name annoyed her. What really needed to happen to Crowfield was a fire. As a teenager she'd often daydreamed about the whole rotten building going up in flames. It was a satisfying notion. Then they could go away and live somewhere normal.

Perhaps, if the house had been sold, like her father had wanted at the very beginning, things would be different. Eric might still be with her. He could be sitting beside her now. She wouldn't be alone.

❧ ❧

John Cullen, the undertaker, was waiting patiently. A tall, thin man in a sober grey suit. He looked exactly as she imagined he would. A perfect go-between, a human bridge between the living and the dead.

"Please take a seat," he said.

Elspeth noted the strategically placed box of tissues in front of her. She sat down and pushed the box to one side. If John noticed, he said nothing.

"So, there are a number of different packages available," he said in a quite business-like tone, before sliding some glossy sheets across the desk.

Elspeth took them in her hands and pretended to flick through them. He can see through me, she thought angrily. He knew that she was not the usual heartbroken mourner. She wished she could suddenly turn on the tears, just to throw him off, but that was a gift she never possessed. Her mother could do it in a heartbeat. Crying at will, that's what she called it. A strange power to possess or use but it served a purpose. All those people, they had such pity for Nora after Eric disappeared. All they saw was the grieving mother, lost in a vale of tears. No one noticed Elspeth.

She glanced quickly through the sheets before her. "I think the second option looks lovely. My mother always loved lilies."

"And you are happy with the casket? You can make changes, of course."

"No. It all seems perfect."

"And would you like a private viewing?"

"Of the casket?"

"No, sorry, of ..." He lost his poise for a moment. "Of the ... of your mother."

Elspeth had known what he'd meant but she had to sting him back, just for the way he'd obviously made assumptions about her lack of grief.

"Yes, better check it's her. Not a bad idea."

Now he looked really taken aback. "No, I meant ..."

"Sorry, black humour. We all have our ways of dealing with grief, I guess. Dr Lacy already certified it was my mother. She thinks it was natural causes, heart attack."

John nodded. "So – what arrangements will I make for the removal?"

"No. No removal. Just the funeral."

Now she had shaken his composure again.

"Very well," he said.

"So, what happens now?" Elspeth asked.

"I'll make all the necessary arrangements and then I'll be in touch."

Elspeth nodded and reached into her bag. "I'll pay you now, if that's all right. One less thing to remember."

And, although he protested slightly, he took the cheque. She watched as he slid it into a drawer and closed it gently.

She reached forward and plucked a tissue from the box.

"Thank you again," she said and smiled.

Elspeth made her way out to the car. Once inside, safe from the world, she closed her eyes. It had been hard, much harder than she'd imagined.

The only thing that had got her through was watching the undertaker squirm. Now there was only one more job to do.

❧❧❧❧❧ ❧❧❧❧❧

She could see the rusted sign through the branches, lopsided and worn, the letters barely visible: *Crowfield House.*

It had pulled her back, of course.

Elspeth turned in through the leaning pillars and drove carefully over the bumpy gravel. She could hear the rasp of overgrown grass against the underside of her car.

Then, as she reached the courtyard, she stopped dead. A shaft of sunlight had suddenly broken through the clouds and like a search beacon it pointed to the heart of the problem – a yellow spotlight, trained on one of the upstairs windows – Eric's bedroom window.

Elspeth looked at the glass, squinting against the evening sunset. For a brief moment she almost expected to see a face or a hand, just a glimpse, but there was nothing there, nothing but shadows.

She turned off the engine and opened the car door. She listened. The once familiar sounds came back to her, the wind in the trees behind the house and the chattering complaints from the rooks and the crows. The rookery, which gave the house its name, stood farther away, on a small hill to the right.

She hadn't set foot in that wood for years and now she wanted to go there. She stepped out and closed the car door in one quick move without thinking about how unsuitable her shoes were.

She pushed open the side-gate at the corner of the house – like everything else it was rusting away and almost fell apart at her touch. She stood there – trying to see the pathway to the rookery but it was completely overgrown. No-one had been this way in years. She began to pick her steps carefully. She could see the tall lines of trees ahead, their shadows stretching like creeping fingers toward the house.

She walked up the slight incline, hugging herself against the wind. It was exposed to the elements here. Why the crows had chosen this godforsaken spot to build, she didn't know, but they'd been here since forever. They'd made their nests of stick and branch long before the house was built and they would probably still be there long after Crowfield House had fallen as well.

She stepped into the ragged circle of trees. Once inside the noise became deafening, overwhelming, with crows taking flight and moving above the canopy in widening arcs. She listened to the branches cracking beneath her feet, all the discarded and broken nests which littered the ground. It was an eerie place but also strangely peaceful despite the noise and fury of the birds. No one had probably been here since her time – *their* time, she corrected in her head. Her and Eric's time. It had been one of their spots. They had so many different places back then, but this was one of his favourites. He was the animal lover, not her. He'd found an encyclopaedia in the library and read the entire section about the corvid family. Then he regurgitated all he could remember, their documented intelligence and how they passed on information from generation to generation.

He'd wanted a pet jackdaw. That was one of the reasons they spent so much time there. He used to hope a fledgling might fall from a nest. Then he could rescue it, tame it, and eventually train the bird to sit on his shoulder, like a poor man's parrot.

Imagine if I could teach him to talk.

Elspeth closed her eyes and allowed the memory to fill her up. It was summer and Eric was beside her, talking, talking always talking. He was telling her his plans, what he was going to call the jackdaw, he was going to call it …

She opened her eyes and looked straight up through the trees, through the dark spiral cobweb of branches and haphazard nests. The sky was dark overhead, too dark. She couldn't pretend it was summer anymore and Eric wasn't two steps away.

She couldn't remember what he was going to call the jackdaw and some days she found it hard to even picture his face. It was all beginning to fade. And now she was the only one left.

She stood within the trees – hearing the bird's angry calls, knowing that in the background there was a shadow, a small flickering shadow, her brother.

She tried again and again to recollect his face. She could see his brown eyes, the sprinkling of freckles across his nose. The way his face went so very white when he was angry. She could see his dark hair, falling into his eyes and his hand pushing it away again and again without pause. But she couldn't put the full picture together.

He was still just a shadow. He'd spent so long shut away, in that box in Elspeth's head, that he'd lost all colour. She couldn't remember the exact shape of his face or his hands. She couldn't recall what his voice sounded like, his laugh. It was all smoke and greyness. And now that she opened the box of memories, she began to cry.

She'd cried of course when he first disappeared but there'd always been that tiny flicker of hope – a small candle burning in a windswept tunnel. Every passing day threatened to blow out the flame but it stayed lit.

They'd never found a body. Despite the search teams and their dogs and all the men and women who'd showed up every day, grim-faced in their determination. An army of volunteers, bolstered with long sticks, poking their way slowly through the bogs and the woods, through the rain-sodden fields but it was as though Eric had simply vanished. A magic trick, the disappearing boy.

Against the odds the tiny flame of hope stayed lit. Perhaps he hadn't fallen into the river that night. Perhaps he was still alive, just lost, in the woods, perhaps.

Her mother took to placing candles in the windows. A ritual Elspeth always associated with Christmas Eve but now it became a sad and lonely thing to do. In her mind she could hear the sound of matches, as Nora went from room to room, lighting them carefully.

It was as though Eric was out there somewhere in the fields playing. He'd just lost track of time, as all eight-year-old boys do. And soon he would look up, push the dark hair off his face and see the far-off flickering illuminations. Soon, he would remember it was time to come home.

Except he didn't. Eventually, the search was called off and the trail, if there had ever been one, went cold. And then it was just Elspeth and her mother, rattling around in the empty house and before long they could no longer occupy the same space.

If Elspeth was in the library and her mother came in, then she would go to her bedroom. Then her mother began spending her days in Eric's room. She sat, vacant-eyed, on the bed, her hands in her lap, saying nothing and seeing nothing, especially her daughter.

Then one morning Nora announced that her father had managed to get her a place at St Catherine's, a boarding school for girls. And Elspeth remembered feeling nothing but relief at the thought of escaping from Crowfield and the engulfing memories it contained. Then she would only have to return for Christmas and the summer holidays.

She knew that was when she first started shutting her life away. Eric was first into a box. She pretended she didn't have a brother when she started school. She didn't want to talk about it. She wanted to talk to Róisín about nail-polish and eyeliner, music and boys. She didn't want to be known as "the girl with the missing brother" and so, even though it felt disloyal and wrong, she started to forget about Eric.

Sometimes, at night, when she couldn't sleep, when the sleeping tablets failed, she carefully unwrapped the box and slowly peeled back all the layers. Then she'd let herself think about him, not on the day he disappeared though, no – she thought about him talking and smiling, playing with her in the fields or at the back of the house, clapping his hands and laughing as the crows rose as one, an angry black cloud, their protesting cries drowning out the sound of their laughter.

Sometimes, she could smile along with the memory. Then other times it was too hard and she would have to shut the box closed as quickly as she'd opened it. Her mother wrote letters, occasionally, mainly about the weather and trivial things. Elspeth read them carefully, looking for hidden messages, searching for signs that were never there. It almost felt as though she'd disappeared as well, that her mother had lost two children. Although Elspeth was certain she never sat on her bed, while she was away, staring into space.

Christmas and summer holidays were just time together that had to be endured. There was no point in putting up a tree or decorations anymore. Instead, they sat, wordlessly, before the television, while Christmas Specials played, people in paper hats blowing streamers and telling silly jokes. They sat together, completely alone, their faces bathed in the shimmering, flickering blue light from the ancient television.

Chapter 15

Adam was still asleep. Heather took the chance to creep down the hall and watch him for a few moments, his face shadowed by the teddy now sitting by his pillow. He turned to one side, muttering, talking to someone in his dream and Heather stepped back quickly out of sight but he didn't waken and she was glad, he needed to sleep. The dark circles beneath his eyes were beginning to look like bruises. He never seemed to get much sleep anymore. He was always restless, calling out in his dreams, every night.

Heather pulled the door closed quietly and went into the kitchen. She poured herself a glass of milk and sat down. She knew if she looked in a mirror she would see the same tell-tale purple marks under her own eyes. Adam wasn't the only one having trouble sleeping.

It all began and ended with Nora Collins and that bloody puppet. Heather thought she'd seen the back of it when she'd left it at Crowfield. She remembered the overwhelming feeling of relief as she handed over the parcel. Walter was someone else's problem. But her plan didn't work.

She could hear Adam stirring, he would be awake soon. Heather had to do something. She knew that much. She had a vague idea, one that was forming slowly in her mind. She discounted it, time and again, but it wouldn't go away. She needed help and there was only one person she could ask. The one person who had ever cared.

Adam came, yawning, into the kitchen. "Hi," he mumbled.

"Morning. I'll get your breakfast."

He tucked himself in at the table.

"At least it's Friday," she said.

He nodded as though that was the least of his worries.

"Would you like a treat after school?" she asked. "Maybe we could go to Patsy's shop and you can get some sweets."

He shrugged and Heather felt her heart sink. This was even worse than she realised.

*

As soon as she dropped him off at the school gates, she made her way back out through the village to Patsy's shop. She pushed the door open and Patsy shouted from the back as soon as she heard the bell.

"*Sorry!*" she called. "*I'm just about to close! Can you come back in an hour?*"

"*Oh, no problem! I'll call later!*" Heather answered and was just about to leave when Patsy poked her head through, to see who it was.

"It's you," Patsy said, coming into the shop. "But I thought you'd be heading there as well."

"Where?"

"To the funeral, of course. They released the body during the week."

"Funeral?"

"Mrs Collins, that poor woman. She's being buried today."

"I didn't realise," Heather said. "Is it here in the village?"

"Yes, at St Luke's. It's on in ten minutes. Do you want to come with me?"

"Sure." Heather nodded. Of course she must go.

"Just give me a minute. I need to get my coat."

"OK."

Heather waited outside on the pavement. She could just about hear the children, their voices, shrill-sharp in the clear air. Was Adam playing with the others? Or was he sitting, like he did at home – curled into a small ball, his face hidden against his knees. He hadn't seemed as withdrawn after Cass died but of course she mightn't have noticed then.

"Well, are you ready?" Patsy was at the door, pulling herself into a bobbled grey coat.

Heather nodded, grateful for the interruption to her thoughts.

Patsy kept up an endless stream of conversation as they walked, telling Heather who lived where, pointing out different houses and commenting on their gardening skills or lack of. It was easy to nod and smile and simply ignore what she was saying.

Heather was wondering who would be at the funeral. The mystery daughter, of course. Perhaps she would be able to talk to Elspeth, explains the situation and ask for Walter back?

Heather felt a sharp poke in her side.

"Are you away with the fairies?"

"Sorry?"

"I was saying we're here."

"Yes, of course." Heather looked around.

They were in the grounds of a tiny church. She'd passed it before on the walks out to Crowfield and thought how pretty it was.

Following Patsy's lead, she went through a heavy wooden door.

Patsy paused for a minute inside, scanning the notice-board, pulling a face as she did. "Nothing new," she said eventually. "Right, come on so. Look, sure there's nobody here."

She was right, the church was almost empty, just a few scattered mourners, dotted about like chess-pieces. And one solitary woman, sitting stiffly, at the very front, close to the altar.

Patsy, a seasoned funeral attendee, nudged Heather and pushed her into a seat halfway up the church. Heather had shown signs of making her way further up to the top.

Patsy blessed herself and knelt forward to pray. Heather sat in her seat, feeling like an imposter at a party, wondering if the woman at the front was Elspeth. All she could see was the back of her head. Her fair hair was twisted up into some sort of an elaborate topknot.

A man in a black overcoat came into the church and was quickly absorbed by the shadows on the other side.

Patsy sat back up on the seat. "That's Elspeth." she whispered, nodding towards the woman at the front.

"Do you know her?" Heather asked.

"Not really, she's a lot younger than me. Of course, she was sent packing off to boarding school after all that business."

Heather frowned. She always seemed to be on the back foot with Patsy who was constantly imparting bits of information piecemeal, as though Heather knew everything already.

Patsy looked at her strangely. "Her brother that disappeared. I thought you knew all about that. Remember I told you to stay away from Crowfield."

Now she was staring at Heather in the half-light as though seeing her for the first time, her eyes shining. For a moment Heather thought she was crying and then realised that wasn't right. It was excitement in Patsy's face – her eyes were almost glittering.

Another clutch of women and a small stooped man came in through the heavy door.

Patsy nudged her. "I'll tell you after. I thought you knew all about it. Why do you think I kept warning you about Crowfield? Oh, he's here." She nodded, elbowing Heather and gesturing towards the priest who had finally made an appearance on the altar.

There was something very wrong about the way Patsy licked her lips before telling you anything, thought Heather, as though sucking the very marrow out the piece of gossip she was about to impart. Heather felt grimy just sitting next to her.

She moved away, slightly to the left. She realised this wasn't the time to ask Elspeth about Walter. It would have to wait.

Chapter 16

Elspeth had never been inside St Luke's church before. She glanced around, trying not to look at the polished coffin poised before the altar. She'd met the undertakers earlier that morning and John Cullen had already explained what to expect. There seemed to be a lot of waiting around involved, so she took her seat in the front row as directed and waited.

She watched the candles flickering in the dull light, throwing shadows of pain against the serene face of the Virgin Mary within her alcove. One expired and a thin grey plume rose stiffly above its blackened wick. She brushed a stray strand of white thread off her black skirt. But, try as she might not to look, her gaze was drawn again and again to the coffin. The one she'd chosen from the catalogue.

It was still early and, as far as Elspeth could make out, she was the only mourner. Behind her rows and rows of seats lay empty. The morning light reflected from their gleaming, polished sides. It was like being inside the belly of long-dead creature. Polished wood, like blackened ribs curved away into the white ceiling overhead and slotted neatly into upright corners. The wooden floor gleamed under countless coats of wax and the smell of incense and lilies hung heavy across the altar. Like a curtain, a veil, concealing, denying the presence of death.

Her eyes were pulled back to the coffin. An artfully arranged spray of lilies sat at the base – a frothy sea of white petals, rising like crested waves before a narrow fishing boat. These flowers were from Elspeth, organised by John, the undertaker. There was also a slim wreath of roses perched atop the coffin and she knew these were from Róisín. At least someone was thinking of her this morning.

The vestry door creaked open and the priest appeared. Glancing quickly over his spectacles, he stepped onto the altar. It might well have been the smallest congregation he'd ever witnessed but, if it was, he showed no sign of surprise.

Elspeth stood, her head thumping, as she gripped the wooden rail in front of her. She was afraid of falling, that the long sleepless nights would take their toll. She sat, then lifted her head slowly and looked directly at the priest – hoping he could read her face, hoping that he had dealt with enough human emotion in his life to understand she was tired and just wanted an ending. She needed it to be over. She hadn't wanted a wake or a removal – the funeral was going to be hard enough.

The priest began to pray and she let her mind drift, barely listening, knowing that he was praying for her mother's soul, but she couldn't concentrate. She was thinking about Eric again and where he lay. Because they'd never found a body there had been no funeral. No goodbye prayers or scented flowers, no chance to grieve openly, no. Instead, there had been whispers in the village and the shops whenever she'd ventured there, until she stopped going. It became too hard to ignore what they were saying.

The priest was praying again and it seemed as though she'd missed something, some cue. She looked around and could see some people in the seats behind. She wasn't the only mourner. A hush descended on the church. The priest was silent, his head bowed low. Then, after a moment, he walked down to the coffin.

Elspeth closed her eyes as the smell of incense filled her nose, choking its way into her lungs.

It was almost over. The priest walked down to her and took her hand between his. His hands were swollen, grotesque, but his face was kind. He was saying something to her, soft and unintelligible words of condolence, while patting her hand gently as though reassuring a shy, wild-eyed child. And Elspeth realised with a shock, *that's all I am, I've never changed, not really. I'm still a fourteen-year-old girl whose brother disappeared.*

"I'll leave you be now," he said, letting go of her hand.

She watched him walk away. The firm set of his shoulders. The beautiful swish of funeral robes as he retreated to the vestry.

Unsure of what to do next, she stood. Her feet unsteady, her eyes fixed firmly on the shining surface of the coffin, she stepped out into the aisle, uncertain.

John, the undertaker, appeared within moments and took her elbow.

Outside, a weak sun was pushing bravely through the clouds and throwing bursts of colour like paper flowers through the stained-glass windows over the altar.

"We never had a funeral for Eric," she said.

"Eric?"

"My brother."

"I'm so sorry, I didn't realise."

Don't lie, Elspeth felt like shouting, *of course you knew about Eric*. But she remained silent – still watching her mother's coffin, the way the light reflected off the shining brass handles.

"I only moved here a few years ago," John said in a low voice. "I'm so sorry about your brother."

"Me too," Elspeth whispered to herself, regretting her impulse to mention his name. "So, what happens now?" she asked, glancing back towards the small knot of mourners waiting at the back of the church.

"As you have chosen cremation, we'll take your mother's remains to the crematorium. It's normally a very short service. You don't have to attend. And I will contact you as soon as your mother's ashes are ready."

Elspeth was standing by the coffin now, her hand outstretched, but she couldn't bring herself to touch the wood. She didn't want to leave a mark on the polished surface.

"I might not go," she said, her voice barely audible.

"I understand."

No, you really don't. Elspeth felt the words, hot in her mouth, ready to be spat out, but again she said nothing. Behind her she could hear voices, low, just a murmur.

"They'll want to pass on their condolences," John said, nodding towards the small group of people who were now standing in the aisle with an air of expectation. "To pay their respects."

Elspeth nodded. It hadn't occurred to her that her mother had people she knew in the village – surely just nodding acquaintances? Nora had always preferred her own company. Why had they come?

"Perhaps if you take a seat?" John gestured towards the front pew.

Elspeth turned, her face burning a little. She felt like a creature on display, an object of curiosity.

As she sat down, John beckoned discreetly to the group then stepped back towards the coffin, to allow the macabre dance to start.

The first was an older woman with her hair pulled severely off her face.

"I'm so sorry about your mother," she said as she took Elspeth's hand, her lips compressing into a thin line. "Such a lovely woman."

Elspeth nodded in acknowledgement.

Then she was gone and the next person stepped forward, a man this time, with a pronounced stoop. She thought she recognised him. Had he done some gardening work for Nora? He said nothing, just took her hand for a moment, nodding his head. And then he left, just as quickly as the tight-lipped woman.

Elspeth continued to take people's hands and listen to their words of sympathy. She looked at their faces, wondering who they were and what relationship they had to her mother. One of the women was young, only in her early twenties with a head of unruly black curls. She somehow looked as out of place in the church as Elspeth felt. She took her hand and leaned gently towards her.

"I'm so sorry," she whispered as though she had done something terrible and needed to apologise.

"Thank you," Elspeth replied.

There was only one man left, a tall man in a black overcoat. He had been holding back, as though he had been waiting purposely, as if he wanted to be the last person there. Now he stepped forward.

Elspeth looked up and she recognised him immediately. The years had not changed him at all. She automatically reached forward to shake his hand and, although his hand was warm and steady in hers, she wanted to pull away. It was as though she had been given a tiny electric shock of remembrance.

Detective Martin O'Neill stood before her. He was the first person she knew in the church, the first person with a familiar name.

"Elspeth," he said. "I was so sorry to hear about Nora."

"Thank you, Detective."

"Not detective anymore. It's just Martin now. I took early retirement a few years ago."

Elspeth nodded. In the background she could see John fussing with the floral arrangement on her mother's coffin. He was trying to catch her eye.

"I think the undertaker needs me," she said, nodding towards the coffin.

Martin nodded. "If you ever want to talk, I can give you my number," he said. "No pressure, just as old friends."

Elspeth paused for a second before answering. "Yes, thank you."

Martin reached inside his overcoat and took out a plain white card.

"Sorry for intruding," John said. "I just wondered what you'd like to do with the wreaths. Some people like to leave them on another grave. A relative perhaps."

She reached out and took the wreaths. "John, I've changed my mind. I will go to the crematorium," she said firmly.

He nodded without question.

"I'll just be a moment though."

And she made her way through the sun-lit door. She wondered if they were all still outside, talking, comparing notes perhaps, but there was no one there. Martin was the only one she could see. He was making his way through the adjacent cemetery. He was visiting a grave.

Elspeth stepped back into the shadows of the porch and waited for a moment, watching him. He stopped at a tall headstone with an ornate cross but he only stayed a moment, reaching down to right an ornament that had fallen over. And then he was gone, lengthening his stride as he walked away.

She knew that grave though she had only visited it a few times when they first came from Australia. It was the Enright family grave where Harry was buried. But why would Martin be visiting it?

She came out of the shadows, shielding her eyes against the unseasonably bright sun and walked across the concrete kerbs and gravel-covered graves till she reached the one with the ornate cross. The letters were barely legible, the name Enright covered in white swirls of lichen. But there was something different about the familiar grave, a new addition, a small heart-shaped headstone positioned to one side of the tall cross. She had never seen it before.

Still holding the wreaths, she leaned down to read the inscription.

In memory of my son
Eric Collins
All the darkness in the world
Cannot extinguish the light of a single candle

Her legs almost gave way and she stumbled forward against the headstone. It was as though she were drowning. She could hear a screaming sound, wind in the trees, a storm and the incessant sound of water, voices crying, her own voice calling – *Come on, come on!*

And then she was in the quiet sun-filled graveyard, holding the wreaths of flowers. She never knew her mother had chosen to erect a marker for Eric. It was something she never mentioned, not even in passing.

Elspeth bent down and placed the wreaths carefully beside the heart-shaped headstone. There were other objects scattered there. A tiny snow-globe with a house inside, a plastic light with a cracked lid and a weathered wreath of silk flowers. It looked as though no one had been tending to the grave for quite a while.

***

Elspeth knew what she had to do as she drove behind the black hearse. It was no coincidence that Martin O'Neill had come to her mother's funeral. Perhaps the time had come to meet him, to try and put the facts together. Her mind freewheeled in circles. Again and again she tried to bring her thoughts back to the present day but she couldn't.

It was 1994 and it was raining, a summer of rain, but that might not be true. It just felt as though it rained all summer. What other things were lies? What other things had her mother decided not to mention? Elspeth always knew that *truth* was a slippery word when it came to her mother. Often, she lied by omission or twisted things and places ever so slightly so there was no certain ground.

Her brother Eric had disappeared. That was a fact. He was eight years old, another fact. And her mother had always laid the blame on Elspeth's shoulders.

The hearse in front slowed down. They had arrived at the crematorium.

Chapter 17

As Heather made her way toward the school her head was spinning. She wished Patsy hadn't waited for her in the graveyard to tell her the sad story of Crowfield, but she had, of course. Patsy was never going to miss an opportunity like that to spread her stories.

Heather cursed herself inwardly. She should have just kept going instead of allowing Patsy to corner her. But as soon as she came out of the church Patsy pounced, appearing from behind a tall weathered headstone. She'd waved and Heather felt she had no option but to wave back.

"Tiny little woman, isn't she? She's never changed, not from when she first came here," she began, riffling through her coat pockets before withdrawing a crumpled bag of bull's-eyes from an inside pocket. Then she'd offered the bag to Heather who'd shook her head.

"Funerals make me nervous," Patsy had explained before popping a sticky-looking sweet into her mouth, then she clutched Heather tightly by the arm as though she needed close contact to tell the story.

They were nearly out of the graveyard when Patsy paused and looked back, pointing at a tall ornate cross. "Oh, of course, I should have shown you the headstone. That would have been the best place to start. Now, he's not buried there, they never found him. Sometimes, I wonder if he's still alive. Sorry, I'm putting the cart before the horse. I'll start at the beginning, well, the beginning of what I know. So the place was a bit of a wreck, to be honest, when the family arrived. They just appeared one day out of the blue. Old Harry was dead a few years by then and we wondered if the house would be sold. He never had any children. There were rumours, of course, but he never married. So, no one expected anyone to turn up but there she was, very glamorous back in the day. Course the years weren't kind to her and what with losing Eric and –"

"*Eric?*" Heather interrupted.

"Yes, she had two children, Elspeth, the little lady there, back in the church, and Eric. The boy who disappeared."

"*Eric!*" Heather breathed to herself. The name she was hearing Adam whisper every night. What had Mrs Collins told him that day in Crowfield?

"Well," continued Patsy, "they arrived at the start of the summer, you know. They threw open that musty old house and she appeared in the village, driving around in Harry's old car. Complete wreck of a thing, moss on the windows, rust everywhere. We all realised quick enough she didn't have a penny to her name and that she must be running from something. So, there they are. All three of them, stuck in that rotten old house, and then Nora leaves. Goes out for the night, apparently."

Patsy's voice had got lower at this point and Heather found herself reluctantly leaning in to catch the words.

"Left those two children alone, in that rattle-bag house. And then there was a storm, a summer storm that came out of nowhere. One of the worst I've ever seen and they went out in it. Some people say she'd locked them out of the house. Punishment or some such. But I don't think so. Turned out she was over at the big hotel looking for a job. Still, those two children went out into the woods behind that house, in the rain and the lightning. Something drove them out, that's what I think."

By then they had reached the shop and Patsy was fishing through her pockets for the keys. She produced the crumpled bag of sweets and handed them to Heather. "You take them," she said with a small wink. "For Adam."

"So, what happened then?" Heather was surprised at her own interest. "What happened to the children?"

"Nobody knows," Patsy shrugged, turning her key in the lock. "Mrs Collins came home. Found all the doors and windows open in the house, footsteps leading into the woods ... "

Heather was waiting, listening intently, hanging on her every word. Patsy smiled and Heather knew this was exactly what she wanted – drama, she knew how to spin a story, you had to give her that.

Patsy leaned forward, pulling her key from the lock, and put one foot inside the door then she leaned back towards Elspeth. She glanced around her and began to whisper furtively. "She found Elspeth, half-drowned by the river in the woods. No sign of Eric, though – gone, like a little puff of smoke ... *pfft!*"

"And they never found him?"

"Nope." Patsy straightened herself up. "Sorry, I have to get back to work. But it was nice to talk to you, Heather. Say hello to Adam. Don't forget to give him those sweets."

And with that, in she went and pulled the door closed and left Heather standing on the street, holding the warm and crumpled bag of sticky bull's-eyes.

Quickly, she turned on her heel and began to retrace her steps. She stuffed the sweets into her pocket and hurried on. She had to see for herself. The graveyard was empty and, as soon as Heather pushed through the heavy double-doors, she was relieved to see the church was empty as well. One fallen lily petal was all that remained of the morning ceremony, their scent still heavy in the air. She went through the side door and followed the path towards the grave with the ornate cross.

The headstone was ancient. She could just about read the name, Enright, which was inscribed in curling letters along the top. There was a newer marker to one side of the cross, a small heart-shaped headstone with much clearer writing. The name in gold lettering stark against the black granite: *Eric Collins.*

So, Patsy wasn't lying or exaggerating or perhaps she was. A boy had disappeared that summer and never been found and now Adam seemed to be dreaming about him every night.

She took one last look around the graveyard. She heard a shout, a child's voice carried from the school, and she knew she had to go if she didn't want to be late for the school pick-up.

They all seemed connected in some way, she thought as she walked to the school. It was like a trail of dominoes falling – one had struck the other and then the next becoming a chain reaction of people and events. For Heather, it began of course with Cass. "*Cass*," Heather whispered her name aloud. Her mouth smiled as she said the soft familiar word. For her it meant home, family, everything she was trying to give Adam. It wasn't perfect, life rarely was, and families often were the hardest puzzle of all. Why do the people who love you cause the most pain? Why indeed?

It was a question she'd always meant to ask Cass but one which had never come up. It was a sad reality that by the time Heather, Cass and Adam were finally living together as a family, Cass was getting ready to say goodbye.

The school-bell was ringing by the time Heather reached the gates. She tucked her hands in her pockets and found the crumpled paper bag containing the sweets. She wondered how much of Patsy's story was true. She looked at the surrounding faces, the other waiting parents. She couldn't ask anyone. They might not even know about Eric.

Adam appeared. Heather looked from his downcast face to the other children. They all seemed to be skipping, hopping, pushing and laughing. Adam looked as though he had the weight of the world on his small shoulders.

"Hi, Adam."

"Hey."

They began the slow walk home. When had it got so bad? Heather couldn't remember the last time she'd heard him laugh. A child's laugh, full of life, the sort of sound that made you smile. She looked at him, his feet slowly dragging through the freshly fallen leaves.

"So, how was school?"

"Fine."

"Did you draw any pictures?"

He shook his head, a tiny barely noticeable movement.

Heather sighed to herself. There was no point talking, so they continued home in silence. The only sound their footsteps, soft and muffled, on the rotting leaves.

Back at the house, Adam shrugged himself out of his coat and bag and disappeared to his room. Heather waited for a moment, making sure he wasn't listening, then she pulled a chair from the kitchen into the corridor and climbed up on it. Then she carefully opened the tiny hatch into the attic and pulled down the folding ladder. She made her way up the creaking treads, trying not to brush against the cobweb-covered sides. The box was exactly where she'd left it. She climbed down awkwardly, carrying the heavy box with her before finally bringing it to her room and hiding it under the tartan blanket.

"Dinner will be ready soon," she called down the corridor. She knew he wouldn't answer. She also knew that if she walked down the corridor and opened the door he would be lying still and straight on his bed – facing the wall, saying nothing.

In the kitchen she busied herself with pots and chopping boards. She was trying to distract her mind, trying not to think about the box in her room. It would have to wait until after Adam fell asleep. She didn't want to run the risk of him seeing it and recognizing the diaries and the Tarot cards. All the paraphernalia that Cass had left behind.

Chapter 18

After the crematorium there was only one place she could go. Home. As she drove slowly, listening to the hedges scrape against her car, she thought, as always, that they needed to be cut back. And then she realised she could phone someone that day and get the work done if she wanted. She no longer had to wait for her mother to think about her suggestions and then politely refuse.

Nora was always wary of any change or any new people working around the house. Her distrust had got worse as the years went by and in the end Elspeth stopped making helpful suggestions and just watched as the house fell further into disrepair. Another box that she'd been glad to close the lid on.

She stopped outside the house and pulled the keys from the ignition. She picked out the key to the house. She remembered her mother giving her the key but the memory was hazy, like so many other memories attached to her mother and Crowfield. She did remember her reluctance as she put it on her keyring – reluctance because of the many implications and the fact it meant responsibility. And that someday her mother would no longer be guardian of the crumbling ruin and Elspeth would inherit it all.

These thoughts flitted quickly through her mind as she stood before the front door. If there ever was a time to stop and leave the past undisturbed, this was it. Her fingers closed around the key and she put it in the lock, turned it and the door swung inwards.

The house lay empty and echoing before her. There would be no turning back now.

For a brief moment she nearly called out, *"Hello, hello, is anybody home?"* But she didn't, afraid that she might get an answer. Fearful that she might even hear footsteps overhead. But the house was silent.

Leaving the door open for light she made her way into the hallway. It was like stepping inside a shaded wood – there was no other light except at the far end. The kitchen door was open but all the other doors were closed. She reached for the light switch but nothing happened. She didn't bother trying it again. If there was one thing she had learned from her childhood at Crowfield, it was not to question anything. A light switch might one work one day and not the next, despite the fact the lightbulb was fine.

Nora always waved away their childhood concerns without really acknowledging them. It's an old house, she'd shrug, what do you expect? So, after a time Elspeth and Eric stopped remarking on the oddities. They became part of their lives.

So when the switch didn't work, Elspeth shrugged in a manner reminiscent of her mother, shut the door and set off down the darkened hall, the oppressive smell of damp already seeping into her nose. It's like swimming through weeds, she thought. She could see the gloomy light at the end but it seemed to be getting farther away, not closer. She stopped and looked back at the front door which by now had closed itself, just another trick of the house. She shrugged again but for some reason she didn't feel quite so confident now. Years of living in normal houses with working electrics and no mystery noises had left their mark.

By now she now knew what normal was, and Crowfield was anything but normal. Still, she accepted it for the childhood home she had known and continued walking. She reached the kitchen and looked back instinctively, knowing that the front door would have opened again and she was right. A bright beam of sunlight lay across the hall.

The kitchen looked the same as ever – the dull green cupboards which seemed to absorb light and a low, yellowing ceiling. This was where she'd died, in this house, sitting at the leather-topped desk in the library. Elspeth was glad it was the postman that had found her mother and not her. She imagined coming in after a long drive on a Friday afternoon, knocking and knocking and eventually making her way inside to find her mother slumped across the desk. No, that was something she would have never wanted to see.

Was that why she'd stayed away? She'd known that her mother was getting frailer and needed more help – and what had been the answer? To bury her head in the sand, of course, and hire a cleaning lady. A fresh set of eyes that could check on her twice a week. A way of postponing the inevitable conversation about care homes and people coming to help her on a daily basis. But none of it mattered now. Her mother was dead and the time for difficult conversations had passed.

Elspeth looked around the room slowly, taking it all in. She could stare at everything now for as long as she wanted without rebuke. It all felt wrong. She was an intruder. She looked around, at the cups and plates on the table, unopened letters, and a badly wrapped parcel.

She walked to the sink and looked out through the tiny square panes into the overgrown garden. Nettles and thistles had overtaken the flowerbeds. She knew she would have to go upstairs at some point but for now the kitchen was quite enough. She filled the tarnished kettle, just for something to do, and then sat down at the table as she waited for it to boil.

She reached forward and began to sift through the letters, normal everyday things, brown and white envelopes with bills inside and bank statements. She put them down and leaned forward to lift up the parcel. It was quite heavy with awkward angles and whoever had wrapped it had done so with no care. It was covered in clear tape with odd lumps and rips in places. Elspeth turned it over in her hands, looking for an address, stamps, any sort of indication as to what was inside. There was nothing on the black plastic – so where had it come from?

The kettle was beginning to boil, steam obscuring the light coming in through the window. She went to the kitchen drawer and pulled it open. It was stiff and heavy, ready to fall apart at the slightest touch. She shook her head as she delved through the mess of cutlery and wooden spools of thread unravelling and catching in the fork tines. Eventually her hand closed upon the scissors and she pulled it out carefully before trying to shut the drawer again. Another dreadful thought dawned upon her as she pushed the drawer fully closed with her hip. The entire house was brimming with stuff, useless, unwanted, broken items. Every cupboard was probably stuffed full. Where was she going to start?

She sat down heavily at the table. The kettle clicked off and silence settled around her like a thick dense fog. I can't do this, she thought as she reached again for the parcel. I need help, maybe a house-clearance company or a fire.

She cut into the black plastic and began to peel back the layers, revealing an electric-blue painted eye and one thin arched eyebrow before pushing the package away. It knocked against an empty cup which in turn slid off the table and fell, smashing into pieces on the stone-flagged floor.

"*Walter!*" Elspeth whispered. The name came to her, like an old friend's, readily and without hesitation. "*Walter,*" she repeated, this time shaking her head in disbelief.

Elspeth didn't want to touch the puppet. She stood and pulled her chair quite a bit away from the table before sitting down again. Walter lay, half-wrapped in his plastic covering, wooden hands crossed over his chest and the same stupid quizzical expression on his face that she remembered from childhood.

Walter! How could she have forgotten about his existence? There was a period when Eric refused to talk to anyone except through the medium of the puppet. God, that had been so tedious! He'd wanted to be a ventriloquist, was that it? Or perhaps he'd just wanted to annoy Nora.

Eric had found Walter upstairs in a wooden packing crate full of junk – old dresses and sunhats, a garden croquet-set pocked with woodworm and then at the very bottom, wrapped in sheets of brittle, faded newspaper, Walter.

Elspeth smiled to herself. It had been a relief when Eric finally came down to breakfast without the puppet draped over his arm.

But where had Walter been? Elspeth tried to remember the last time she'd seen him. He used to sit on Eric's bed. And, at some point, after Nora turned the room into a shrine, Walter had been promoted to sitting tucked in bed like a grotesque Eric replacement.

She remembered first noticing this on the morning she was leaving for boarding school. She was on the landing, waiting for her mother to help with the suitcase and then she'd ventured towards the shrine, thinking Nora must be in there, sitting on the bed, staring into space as usual, but she wasn't.

That was the last time she'd been in Eric's room and she'd only made it as far as the door before a feeling of paralysis had come over her. She'd stayed frozen on the threshold – her eyes scanning the torn pictures and drawings that had been thumb-tacked over the fading, rose-patterned wallpaper.

Their mother had promised their rooms would be painted, as a matter of priority, when they came to the house that summer. At that stage Crowfield was being touted as a holiday home and no longer just a little break to sort out Harry's estate.

So, one day a man from the village arrived with a stepladder tied to the roof of his van. Tall, in paint-splattered clothes, and a shiny bald head, he never even got so much as a brush out of his little van. Instead, he'd wandered from room to room, looking and measuring, while Nora told him her plans and colour schemes, the wallpaper designs she liked. And then they'd gone to the kitchen to discuss the decorating further. Eventually the shiny-headed painter had gone off whistling and never returned.

Elspeth shook her head at the memory. Another piece of the puzzle that was her mother. How many things had she blocked out from her past? How many more memories were hidden, just waiting to be uncovered?

Feeling braver, Elspeth reached forward and pulled some more plastic off Walter. She half-expected him to be wearing an old cut-down pair of Eric's pyjamas but of course he wasn't. He was dressed in the familiar worn grey suit with elbow-patches and crumpled trousers. She pulled him fully out of the package, thinking about his previous resting spot, Eric's bedroom, which was just above her head. She looked upwards almost expecting to hear footsteps or a creaking board but the house remained silent.

There was a piece of paper tucked into the breast-pocket of Walter's jacket. She hesitated for a moment before pulling it out delicately with two fingers.

Dear Mrs Collins
Thank you so much for this thoughtful gift for Adam but he is a bit young for a puppet unfortunately.
Regards
Heather (The Cleaner)

Elspeth folded the paper again and put it back on the table. There was no date and no indication of when her mother had given Walter to the cleaner. What had her mother been thinking?

She remembered the cleaner, Heather, phoning and leaving a message a week after she started, saying she could no longer do the job, how she was sorry that it hadn't worked out. But she had called to Crowfield for two days at least.

Elspeth looked around. The kitchen seemed just as dusty and cobwebby as before, the window was possibly cleaner but that was all. Perhaps this Heather had called just like that shiny-headed painter from years before and merely took tea in the kitchen before leaving on her merry way with Walter under her arm.

There was a sound from upstairs, a tiny creak. Elspeth recognised the noise. The loose floorboard in her mother's room. Another childhood memory, one she really didn't want to think about, so she stood up. It was time to go. The evening was starting to close in and she didn't want to stay at Crowfield any later, not in the dark.

Out in the weed-choked courtyard she paused for a moment before getting into the car. She wanted to look up at the third window from the left, Eric's room. But she was afraid of what might be watching from the shadows, so she got in, closed her car door and drove away.

She glanced in her rear-view mirror when she was safely on the drive, the house behind her lost in the growing darkness.

Chapter 19

Later that night, safe in her own apartment with a glass of wine and the familiar sounds of her neighbours around her, Elspeth let her mind travel back to that summer at Crowfield.

Those early days were just a hazy recollection now. One day seemed to bleed into another and the first weeks were dreamlike, surreal, like one long endless day.

She clearly remembered their very first morning. How when they woke, curled together on the lumpy couch, Crowfield had seemed like a magical forgotten place, where time had stopped. No ticking clocks, no other world existed outside the boundaries of the house. It was the centre of their universe, for now.

The face in the alcove seemed a ridiculous thing to Elspeth in the clear sunshine. She convinced herself that it had been an imagining. Perhaps there was something on the wall that had caught the light and looked like a pair of eyes. Perhaps it had been her own face reflected in the mirror. But she didn't want to check again. She didn't want to recreate that look of fear on Eric's face. No, it was better to just forget about it.

Nora groaned as she tried to move her arm from beneath a still-sleeping Eric. "My arm is dead," she whispered to Elspeth. "I don't want to wake him yet. Look, he's like an angel, isn't he?"

Elspeth failed to see the comparison. Eric was just a grubby, dirt-stained boy, with a gappy smile and freckles sprinkled across his face.

Nora cautiously pulled her arm free. "You stay here with him. I'm going to see if there is any food in the kitchen."

She extracted herself carefully from the remaining tangle of limbs on the couch and pulled on her shoes.

Elspeth listened to her mother's retreating footsteps with annoyance. She hadn't been quite so brave the evening before. No, it was Elspeth that had been pushed into the darkness of the house in search of candles. Still, at least it was warm here, sitting in the heat of the morning sun. She stretched carefully like a basking cat and then froze.

She could hear footsteps. Was her mother coming back already? But these steps were coming from somewhere else, not the hall. Maybe there was a basement beneath the house? But it was something about the sound that was wrong. These were stealthy, creeping steps, coming closer, then stopping as though the person didn't want to be heard.

Even though she was sitting in a warm patch of sun, she could feel goose-bumps begin to prickle down her arm.

It was silent for a moment. Then another stealthy step. Elspeth strained, trying to quiet her thumping heart, listening hard, trying to locate the sound. Another step. Yes, it was directly beneath her and heading towards the corner of the room, where she had seen the face the night before.

"Well, I managed to –" Nora began.

Elspeth screamed and jumped. She hadn't noticed her mother returning to the room.

"*Elspeth! What is the matter with you?*"

Eric woke and rolled off the couch onto the carpet with a heavy bump. Elspeth stood up immediately and turned to face the corner again. Was the face back? No, just shadows.

"*Elspeth! Do you hear me? What has got into you?*"

Eric was howling now and Nora was kneeling on the floor before the dead, grey fire, trying to comfort him. He was also straining his head, trying to see what Elspeth was looking at, but there was nothing to see.

Nora continued to shush him as though he were a baby, and Elspeth tried to block out their noise.

"Elspeth. We need to discuss this. I will talk to you later," her mother said, in the iron voice she normally reserved for their father. Then she pulled Eric up and reinstated him on the couch.

As soon as the crying subsided, Nora told them all she had found, good and bad.

"Well, I found the kitchen. It's just down the hallway but there's not much in the way of food. Unless you fancy some tapioca for breakfast."

"What's tapioca?" Eric asked.

"Not breakfast," her mother replied, pulling a face. "Now, why we don't we change and walk to the village. It's not too far from what I remember."

"Did you live here for a long time?" Eric asked.

"No." Nora shook her head. "Just a couple of months. Uncle Harry was quite eccentric and he didn't really like children, to be honest."

"Imagine that!" Elspeth whispered under her breath.

❦

Not long after, they began the short trek to Glenfeale. As they walked Nora told them what she could remember about her time at Crowfield. Harry was born there but had no interest in modern life or making any improvements to the house, so nothing had been updated in years. He had begrudgingly got electricity in to the house when his mother insisted and then, some years later, the enormous black rotary-phone was installed.

Elspeth had already noticed the phone in the hall and she wondered if it still worked. Perhaps she could call her father if she got the chance.

"Unfortunately, the phone is dead and the electric seems to be cut off too. But I'm going to make some calls today and soon we'll have the house to rights," Nora stated, as though she'd read Elspeth's mind. "At least we have a kitchen and a bathroom. We'll sort out the bedrooms next. It'll help us get settled in."

Elspeth pulled a face behind her mother's back. Now she was talking as though they were moving in.

As they walked to the village Nora ran through her plans. The first thing on the list was to get the power and telephone working again. Then they were going to pick out colours and wallpaper for their bedrooms and start planting seeds in the garden, maybe harvest the crab apples in the orchard when they came in.

"I've always wanted to make crab-apple jelly," she announced gaily.

Eric began to lag behind – dragging his feet and letting his hands trail through the giant white-weeds growing in the hedgerows. He was singing about Fred, who had lost his head and was better off dead, poor old Fred.

Seeing her opportunity, Nora sidled back slowly to Elspeth.

"What is wrong with you?" she asked quietly.

Eric was still singing loudly.

"Last night, screaming about nothing and the same this morning. You're like an old lady with the vapours."

Elspeth was silent.

"*Well?*" her mother hissed.

"There's nothing wrong with me," Elspeth answered sullenly.

"Really, I'd say different."

Elspeth bit her lip. There was a lot of things she could say but it wouldn't end well.

"I know you're angry with me, Elspeth. You've made that very clear," her mother continued in the same cold voice. "But, fortunately, I am the adult here and I would appreciate it if you would stop scaring Eric. He's just a child."

And what am I, Elspeth felt like shouting, but she remained silent. Long experience had taught her that there were no winners in any arguments with her mother. Why had she come on this journey of madness? Why hadn't she said no, for her sake and for Eric's?

"Have you spoken to Dad yet?" she asked, knowing this would upset Nora further.

"I'll phone him today. He knows we're here, just in case you think otherwise. I'm not a complete incompetent, Elspeth."

Eric had stopped singing and was looking at them both.

"So, what will we get for tea?" Nora said. "We think sausages might be a good option, Eric. What do you think?"

"With gravy?"

"Yes, we can manage a bit of gravy," Nora said with a smile.

Elspeth walked on.

The village, Glenfeale, was tiny: a church, two shops, a pub and an undertaker.

"What's an undertaker?" Eric asked. "What do they take?"

"I'll explain later," Nora answered.

She was busy with her list again and her brow seemed to be permanently creased as she read and reread the piece of paper in front of her.

"Right, I need to make a phone call," she said, nodding towards a cream-and-green telephone box with thick glass panes and a mould-covered roof.

"Why don't you take Eric to the graveyard, Elspeth? See if you can find our relatives there. Look for a headstone with Harry Enright on it, or maybe just Enright."

"We have relatives here?" Eric asked.

Elspeth said nothing, just looked at Nora, but she was already gone – marching towards the phone box. You didn't need to be a child-genius to know who she was planning on calling and why she wanted them out of the way.

Elspeth didn't want to go to the graveyard with Eric. She wanted to stay and eavesdrop on the conversation. What would her father say to her mother? Did he realise by now where they were? Was he worried? What she really wanted to do was march to the phone box with a determined step, just like her mother and wrench open the door and demand to speak to her father. She wanted to explain that her mother had made them come. That they wanted to go home, that it wasn't their fault – they were hostages to their mother's insanity.

But Elspeth knew she could say nothing, it wouldn't help, it would only make things worse.

So, she took Eric by the shoulder and steered him in the direction of the graveyard while trying to explain what their mother had meant by relatives.

"So, are these real people then?" Eric asked, almost as though he expected to see a welcome party in the graveyard.

"Of course they were real people. Once."

"How long ago though? What did they die of? Battles, I suppose, or maybe –"

"Old age, most likely," Elspeth interrupted. She put her hand out to quiet Eric – there were other people in the graveyard already.

The woman wore a straw hat and had a notebook in her hand. Every so often she bent down beside a headstone, and began to write in her book. The man had a sheet of paper in his hand and he kept folding and unfolding it, as though it were a treasure map with secret symbols. He looked at the children, smiled and tucked the folded paper back into his shirt-pocket.

They waited on the footpath, Elspeth still with her hand on Eric's shoulder. She wasn't sure what to do, she didn't want to intrude.

"What are they doing?" Eric whispered.

"Looking for their relatives as well, I guess." Elspeth shrugged.

"*Elspeth! Eric! Where are you?*" Nora's voice broke through the heavy, still air. She didn't sound happy.

The woman with the straw hat looked up, expectant, from her notebook.

"*Well, what are you waiting for?*" Nora shouted. "*Let's go!*"

She began to walk up the gravel path before noticing the couple in the graveyard. "Children, there you are!" she said, smiling before turning away from the woman and grabbing at Eric's hand. "*What are you doing?*" she hissed at Elspeth. "*Didn't you hear me calling?*"

"We were looking for our relatives, like you said," Eric replied. "But we couldn't. There were people here already."

"Oh, there probably isn't even a stone over old Harry's head," Nora muttered to herself. "Ran out of money, most likely!" She laughed but it wasn't a happy sound. "I don't know what I was thinking. Well, let's go to the shops and get some food, I guess, and then home."

On the way back, Eric took to dawdling again in the ditch. He had found a stick and he was busy beheading all the weeds along the way. Bee-drone accompanied them and Elspeth felt an enormous wave of tiredness and lethargy steal across her. Her feet began to drag and soon she was as slow as Eric, lagging further behind with every step.

"*It's like a death-march with you two!*" Nora shouted. "*Hurry up!*"

Elspeth looked at Eric and smiled as their mother walked around the bend in the road and was lost from sight.

"Eric!" Elspeth said. "Eric, are you listening?"

"What?" Eric asked, red-faced and sweaty from his war on weeds.

"Will we hide? Just to scare her."

Elspeth watched the slow smile creep across his face. "Come on then! Let's go!"

She grabbed Eric's hand and pulled him into a gateway to a field. They crouched down among the bee-sounds and broken stems.

In the distance they could hear Nora, still complaining, still grumbling. "*Will you just hurry-up!*"

Elspeth watched a bee crawl carefully into the speckled mouth of a foxglove. She had a sudden urge to reach out and seal the flower shut. But before she could stretch her arm, she heard footsteps.

Her mother must have turned back to find them.

"Really, Elspeth! Can I not trust you to do anything?"

Elspeth felt the familiar surge of anger begin to rise within her chest but said nothing. Her mother glanced from the mess of saucepans on the floor to Eric, standing in the farthest corner, doing his best not to look at anything or anyone.

"Eric, please come with me," she said, holding out her hand. "Elspeth, you will finish dinner and tidy this mess."

Eric stepped carefully over the upturned lid and went to his mother.

"Half an hour should be more than adequate," Nora said to Elspeth's back as she left the room.

Elspeth stood at the sink, biting back the anger, watching the saucepan fill with water. The tap was incredibly slow, nothing more than an extended drip really. She concentrated on the moving water, the trickling sound it made.

Chapter 20

Adam was finally asleep. Heather left the bedroom – cautious and mindful of every step, her bare feet sticking to the boards, making soft kissing sounds with every step. She winced each time it happened but he didn't wake. She quietly closed the door and tiptoed down the corridor.

In her room she took the blanket off the wooden box, knelt down and opened the lid. It was full to the top with notepads and books. She scarcely remembered packing them away. They all belonged to Cass. She'd gone to the old house, a few days after the funeral – Teresa had grudgingly offered to babysit Adam for a few hours.

She remembered the feeling of emptiness and stillness when she entered the house. Cass had been such a life force – not a whirlwind, more like a soft rain, a constant presence, never-failing – and now she was gone.

At that stage Heather hadn't fully made up her mind what to do. Teresa said they were welcome to live with her and she almost sounded like she meant it. Heather was watching Adam play as Teresa droned on, telling her that she was too young to be alone with Adam, how he needed a steady influence in his life. Adam was ignoring them, busy playing with his farm animals. A menagerie of tiny plastic creatures marched across the cream tufted carpet in Teresa's immaculate sitting-room.

Heather was thinking about all the times Cass had called to visit her, bringing presents. A tiny welcome from another world until the day she brought no presents, only news.

"I've a bit of a surprise for you, Heather."

And Heather waited, afraid to speak, afraid to hope – dreaming that her mother had found a house, a home of some sort and they could live together like normal people, a family. But that wasn't the news.

Instead she told Heather about the baby, while holding her hands splayed across her tummy with its non-existent bump. She was smiling.

"How long?"

That was the only question Heather managed to ask.

"Not too long. Only four months to go."

After Cass left, she found a calendar in her school journal and counted forward. Four months, a Christmas baby. And then she cried – tight, bitter tears. It was as though Cass expected her to be happy about this. She'd just sat there the entire visit, smiling and talking about who the baby might look like.

Downstairs she could hear Teresa. She wasn't even bothering to lower her voice.

"And if she thinks that I'm taking in another brat while she wanders the country, forget it! It's not happening. She's damn lucky I still give the first one house-room!"

Uncle Dan mumbled something inaudible in response and then Michelle started, her voice just as loud and angry as her mother's. "*Probably another weirdo! Just like her!*"

Dan muttered again and Heather wrapped her pillow around her head. She didn't want to hear any more.

Christmas came and went that year without any visit from Cass, not even a card. She was afraid to ask Teresa if she knew anything. They all seemed to have entered a pact of some sort and were busy ignoring her, even Uncle Dan. Well, they talked but only in small ways. *Have you done your homework? Dinner is ready. It's time to go to bed.* Those sorts of things but otherwise Heather felt she was in danger of disappearing altogether.

Whenever a teacher called on her to answer a question, her voice, rusty and hoarse, surprised her by still being there. One day she was sure it would simply stop working altogether.

Then, on a bitterly cold January morning, she came, no fanfare, no advance call. A rattling old taxi pulled up outside the house. It was a Saturday and the house was empty except for Heather. She remembered hearing the car and then the knock at the door.

She went downstairs and there she was, Cass, thinner, older and some of the light had left her eyes. Heather heard herself talking in her rusty voice, sounding like an old woman, like Aunt Teresa, asking Cass how she was? Did she want a cup of tea? It was her polite but distant voice, the one Teresa always used with Cass.

And then Cass handed over a tiny, wrapped bundle. "This is Adam," she said.

And Heather realised that was where the light had gone, into his eyes. They were the deepest shade of blue she had ever seen. He was perfect and she felt all the hardness and bitterness roll away. Why was she so angry? He was just a baby.

"Hi, Adam," she heard herself saying. "I'm your sister. I'm Heather."

She found out afterwards that both Cass and Adam had nearly died – the cord had got wrapped around his neck.

"I asked Teresa not to say anything. I didn't want to worry you," Cass explained. "And I'm so sorry I couldn't get in touch sooner. But I have some other news as well."

And this time it was the news Heather had always hoped for, the dream she always held within her – a house, a home, a family. Cass explained that she was trying to find a house to rent beside Teresa so Heather could stay on at school.

"But what about your job?" Heather asked.

"I can still help others. It's time for my family though. People will just have to come and see me, not the other way around."

***

And they had. As Heather took out the notebooks and the diaries from the wooden chest, she thought about the people who had come to see Cass. They arrived in a steady stream. Looking for help, guidance, reassurance – and, whether or not Heather believed, here she was, just the same as all the others before her – hoping to find a solution in the cards.

She was nervous, unsure of her abilities. She wondered if it was because she hadn't grown up with the rituals, the candles and cards, the whispered words and intonations. Instead, she had been sequestered away, with Aunt Teresa and her safe, normal, clean-lines life, while trying to maintain her sanity.

She hoped she wouldn't fail.

She checked that the door to Adam's room was still closed. She didn't want him to see what she was about to do, not only for fear of stirring memories but also because she had no idea what she was doing. She had no answers if Adam asked any questions.

Then she went to the kitchen, carrying the necessary bits in her arms and positioned herself at the kitchen table.

She took a deep breath and lit the purple taper that had been in the box. The wick spat and crackled, refusing to light. She lit another match and held it close again, willing the flame to take hold. She knew it was important to have it burning bright and clear. The match began to scorch her fingers and she pulled it away. The taper stayed lit but the flame was guttering. She waited, holding her breath, and slowly it took hold, turning green and then yellow before settling into a deep purple colour.

Heather slid the taper carefully into the centre of the table. The flame burned steadily, a good sign, an omen. If Cass had been there with her, she would have smiled and clasped her hands together. "*The signs are good*," she might have whispered.

What signs though? Heather felt the fear surge within her again. She looked around the room, checking she had all she needed – and then she realised that Poe was missing.

Cursing softly, her nerve already beginning to fail, she went in search of Poe. If he was in Adam's room she had no hope of getting him. She knew that she would wake Adam if she tried the door again. Then she remembered Poe was in her room. Adam seemed to have lost interest in so many things and Poe was there, abandoned, forlorn, dust gathering on his glossy wings.

In the darkness she could see the dull, metal glint of the cage and through the window she could see lights in Patsy's house. She had to stifle a nervous laugh. What if Patsy was snooping around the house and saw her? What if she succeeded in contacting the dead?

Heather shivered and carried Poe back to the kitchen. The candle was still burning, the strong purple flame shining bright. She positioned Poe beside it and took out the worn pack of cards. Then she picked up a notebook. It was crammed with Cass's neat writing and it seemed to decipher all the cards and their meanings. She could just about remember the proper way to shuffle and the formation to lay the cards in.

In her head she could hear Cass's voice, her quiet way of explaining the process. Heather was silent, holding on to the cards and holding on to the memory. She'd never seen her do an actual reading for someone and she'd only tried the cards herself one time under Cass's instruction, a test to see if she'd inherited any abilities. She remembered trying to keep her face neutral as Cass spoke about the energy flow and what the different colours of the flame meant. It hadn't gone well. The cards had continually stuck together and bunched themselves into little piles as soon as Heather touched them.

The wick guttered and hissed before expiring and Cass sat, quiet and still, as though waiting for a miracle, some sign that she'd passed on her gift.

"Never mind," she said eventually, when it was apparent that Heather had no feeling for the cards. "Your strength is in you. I can see that. I can feel it. You are a good person and that will always be your guide."

Heather felt as though she'd failed a very important test, proving there was no true bond between them. That she was forever cut astray. And for some reason it felt as though it was her fault and hers alone.

Now, sitting before the deep purple flame, she wondered would she pass the test this time? Cass wasn't there to help her – or was she?

She took the cards from their velvet wrapping and knocked them carefully against the table, wincing at the sound, hoping the noise wouldn't wake Adam. It felt like knocking on the door of another world.

She closed her eyes and held the cards loosely in her hands – trying hard to concentrate, to ask the right question, the one with the fewest words and the clearest meaning. Except, she realised, it wasn't a question she wanted to express but an instruction. One she hoped the right person would hear.

"*Please help Adam.*"

That was all she could think of. She wanted to shout Cass's name, to ask if she was there? But she was afraid that she might get an answer. That there might be a faint little knock on the underside of the table, an answer from another world.

She tried to clear her mind and think of Cass. Her image came to her, swimming upwards, as though from an algae-covered pond, her clear, blue eyes, her heavy, dark hair streaked with grey.

"*Please help Adam.*"

Then she began to lay out the cards. They didn't stick or clump together. And this time the candle burned clear, the flame stayed straight and true. She placed the cards face down, as Cass had shown her. She put the deck to one side and began to turn over them over, one by one. There was one card that she was pulled to, that she couldn't take her eyes from – a tall grey tower with flaming windows and people falling to the jagged rocks below.

"*The tower,*" she whispered.

She opened Cass's notebook, the pages soft and warm beneath her fingers. There it was, the tower. Cass had drawn a sketch of the card, with razor rocks and fire exploding from the narrow windows. A single thunderbolt erupted from black clouds.

Heather began to read.

A necessary change is about to occur. A situation or conflict will be resolved. Life may become difficult or overwhelming but this needs to happen. All will be altered.

Chapter 21

Elspeth didn't want to wake. She could feel the early morning sun, hot against her face. She closed her eyes tighter against the burning brightness. It felt as though she hadn't slept at all and she knew if she looked in a mirror her eyes would be bloodshot. She opened one eye slowly to see what time it was, though it made no difference, there was nowhere she needed to be. Well, there was one place.

She rolled over and pushed herself off the bed, feeling much older than the previous evening. Her head was throbbing as though she'd consumed a full bottle of wine the night before instead of a single glass. Her thinking was scattered and unsure but the memories from her childhood were still there, intact, just hidden beneath a lot of dust.

All the years spent taking sleeping tablets and shutting memories away hadn't worked. Her childhood at Crowfield remained, perfectly preserved, like an awful thin-veined and transparent creature, immortalised in a glass jar of saline. All she had to do was unscrew the lid and the whole slimy mess would slop right out.

She stood up and reached for her dressing-gown. The normal life, the one she'd tried to pretend was hers was gone now. She would have no peace until she solved the mystery or tried to at least.

Her phone call with Geraldine was simple. No drama. Of course she could take some time off work, she had quite a bit of annual leave built up. No, there was no problem. That overused phrase "as much time as you need" was bandied about and eventually Elspeth hung up, feeling dismissed and unneeded. Even the career she'd so carefully managed and devoted time to seemed a distraction now. Just a game she'd been playing at while she waited for the right time to begin her life or rather take up the threads of her old life and see what would happen.

She took a quick shower and packed a week's worth of clothes. She didn't know, as she'd told Geraldine, whether she needed a week or a month. Part of her felt that a week would be more than adequate. She knew the answer had to be at Crowfield and she'd always known that. From the moment Eric disappeared she felt that he'd never left Crowfield. It was just something that she knew, deep down. It was as though she could still sense him there, a faint unseen presence, one that must never be talked about but a presence all the same.

As a teenager Elspeth had tried to tell Martin O'Neill her feelings but Nora intervened, as always – shutting her down, shutting her up, telling Martin that Elspeth was nothing more than a seasoned teller of tales. "*More deceptive than Salome*," she whispered, shaking her head, looking at Elspeth with a wary eye.

Detective O'Neill persisted though. He'd tried, again and again, to get Elspeth to open up and talk about her "feeling" and what had happened that night, until Nora became incandescent with rage and banned him from the house. By then it had been over a month since Eric's disappearance and the case had reached the stage where hopes of finding him alive had completely faded. At that point they just seemed to be hoping to find a body and a reason.

Was the case ever closed? Elspeth didn't know for sure. The stand-up screaming match between her mother and a strangely silent Martin O'Neill had signalled the end of something. They were left alone after that and the people in the village began to turn their heads and whisper, whereas before they'd been interested and sympathetic.

Elspeth pulled the zipper closed on the bag and began to search for her black coat. The card was still in her pocket, just a plain white card with his name and phone number printed in black ink. Did he make a habit of handing them out to people whose cases were unsolved, she wondered. She turned it over – there was nothing else on the back, just his name, Martin O'Neill, and a mobile number. Had he ever really retired at all?

When he closed his eyes at night, did he see their faces? The ones whose fate had never been revealed. How many more like Eric? How many missing children?

She tucked the card into her pocket and swung the bag over her shoulder. There was no point in dwelling on it but, as she pulled the door closed on her tidy, clean, well-lit apartment, she knew that she was stepping into the unknown. And she had no idea what ghosts were waiting for her at Crowfield.

***

The draining sense of loss and uncertainty was back and growing stronger as she drove towards Glenfeale. The day was already beginning to darken and gradually the sky turned black overhead with great tumbling clouds continually rising across the horizon. She kept her hands steady on the wheel as though she were steering a ship through unnaturally calm seas. There was nothing to see, for now all was still, but the storm was building and she could almost taste it.

Her mind began to wander, her thoughts idling, thinking of nothing and everything. Skeletal tree branches and bursts of orange leaves passed her in quick snapshots, barely registering. Her mind was fully on the past again. She was back in Crowfield.

She was fourteen and Eric was eight and her mother was smiling – real smiles, ones that lit up her face and crinkled her eyes. With hindsight, as an adult, Elspeth wondered how long had she been unhappy, how many years had she hated Frank, wishing herself away. The crazy midnight decision to leave hadn't really happened overnight, it had been years in the making and then she'd come to Crowfield.

Her father was an important man, at least that's what Nora always said to them every time they had to move. As a child it seemed that just as she'd settled into a new school, made new friends, finally acclimatised to a new house, they would be packing up again.

"Your father is important and he's needed elsewhere," her mother would explain in an abstract fashion as though the moving was of no real consequence, it was just a fact. This was the answer to every question and covered all eventualities. As she grew older Elspeth realised that it was just his job. He was a project manager and had no choice – he just had to go where the company needed him. For a long time, she wondered why he dragged his family with him and she had no answer. Perhaps he was lonely. Perhaps Nora was the driving force in wanting to keep their little family together. Perhaps there was no reason – it had simply not occurred to her parents that their lives could be different. They didn't have to choose this strange nomadic existence. They could settle down in one place and the world wouldn't end.

All she knew was that, as she grew older and more aware, she noticed the silences between them more and more. At dinnertime, as Eric chattered on, filling every void, every protracted silence with tales of bravery and school shenanigans, she couldn't help but notice how they did not speak to each other.

Had it always been like that, she wondered. She did remember a Christmas when she was younger and her parents had danced in the dining room after dinner. It was a new house, in a new location. She knew now that the weather was much too warm for Christmas food and paper hats but they persevered in all the usual traditions. And when a waft of festive music from another party reached in through the open windows, her mother smiled in recognition at the tune and her father stood and took her hand.

Eric was just a toddler at the time, content in his high-chair, babbling and waving a plastic spoon. And Elspeth had watched them as though they were other people, not her parents, not a very important man and a woman in a sun-dress, but a couple from a postcard or a movie scene. One small moment of romance, forever immortalised in her mind.

But those moments had long passed by the time Elspeth was a teenager and all Eric ever knew of his parents was two people who seldom spoke.

Nora had changed, though, after they came to Crowfield. She started smiling more, even though their lives were chaotic and unplanned. The tension had lifted from her shoulders. She seemed younger and more carefree, despite living in a falling-down wreck of a house.

It all came back to the house, Elspeth decided. Her mother was definitely happier there and Eric viewed Crowfield as some great adventure playground. But she had often felt that someone was watching, a constant unseen presence.

Once, in the library, she'd come across old photos and newspaper articles tucked away. She made up names for the faces in the pictures. She didn't dare ask Nora who they were because then they would be spirited away, never to be seen again. Her mother didn't like questions and she certainly never liked answering them if she could help it. Why the secrecy, Elspeth wondered. Was it because Nora didn't know anything about her long-dead ancestors? She remembered studying them closely, trying to see any family resemblance. She had no idea who the woman in the high-necked blouse was, sitting straight-backed and clear-eyed, staring resolutely at the camera. She was in so many of the photos, first as a young woman, and then as the years passed lined and worn. Elspeth decided to call her Maggie – she looked like a Margaret – but Maggie to her family.

She also managed to find photos of Harry, her distant relative, the man who shunned technology. He was a tall man with grey whiskers and overlarge eyebrows. He looked unkempt, uncared for. There were many newspaper clippings about Harry, mentioning his stables, and some had an accompanying picture of the wild-eyed man. In some photos he had a pipe, clamped firmly between his teeth, lost in the tangle of his beard.

The articles were never interesting. They were mainly about horses or geldings or yearlings. There was talk of guineas and hands and some of the horses had long tongue-twisting names, the Last Lass of Eventide, Promise of a Summer Sun.

Elspeth couldn't work out the dates they referred to. All the newspaper articles had been trimmed out neatly with no surplus print attached. There were some other pieces about a local exhibition and a woman who specialised in painting horses. One of her paintings was pictured and Elspeth studied it closely – looking at the grainy dots, trying to ascertain if it was any good – and if it was the Lass of Eventide or Promise of a Summer Sun – but there were no dates. It was just another clipping shoved in amongst the rest.

Then, the last one, the strangest piece of all. It was about Harry, a memorandum recalling his passion for horses and some lines about his time with the local hunt. How he had lived a long and dignified life. The word "distinguished" was used six times. But who had cut it out? Who had placed it in the library with all the other bits after Harry died? Who else had lived at Crowfield?

Chapter 22

The house looked like a dead thing. No flickering lights in any of the windows. Elspeth sat in her car, the door open, but the lights and engine switched off. She could feel the chill in the autumn air. She watched leaves from the enormous beech tree spiral and twist as they fell through the darkening sky before beginning to pile up in the corners of the weed-choked yard. It was so quiet, so still, as though the house and trees were waiting to see what she would do. Who would blink first?

She stretched her head backwards and looked down the overgrown driveway. She closed her eyes briefly. She had to move, now or never.

The front door didn't want to open. Elspeth checked the keys again – yes, she had the right one. It had opened the door just fine the last time. She looked closer at the keyhole. Was it a new lock? It seemed bright and tarnish-free – but who would have changed the locks? She was wrong, she was imagining things. She pulled the key from the lock, checked it again, and tried once more. This time the key spun easily and the door opened into darkness.

Using a bag of groceries, Elspeth propped the door open. Then she went back to the car to fetch the rest of her things. She was in no rush, pausing momentarily each time she had to cross the threshold. Her mind kept returning to their very first night at Crowfield. How she'd entered the house alone and left Eric with Nora in the doorway – standing, waiting, just two shadows in the night.

Finally, all was unpacked. She locked her car though she knew it was completely safe and she watched the lights flash briefly, a warning, a sign. No, it was just the car signalling it was locked, a thing it always did. But now, as she stood in the open doorway, her mind was racing. She was looking for signs where there was nothing to see. There was no danger here, it was just a house.

Once inside, she closed the door behind her and turned the key, listening to the satisfying click of the locking mechanism. She looked down the hall, wondering if the kitchen door would open by itself but it didn't. So far, so normal.

She glanced up the stairs and wondered how dusty the sheets were on her old bed. She'd packed the heavy patchwork quilt from her own place, just in case. It might be easier to sleep on the couch for tonight, just like that first night, so long ago.

There was no point in unpacking, not yet, it would be easier to do it in the morning. She picked up the groceries she'd bought in the village and carried them down to the kitchen.

Walter still lay, half-unwrapped, on the kitchen table. The overhead light was buzzing, as though it were full of flies. She walked back to the doorway and switched it on and off, listening, wondering what the sound was? Then it stopped abruptly.

In front of the darkened window, she stood at the sink and waited for the kettle to fill. She was trying to make a list, trying to decide how to pass the evening. In the blackness outside she could see the room clearly reflected behind her, the open door, the table, her groceries waiting to be unpacked and Walter lying there, one hand hanging off the table's edge, his eyes shut tight, a sleeping heirloom of the past.

The kettle was full and Elspeth carried it over to the corner and plugged it in. It started spitting and crackling immediately but that was also normal. How many times had she listened to it, creaking slowly to the boil, while her mother sat, vacant-eyed, waiting.

She glanced over at the table, almost expecting to see her there, but it was just Walter. His electric blue eyes staring, watching her. But wait, his eyes were closed when she was at the sink, filling the kettle. She looked at the dark window again, watching Walter's reflection, holding her breath, waiting for him to move but he didn't. His eyes were open and they stayed open, vibrant, watchful.

The kettle began to whistle and scream. She found a clean mug beside the sink and got a jar of coffee from the shopping bag. She would move Walter tomorrow, she decided – he could go back up to Eric's room, that was where he belonged. Then she left the kitchen, mug in hand, pulling the door shut as she went.

She went into the sitting room and placed the mug on the coffee table in front of the fire. Then she fetched her quilt from the hall.

The sitting room was covered in grey dust. As soon as she sat on the couch, puffs of ash rose in dust clouds around her. She wrapped her cold hands around the coffee mug and tried to absorb what little heat it held.

There was an open fireplace. Perhaps she could manage to light it. Her mother had always lit the fire in the evenings and everything was still waiting for her hand. She began to crumple papers into little twists, arranging them in the empty grate. Then she set a match to the nest of paper and twigs. It caught immediately, one or two gusts of choking smoke blew back from the chimney but then it settled. She placed some smaller logs on the fire and soon she could feel heat begin to radiate into the room.

It was as though she were thawing after a great frost. She sat on the very edge of the wing chair, close to the fire. This had been her mother's seat and if she reached underneath she knew she would find a mending-basket, piled with socks to be darned, knitting needles, a stray ball of wool or some other half-finished project.

Elspeth drank her coffee and watched the flames take hold. She glanced at the darkened corner beside the bookcase, once, maybe twice. Then, as the fire began to die, she curled herself carefully into the heavy quilt on the old couch. She closed her eyes and tried not to think about Eric, or her mother or the brief time they'd had together at Crowfield.

She'd never been alone in the house before. This was a first. There'd always been another person with her, except for that morning, the one in the bathroom. And, all of a sudden, the memory came back to her, tumbling out of the box where she'd keep it locked away for so many years.

Chapter 23

They'd only been at Crowfield a week when Nora announced that she was going to Glenfeale, alone. She needed some things from the shop and they were to stay in the house, while she was away.

Elspeth didn't mind. It was a bright sunny day and they'd already been to the village several times. There wasn't a lot to see or do in Glenfeale. There didn't even seem to be a hairdresser or barber and Nora had already muttered that she would need to take the kitchen scissors to Eric's fringe shortly.

After she left, Elspeth persuaded Eric to go outside and search for squirrels in the walled garden. She wanted to have a bath in the swimming-pool-sized monstrosity upstairs and she didn't trust the bolt on the door.

The key was missing as were all the keys to all the doors. Nora had already searched all the usual places where keys might be stored, with no luck. The only ones she had were for the front and back doors, which had been posted to her by Uncle Harry's solicitor months before.

"It's very strange," Nora said a few times after pulling out kitchen drawers and checking cabinets in the front room before deciding they didn't really need keys anyway, the ones they already had were more than sufficient.

That morning Elspeth waited until her mother disappeared around the corner of the driveway. Nora had dressed very carefully – a silk dress with pink flowers dotted all over. She was also wearing a very determined look on her face when she set off.

Elspeth guessed that she wasn't just going shopping but that she was going to try and phone their father again. Nora had gathered as many coins as she could find around the house and tucked them into her purse before she went.

Elspeth wondered if her father had even noticed they'd left. Would he miss Eric singing and shouting, trying to swing out of the stair bannisters? Did he miss her? Perhaps he was still away on the neighbouring project?

Eric came bouncing into the hall, shouting about squirrels again. He had seen one the day before and decided it would make a brilliant pet, even better than a jackdaw, if only he could get close enough to catch it.

Elspeth persuaded him to take the ancient jar of dried-up peanut butter to the walled garden – that way the squirrel wouldn't be able to resist. He wanted Elspeth to come as well but she convinced him that he would have better luck on his own, squirrels were notoriously shy.

Eventually he skipped off to the walled garden with the jar and Elspeth made her way upstairs. This was the first time she'd been free of Eric bothering her since they had set off on their "journey of madness" as she liked to call it. She'd been watching her mother carefully for more signs of possible breakdowns but the country air and the fact she wasn't fighting with their father very night had improved her mood greatly.

Of course, they seemed to be running out of food and money – that was what the phone call was about, most likely. Still, it didn't really matter to Elspeth – she'd already made up her mind that as soon as she was old enough to get a job and leave, she would. She didn't like to think about leaving Eric alone with her mother but she would worry about that another time. Right now, she had an hour of free time and she intended to enjoy it.

Only the day before she'd found a tin box filled with bath-salts and tiny, foil-wrapped soaps in one of the bedrooms. They'd remained intact and perfectly persevered in the metal tin, their perfume still strong and potent. She'd tucked them back where she found them, wondering when she would get a chance to use them. Now this was an opportunity too good to miss.

As she went upstairs, she checked the windows overlooking the walled garden at the back of the house. Eric was sitting cross-legged before the ancient crab-apple tree, the open jar of peanut-butter propped at the base of the stunted tree. She smiled to herself and carried on to the enormous bathroom. Nora guessed that it had been a bedroom at one point and Uncle Harry had just got it repurposed into a bathroom.

The oversized cast-iron bath sat alone in the centre of the space, a frosted white island in the middle of the room. There were no curtains or frosted-glass on the windows. Just tarnished mirrored panels dotted about the walls – reflecting the light, making it seem like a hall of mirrors.

Elspeth closed the door and set to work. She wiped out the bath with a soft damp cloth till it shone and then she turned the heavy taps to full. There was plenty of hot water from the downstairs stove which they lit every evening. She knelt by the taps, swirling her arm through the greeny depths, listening to the sound of water rushing in a steamy waterfall, the pipes rattling and banging in the walls, high above her head.

By now the bath was getting dangerously full so she twisted off the taps. Through the open window she could hear birdsong and a soft summer wind sighing through the stunted apple trees.

She stood for a moment and listened to the tinkling *drip, drip* of the cold tap. Now she could hear Eric's voice. He was singing. Knowing Eric it was probably meant to lure the squirrel into his trap. Elspeth smiled. At least he was happy – happier than listening to endless rows and arguments. Maybe it would all work out.

She crossed the floor, wooden boards squeaking in protest, to check the door one last time and peek through the window at Eric. She could just about see him, still under the tree, tall grasses surrounding him. He had stopped singing but he seemed content, watching his peanut-butter trap, waiting.

The bathroom door was a great battle-scarred slab of wood with paint flaking off at the edges and grubby marks along the door handle. Elspeth put the latch down and rattled the door. She knew it could be opened from the outside by putting just the right amount of pressure on the bottom panel, then the door twisted and the latch slipped up, like a safety-valve.

They had found this out by accident after Eric locked himself in one evening. Nora had pushed the bottom corner in frustration while he fumbled with the latch on the other side. Then when they'd got the door open, they tried the trick again and it worked.

Elspeth agreed to lock herself in the bathroom and then Nora and by the end of it all Eric was laughing and smiling, his fright forgotten, just another oddity in the strange old house, like the locked doors with no keys, the empty rooms and dusty curtains hanging over blank walls.

She gave the latch one final ratttle and, satisfied that she was alone, she undressed. The bathroom air was chilly, raising goose-bumps on her arms and legs. As she stepped into the bath the water rose with her, threatening to spill unto the wooden floor but then it settled along the very edge.

Elspeth sank deeper into the green water, feeling the gritty residue from the bath salts along the bottom. She held the rose-petal soap in her hand, squeezing it, and she could feel it begin to soften between her fingers. Then she closed her eyes and lay back, the warm, scented water making her drowsy and content.

Eric had started to sing again. She could hear the words more clearly now, his voice coming in through the open window, echoing within the room.

"Come little squirrel,
Come and be my pet,
Come little squirrel,
I'll fed you peanuts from a net!"

Elspeth smiled again. She closed her eyes. She couldn't hear Eric anymore. She could hear the water pipes banging, far-away tinny drums, and her heart, beating, slow and steady, the blood pushing through her body.

And then she heard footsteps. She froze, listening, her heart beginning to thump louder in her ears.

The steps were coming closer. It must be her mother. Maybe the phone box was broken. Perhaps her father hadn't answered the call.

The footsteps were upstairs now – walking down the corridor, tapping along the wooden boards. The sound getting louder with each step. Elspeth opened her eyes and looked at the door. Maybe it was Eric, maybe he'd caught the squirrel.

Her heart was a racing drumbeat. The footsteps stopped. They were outside the door. Her mouth was filled with dust, she couldn't speak. She watched as the handle began to move downwards, slowly, very slowly.

Then two things happened at once. A noise, screaming, from outside the window. And the door handle was released, flying upwards.

That broke the spell and Elspeth could move again. She pulled herself out of the water, grabbing the towel from the floor. She knew the scream – it was Eric.

"*Eric!*" she shrieked. "*Eric, I'm coming!*"

With wet, shaking hands she pulled up the latch on the bathroom door. She didn't even wait to think about who was on the other side. She had to get to Eric. He was still screaming, the sound echoing through her head. She pulled the door open and burst into the corridor. It was empty.

Without stopping to wonder why, she took the stairs two at a time, holding the bath sheet wrapped tight about her, her wet feet skidding and sliding on the wooden floor. She pulled open the back door and ran through the long grasses to where Eric was standing in the walled garden. He was holding one of his hands. Tear-marks streaked his cheeks. At least he'd stopped screaming.

"What happened?" Elspeth said as calmly as she could. It looked like he was in shock and she didn't want to frighten him any further.

"It was ... it was ..." Eric gulped, nodding towards the jar of peanut-butter.

"The squirrel?"

"No," Eric sobbed.

"Then what? What was it? Are you hurt? Show me your hand!"

Eric shook his head and pulled away – still holding his hand tightly with the other.

Elspeth knelt down beside him. "Eric, I can help, OK? I heard you screaming, from all the way up there."

Elspeth turned to look at the bathroom window so she could show Eric how far away it was. And she saw him, a man, standing in the shadows. Watching them from the window – just as she had watched

Eric earlier. Then the face was gone and there was nothing to see, just a blank pane of glass.

Reluctantly, Eric was holding out his hand. "He was trying to eat the peanut-butter," he said.

"Who was?" Elspeth asked, looking up at the window, at the darkness where the face had been moments before.

"The bee."

She dragged her gaze away and looked at Eric. He was holding out his hand. One finger had turned red and was nearly double in size.

"*I had to stop him eating the peanut-butter and then – then he stung me!*" Eric sobbed.

"OK."

Reality kicked in and took over. Was Eric allergic to bees? She couldn't remember.

"We need antihistamine," she said, her voice much calmer than she felt. "Do you remember the ants? When we lived in the blue house, remember? It's just a sting. The same as the ants. Come on!"

Elspeth stood up, uncertain if she wanted to go back into the house but knowing that she had to.

Then her mother appeared and she was smiling – at least until she saw them.

In the kitchen Nora took over, sending Elspeth upstairs to get dressed. She was busy fussing over Eric.

"It's only a little sting," she kept saying. "The bees here aren't dangerous. Now let me see it, Eric."

Elspeth left them to it and went back up the stairs. Her wet footprints had dried already but she could still see the tracks of where they'd been. She walked slowly to the bathroom door and pushed it open. The floor was still wet from where she'd jumped out of the bath, and there, just in front of the window, right where she'd seen the face, was a wet footprint. It wasn't one of hers, not a bare footprint. No, this belonged to someone who was wearing shoes.

She wanted to shout, to call her mother and Eric, to show them the evidence – but she didn't, something stopped her. She thought about Eric's face and how scared he'd been on the very first night, so she just stood there – watching the morning sun falling through the window.

In less than ten minutes the footprint would be gone forever. All tangible proof lost, dried with the heat of the sun.

***

"Elspeth, do you believe in ghosts?"

It was a half-whispered question and one that she had to strain to catch. She looked at Eric, curled up on the dusty old couch in the morning room. He was watching her intently as though he hoped to catch her out if she tried to lie.

"No," Elspeth answered slowly. "Why? Do you?"

Eric turned towards the open doorway – checking that Nora wasn't on her way. There was a distant clatter of plates – she was in the kitchen, making supper.

Eric nodded, his eyes nearly as big as the dinner plates Nora seemed to be throwing around the place.

Elspeth looked at him, saying nothing, buying time.

Then at last she said, "How's your finger?"

"It's fine now."

"So why are you still wearing the plaster? It's been over a week."

"It's still sore at night."

"I see."

Elspeth knew why he was still wearing the bandage and why he was reluctant to take it off. As a treat he'd been allowed to sleep in the pull-out bed in Elspeth's room, just until his finger got better. Nora made the arrangements just after the bee-sting episode.

"Now this is only while you're out of sorts," she'd said, smiling, brushing his overgrown fringe to one side. "That's fine with you, Elspeth. Isn't it?"

"Why can't he stay in your room?"

"I'm such a light sleeper, it wouldn't work. And this way it will be fun for you both," Nora declared. "Like a little holiday."

Elspeth had bitten her lip at that point, the angry words ready, but she said nothing. Instead, she asked how their father was.

"He's fine," Nora answered swiftly. "Hoping to get some leave soon and come to visit us. He misses you both so much."

"Does he really?" Eric asked.

"Yes. I was telling him all about your adventures, Eric. He said he was the very same as a boy, out fishing and playing in the woods. He can't wait to see us all again."

This was the new line. Apparently, the holiday had been extended indefinitely and their father couldn't wait to come over too. Elspeth had no idea if Nora had even managed to contact him, but she seemed happier with each passing day, so she decided to play along. Life was always easier if you went along with Nora's games.

Nothing strange had occurred since the face at the window. Sometimes Elspeth thought about the footprint and the face and decided it was easier to pretend it never happened. She was her mother's daughter, after all.

"*Supper's ready!*" Nora shouted from the kitchen, her voice making both children jump.

"Come on, Eric. I'll explain why ghosts aren't real this evening, I promise," Elspeth whispered to him as they left the room.

Eric nodded and they went across the hall to the kitchen together.

After supper, Nora made a big fuss of unwinding the bandage on Eric's finger. "Why, look, it's all healed up!"

Eric immediately began to protest. "But it's sore at night, honest! Really, really sore!"

"Well, your sister has been very good to let you have a get-well holiday with her. But you need to go back to your own room now." Nora looked to Elspeth for confirmation.

"I can still see a red mark," Elspeth said.

"Where?" asked Nora.

"Just there." And she pointed at the invisible puncture marks from a week earlier. "But maybe it is time you went back to your own room, Eric."

"But, but –" he began.

"Or why don't I visit you for a sleep-over instead? We can tell stories and –"

"No scary ones," Nora interrupted. "But that's a good idea, Elspeth. That sounds like fun. What do you think, Eric?"

Eric was nodding in agreement and wrapping the plaster back on his finger.

"Can we can make a fort as well?" he asked.

"Of course!" said Nora.

She agreed they could make popcorn later and then she disappeared into the woods, for her evening walk. It had become a new habit with her. She'd found some old ordinance-survey maps in the library and she was trying to figure out where the boundaries of Crowfield lay.

As soon as she left, Elspeth and Eric went upstairs to make a fort with bedsheets and cushions and pillows. Soon they'd piled them all in the centre of the room.

"It's not enough," Elspeth said, frowning.

"But there's no more," Eric shrugged.

"We could go into mother's room," Elspeth said. "Or Uncle Harry's room, the one down at the end."

"But it's locked, isn't it?"

"No, I think she found that key. It was in a desk drawer in the library."

Nora had found a big bunch of keys a few days before and told them she would try all the locked doors at the weekend, then promptly seemed to forget all about it.

"Come on, let's see!" Elspeth said.

"I don't know if I want any of Harry's pillows," Eric said. "Or even if I –"

"Come on," Elspeth said, catching him by the hand. Suddenly she felt reckless – her mother was out of the house and would be gone for hours if this was like any of her other evening walks.

Eric pulled his hand away from Elspeth.

"Fine," she said. "You wait here, I'll get the keys."

"No, don't leave me. I'm coming with you."

The library was at the front of the house. Elspeth opened the door and crept inside. The wood-panelling and shelving were all stained a deep mahogany colour, making the room feel dark and oppressive. A hooded, green lamp stood on the leather-topped desk. She pulled the hanging chain, hopeful, but of course it didn't work, it was merely an ornament, no longer functioning, much like the rest of the house.

Eric stood in the open doorway. He seemed hesitant to pass the threshold.

"*Hurry up!*" he hissed at Elspeth.

But Elspeth was still feeling giddy. She had to try not to laugh at Eric, his face solemn as he waited for her. She pulled a few drawers open before finding a large bunch of grimy keys tied together with a piece of red twine. She pulled them out.

"This must be them," she said and lifted them high so he could see, the keys jangling and rattling in her grasp.

Eric winced at the noise, as though fearful their mother might hear their disobedience from all the way across the woods.

"*Come on! Let's play hide-and-seek. You're it!*" Elspeth laughed.

She skirted by Eric and slid right by him, the keys still jangling in her hand. Eric had to run to keep up. Elspeth was on the landing and now she was at the top of the stairs. She laughed, skidding on the varnished boards in her stocking feet. She had a good head-start on Eric and she quickly ran down the corridor, holding the keys tight against her chest now so they made no noise. She ran as fast as she could, past the moth-eaten curtains that covered nothing. Uncle Harry's room was at the very end. She came up against the door and turned the handle, wondering which of the keys would unlock it.

But it wasn't locked. She put a hand to her mouth, trying to contain the laughter which was threatening to bubble over. She could hear Eric at the top of the stairs. He was calling her name.

She slipped in through the door. The room was pitch-black, the heavy curtains pulled across the window.

She could hear Eric running, his footsteps a whisper on the wood.

Then she heard her mother's voice. She was talking to someone, outside.

Father, Elspeth thought. *He must have come!*

She rushed to the curtained window. Her mother was still talking but she couldn't hear another voice. It seemed to be a one-way conversation.

She gently pulled back the velvet curtains, dust rising as soon as she touched them. She put her hand across her nose, trying not to sneeze. The window was slightly open and she could see down into the walled garden, all the way to the end, to the high crumbling wall and the narrow gate to the orchard. But she couldn't see her mother. Then she heard her voice clearly again. She was saying goodnight to someone.

Elspeth waited – watching, trying to see where she was. Then she heard a metal bolt being pushed back and a loud, squeaking noise. The locked gate swung inwards and Nora appeared. She was smiling.

The door in Harry's room opened with a tremendous crash.

"*I found you!*" Eric shouted.

And Nora, hearing the noise – looked up at the window to see Elspeth watching her.

Chapter 24

Heather slept better that night than she had in weeks. Maybe she was just incredibly tired and all the madness had finally caught up with her. Perhaps going through the motions of asking Cass for help had settled her. She didn't care which really – it had worked. When she woke, her mind felt clearer than it had been in weeks.

Across the hall she could hear Adam stirring in his sleep. She braced herself to hear the words "*Walter*" or "*Eric*" but he didn't say anything – instead he laughed, a sound she hadn't heard in weeks.

That's a better start than the last few mornings, she thought, and got out of bed. In the kitchen she pulled the curtains open– it was a bright clear day. As though overnight all the trees at the back had turned orange and there was a sugar-dusting of frost across the grass. The sky was an endless canvas, a pale wash of blue. She could see the outline of Crowfield through some of the newly bare branches and a thin spiral of smoke, creeping skyward. But there was no one living there now. It must be another chimney, a different house.

It was going to be a perfect autumn day. We can go for a walk, she thought, out of the village and past the graveyard to the wood, the one with the stream running through it. The fresh air will do us both good.

In the kitchen, she tidied away her cup from the night before. Cass's box of tricks was already stored away safely in the trunk in her room, the red tartan blanket covering the box completely. She still wasn't sure what the cards were trying to tell her the night before. She had spent more time than she cared to admit looking up notes in Cass's book. In the end she decided that a change was coming, nothing more sinister than that. And, hopefully, a change for the better.

Adam came into the kitchen just as Heather was taking out the frying pan.

"Morning," she said, smiling. "Pancakes?" She held up the pan.

"Yes, please," Adam replied and then without another word he came up to Heather and wrapped his arms around her.

"Thank you," he whispered.

Heather bent down awkwardly, still holding the pan, and hugged him back. It was like Walter and Mrs Collins and the rotten old house had never happened.

As they ate breakfast Adam told her how a witch's cat could stay put on a broom – the secret was magic claws, apparently. The cat could also twist his tail around and around the wooden handle as well. Then they talked about the party in school, the fancy-dress one for Hallowe'en.

Adam didn't know what he wanted to be but Joe was going to be a werewolf so he could chase people and bite them. Adam thought that Joe should really dress up as a dog, that way he could fetch sticks as well.

After breakfast they got dressed and packed a picnic. Adam insisted on using his school rucksack. Heather waited by the door as Adam hoisted the bag on his back.

"All ready?"

He nodded and began to walk towards the door before stopping abruptly.

"No, wait. Poe, we need Poe."

He ran back inside and Heather could hear the buckle on his backpack jingling against the metal cage.

Why not, she thought. She wasn't going to start arguing with him over something so silly.

"I'm sure Poe could use some fresh air too," she said, pulling the door closed after them.

As they began heading towards the village, Adam was still talking non-stop, Poe swinging by his side. Heather was nearly beginning to miss the long silences of the past few weeks. They were almost out of the village, just Patsy's shop left to pass.

Adam stopped walking.

"Why don't we get some sweets, for our picnic?"

Heather sighed inwardly. "That's a great idea, Adam."

The little bell wheezed half-heartedly as they pushed their way in through the heavy door. As usual, the shop was deserted, one tiny ray of sunlight piercing its way through the shop display window. Heather could hear Patsy making her way from the back.

"Well, if it isn't Adam and Heather!"

She smiled at them both, a warm, friendly smile, making Heather almost feel guilty for avoiding her.

"Haven't seen you in so long, Adam. You're getting so big but it's important to get lots of sleep, isn't it?" She looked at Heather with a pointed smile on her face, then back to Adam. "I see you brought your pet for a walk."

"He's not a pet."

"Sorry, that's right. He's your familiar."

"Not me. He belongs to Cass."

"Oh, right!" Patsy nodded as though she wasn't too bothered. "And what can I get you, young man?"

"*Em*, jelly snakes and some of those stripy ones as well, please."

The sweets were rattling and falling into the scales and Adam was waiting, his fingertips on the edge of the counter. A small cloud of sugar-dust rose from the jar as Patsy poured the sweets. Adam stuck out his tongue, tasting the sugar cloud and glanced back at Heather, waiting for a reprimand. She said nothing.

As they left, Patsy smiled again. "Bye, Adam. You're my favourite customer, you know."

Adam returned the smile and waved – his mouth full of sweets.

As they made their way along the road again, Heather wondered what Patsy meant about getting lots of sleep. Had she been watching their house at night? She needed to get curtains. How much could Patsy have seen? Would she have dared sneak around the back of the house to the kitchen window? How many people has she told? Probably everyone in the village. She could hear her now: *You know that new woman. The one with the little brother. Do you know what she spends her time doing? Lighting candles at night and trying to talk to the dead. I've seen it with my own eyes!*

Heather remembered the way Patsy licked her lips before telling the story about the little boy who went missing at Crowfield. She'd enjoyed telling it. That was another person's life, another person's sadness, but to Patsy it was just gossip. A grim tale to be repeated. A warning to others, but of what?

Adam was pulling at her sleeve, trying to get her attention.

"Sorry, Adam. I was miles away."

"I was asking if we could visit Walter?"

Heather didn't know what to say. *Walter.* And they'd been having such a nice morning too. Well, apart from calling in to Patsy's shop.

"*Hmmm,*" she replied, thinking.

"It's Poe's idea," Adam continued. "And we're getting quite close to his house, aren't we?"

Heather looked up and realised that, yes, unfortunately they were nearly at the entrance to that rotten old mausoleum, Crowfield. Any moment now the rusty sign would appear, creaking on a tree branch.

"But what about our picnic?"

"We can have it on the way back."

"I don't know, Adam. There mightn't be anyone home."

"Please!" he said, swinging Poe up towards Heather's face, as though he was making a case for the visit as well.

Heather shook her head. Then she thought, why not, it's not like Mrs Collins was going to answer the door, was she? She heard the familiar squeaking sound and the metal plaque appeared, swinging gaily in the autumn sun.

"Look, we're here!" Adam said, pointing at the sign. "This is it, isn't it? And we can see the knight as well. Can we call, please?"

Heather looked down at him, at the light dancing in his eyes and she remembered him laughing in his sleep earlier.

"Fine, we'll walk up to the house but it might be empty, OK? There might be no one home."

"*Yay!*" Adam shouted and then he started to sing the stupid rhyme about Fred and how he'd lost his head.

They began to make their way up the drive. Of course, there would be no-one to answer the door and then what would happen? But a wild plan was beginning to form in Heather's mind.

What if the door wasn't locked? She could go in and take Walter back. She was certain the house was empty. That little bird-lady, Elspeth, looked like she couldn't wait to leave when she saw her at the funeral. And, besides, it wasn't really taking anything back – Mrs Collins had given the puppet to Adam. She was just fixing her mistake, that was all. Perhaps Cass had heard her plea for help and it was all going to work out.

They had reached the limestone pillars. Adam stopped singing.

"Look, a car! Mrs Collins got a car," he said, pointing.

Heather stopped in her tracks. This wasn't part of the plan.

"*Adam!*" she called. "*Wait a minute!*"

But it was too late. Adam was already running towards the front door.

Chapter 25

Elspeth woke, and for a minute she didn't know where she was. The room was still in semi-darkness and she could hear crows outside. Then it dawned on her, like a horrible nightmare. She was back home, in Crowfield.

She remembered settling down here on the couch the night before, trying not to think about the past, when more memories came back.

It seemed that no matter how hard she'd tried to forget, they were all still there. But how much was real?

"You're such a storyteller, Elspeth," her mother always sighed. "This imagination of yours, telling tall tales, trying to frighten Eric. Why?"

But had she really imagined these things or not?

She sat up and pulled the heavy quilt tighter around her. The room was freezing despite the weak morning sun. No, she decided, there was more to her recollections than tall tales and false memories, much more. Her mother had always been keen to silence her and paint her as a dreamer, a fantasist. But the evidence was there and always had been, despite the many times she'd tried to ignore it.

They weren't alone at Crowfield that summer. There was someone else there as well – not living in the house but he had access to it and came and went as he pleased. But who?

Elspeth tried to see the face from her memories but the image was shrouded in smoke. A flickering picture that she couldn't see properly. He was a young man, of that she was certain, with shoulder-length dark hair, in his twenties perhaps.

And Nora knew him. That was who Nora was talking to in the orchard. His was the face at the bathroom window, and the reflection in the mirror on their very first night at Crowfield.

But who was he? And why had Nora wanted to keep him secret? And after Eric disappeared, the man disappeared too. Why? What had happened?

She shrugged off the eiderdown and stood up. At fourteen, had she believed he was a ghost? She shook her head. No, but there were still gaps in her memory. For instance, she could not remember any of the night Eric disappeared. In fact, the entire day seemed to have been erased completely from her mind, scrubbed clean.

She knew bits of the story, but only from her mother. Otherwise, she had no recollection at all. She had been ill with pneumonia and she vaguely remembered the hospital. The whirring hum of a ventilator and a burning brightness from the overhead lights, a light so intense it hurt her eyes, an array of tiny suns, reflected a thousand times off the polished floors. There was no darkness, no shadows, nowhere to hide.

Even now she wasn't sure how long she'd been in hospital – days or weeks. She did remember coming home, in a taxi, her mother silent beside her. They'd only just arrived back at Crowfield when Martin O'Neill called.

"Just a few questions," he said to Nora. "It won't tire her out."

Elspeth had been upstairs in her bedroom with the door open so she heard their voices clearly in the hall. She remembered being afraid of him. Why, though? She had no memories, nothing that would help find

Eric, she was useless. Then her mother started screaming, saying that she wasn't going to lose two children and she wanted him to leave the house and never return.

Martin mumbled something inaudible in response, but Elspeth could tell he had admitted defeat. She heard the door closing and knew her mother had won the battle. There would be no more questions. The case was closed.

Her father was at Crowfield that morning as well but he had more sense than Martin. Frank had waited, safely ensconced in the library, until he left. He had come to Ireland as soon as the news reached him about Eric. She remembered him visiting her in the hospital, or perhaps she'd been dreaming, she wasn't sure. He was staying in some hotel nearby, not at Crowfield.

Elspeth had a sense her parents were both trying to keep each other at arm's length, for fear of the damage that might occur if they came into closer proximity.

She then heard her father asking politely if he could see her before he left.

She expected another shouting match to take place in the great, echoing hall below but it didn't. Her mother agreed in the same polite distant tone and mentioned something about not wearing her out. Then she heard him coming slowly up the stairs.

He knocked gently on the open door before coming in. He'd aged ten years in the two months since she'd last seen him. His hair had traces of grey among the black and his suit jacket hung much too loose upon his shoulders.

"Elspeth, I hear you're on the mend."

She nodded.

"Well, I'm afraid I have to go. Duty calls."

And Elspeth nodded, glad that he was still an important man, even if his hair had turned him old.

"We must see about schools or getting you settled somewhere. What do you think?"

"I don't mind."

He nodded and turned back towards the open door before stopping again.

"Elspeth, are you happy here?"

She knew in that moment what he was asking and for a brief second she wanted to say, no, I want to come with you. Then she thought about the empty room next door.

"I think so, I guess."

And her father turned away.

<hr/>

Elspeth picked up the quilt and folded it. She had an ominous feeling that the longer she stayed in Crowfield, the more memories would surface.

But was she ready?

She found her shoes under the couch and went out to the kitchen. She was just about to fill the kettle when she heard the knock. She put the kettle down and turned off the slow, creaky tap and waited. She wondered if she was hearing things. She was already beginning to tune into the mindset of Crowfield – hearing things, seeing things. She shook her head as though trying to dislodge the strangeness of the house.

There, a knock again, at the front door.

She looked around the kitchen. Walter was covered with a tea towel – sleeping. Elspeth was planning on wrapping him up with a bigger towel and taking him upstairs later. But she needed some coffee before she could bear to touch his wooden joints, feel the soft limpness of his wood-wormy carcass in her hands.

She waited, looking around the kitchen, looking everywhere except at Walter. She needed to hear one more knock before she went to the door, then it would be real. She'd always knocked in threes when she came to visit her mother. Three smart knocks, pausing to count to three between each knock. It was only polite, really.

"Why don't you use your key?" her mother would say as she answered the door, letting the gloominess of the hall escape and wash over Elspeth.

"But I don't live here. It doesn't feel right."

"*Phft!*" her mother would reply, before beginning the slow walk down to the kitchen. "This is your place, Elspeth. Use your key. It's your home too."

At that point Elspeth always felt like screaming, *No, this is not my home and never will be!* But she didn't, instead she just followed along, head down, nodding in agreement, rolling her eyes like a teenager, knowing her mother couldn't see the gesture.

Once, Elspeth had thought about breaking with tradition and using the bloody key, just to see her reaction when she appeared in the kitchen doorway, but she knew she wouldn't win, regardless. Then she would be "taking liberties" so that was why she'd always stood at the door, knock once, and hope she heard, knock twice, to make sure she heard, knock three times to be certain, then stand back and wait.

And there it was, the third knock upon the door.

Now Elspeth had no choice but answer whoever it was. She wiped her wet hands on her trousers, feeling the water leach through to her skin, and began to walk down the dark hall. She could see sunlight struggling to enter through the grimy windows. Perhaps it's me, she thought. Perhaps we've changed roles in the night-time. I'm my mother now and I'm answering the door to me. What will I say? Will I ask me in?

Elspeth passed the tarnished, silver mirror beside the suit of armour and resisted the urge to check if it really was her own reflection.

Now a knock came again, gentle, a small hand upon the door, a fourth knock.

Elspeth opened it and a child stood there, his mouth open.

"You're not Mrs Collins!" he said.

"No, I'm Elspeth, her daughter," she heard herself reply.

A young woman was making her way to the door, looking equally astonished. "I'm so sorry," she said, putting a hand on the child's shoulder as though to pull him away.

Elspeth looked again. The boy was holding a stuffed jackdaw in a wire cage. Perhaps it was a Hallowe'en costume, if a bit early.

"I'm sorry. I don't have any sweets for trick or treaters yet. But perhaps you can call again, closer to the day." She looked at the woman for confirmation. There was something familiar about her face.

The woman was still holding the boy by the shoulder, still trying to turn him away from the house.

"Do I know you?" Elspeth asked. "Have we met before?"

"I don't think so," the woman began. "I –"

"Yes, you were at my mother's funeral. I remember shaking your hand and –"

"*Funeral!*" the boy interrupted. "*What happened to Mrs Collins? You never said she died!*"

Elspeth watched as the younger woman began to blush, a high, red colour starting to creep across her cheeks.

The young woman bent down, taking the boy's hands in hers. "Adam," she said gently, "I'm sorry. I just didn't want to upset you."

"Like Cass!" He nodded. "She sang the song too and then she went away!"

"I'm so sorry about this," the woman said, standing up. "We shouldn't have come. I'm sure you have enough to –"

Then the boy interrupted again, all sadness instantly forgotten, his finger pointing. "Look, Poe! It's the knight!"

Elspeth turned and followed his gaze to where the armour stood, keeping watch over the same dark dusty corner, as always.

"Can we visit Walter?" the boy asked.

Elspeth didn't know what to say. She could feel all the tiny hairs beginning to stand on her arms. It was something about the way he spoke about Walter and the suit of armour, familiar, as though they were friends. She turned to look at her visitors again.

"Perhaps we should start over," the young woman said. "I'm Heather. I used to clean for your mother and this is Adam, my brother. We spoke on the phone before. You made the arrangements but I only called twice and then I had to leave."

The boy nodded. "She gave me Walter."

"Yes, there was a note in his pocket," Elspeth said. "He's still here." She was thinking of Walter, sleeping under his tea towel on the kitchen table. She wondered if his eyes were open or closed? Was he listening to the conversation? Could he hear them talking, all the way down the hall? "But why did you bring him back?"

The young woman flushed again. "Well, we couldn't accept such a kind gift so –"

"*You said Mrs Collins wanted him back!*"

"Well, yes, Adam, she did. I'm sure she didn't mean for you to keep Walter at our house. Perhaps just to play with him at her house."

"She did!" Adam said, his voice loud and clear in the morning air. "She said I was a special boy and that Walter needed a friend. And that if I talked to Walter and we became friends then Eric would be my friend too!"

Elspeth stayed silent in the doorway but her eyes met Heather's. In that moment she realised that Heather had been pulled into the madness that was Crowfield. Now she could see the darkness across her face, the soft purple beneath her eyes, like bruises, an actual physical mark. It was all too familiar – another person who couldn't sleep. Another life touched by the insanity of her mother.

"I think you'd better come in," Elspeth said, standing to one side. "Maybe a coffee?"

"We can see Walter now," Adam whispered to Poe as he walked down the hall.

"Thank you," Heather said as she stepped inside.

Elspeth nodded. What else could she do? Adam seemed to know where he was going. Questions quickly ran through Elspeth's head. Why had her mother given Walter to the boy? Why had she mentioned Eric to him? Did she tell him something about what had happened that night so long ago and what exactly did he mean about being friends with Eric?

But she said nothing. She didn't ask any more questions. She had a feeling that Heather knew very little as well. She'd seen the confusion on her face when Adam told them about Walter so Elspeth followed them down the length of darkened hall and into the green gloom of the kitchen, saying nothing.

Walter was still "asleep" under his makeshift blanket.

Adam immediately made a beeline for the table and pulled out a chair. He placed Poe gently on the table, then slid Walter onto his knee and began to arrange his wooden limbs carefully.

The two women locked eyes and it was hard to say which of them looked more horrified as Adam began to talk to Walter. Although Poe was relegated to the table, he seemed to be part of the conversation. While Adam whispered into the puppet's ear, the bird seemed to be listening too. His head cocked to one side, regarding Walter and Adam with a quizzical air.

"Some coffee then," Elspeth said, trying to rein the proceedings back to some sort of normality.

"Please," Heather replied, as she pulled out a kitchen chair and sat opposite Adam.

Adam was still whispering to Poe and Heather was trying very hard to ignore them. Just another normal day.

The kettle began to rattle and bang.

"Sorry, it's very noisy," Elspeth said loudly. "It's old, you know. Probably should just go and buy a new one. Think this one predates the house."

Heather nodded, the pained look of ignoring Adam still on her face.

The kettle stopped banging abruptly and the heavy switch clicked off.

"Could we, perhaps, have the coffee outside or ..." Heather trailed off.

"How about the morning room? It gets lovely sunshine this time of day," Elspeth suggested.

"Perfect. Why don't you stay here, Adam?"

Adam nodded, only half-listening. He was humming now, the song about Fred, losing his head.

"This way," Elspeth said, holding the kitchen door open. There was something vaguely familiar about the tune Adam was humming but she couldn't remember where she'd heard it before.

The morning room was a bright oasis of sun and warmth after the dark kitchen and hallway. Elspeth pulled the quilt to one side before sitting down. If Heather noticed that she seemed to have slept on the couch the previous night, then she was polite enough to say nothing.

"So, you knew my mother?"

"And Walter," Heather said, getting straight to the point.

"Yes, Walter."

"What is wrong with that puppet? Is it possessed?"

Elspeth put her cup down. This was all going too fast, getting too strange, too soon.

"Heather," she said in a calm voice that was nowhere close to how she really felt. Her heart was actually banging inside her chest so loudly that she wondered why the young woman couldn't hear it.

Heather nodded, waiting to hear her out.

"I need you to know something – there are no ghosts," Elspeth said firmly.

Heather was staring owl-eyed at her. It was as though she'd only just realised what she had said about Walter being possessed.

"Yes, I know that," she replied eventually. "It's just –"

"Strange, I know. And I agree with you. In fact, this whole house is quite strange, but there are no ghosts. Absolutely not."

Heather was nodding, her whole body moving back and forth – as though she wanted to agree with her and yet ... She began to speak again, hesitantly, uncertain. "I, *em*, Adam has, you know ... been talking in his sleep ... he dreams and ..."

Elspeth was silent, waiting. She knew what was coming, she knew the words Heather was about to say. She wanted to stop her, to stand up and scream. *Weren't you listening to what I said? There are no ghosts, none, not here, not in this house or these woods, not anywhere!* Just like she'd told Eric, all those years ago. There are no ghosts, nothing that could hurt you, nothing real, just little things that were odd. Things you might glimpse from the corner of your eye. Sounds you might hear, that might or might not be the house, settling, closing its doors, straightening its timbers, stretching its rafters, smoothing the roof slates after a hot day baking in the sun. Just normal everyday things that every house does, just sounds, nothing that could harm you. But no ghosts – they can't hurt you – people however, that was a different matter entirely. People could definitely hurt you.

She couldn't stop Heather talking though. She knew that. So she sat and waited to hear the inevitable words, his name upon her lips.

"He talks about Eric," Heather continued in a low voice.

Elspeth swallowed slowly, then spoke, her voice also low, just a whisper, as though she didn't want the house to hear. "Eric was my brother."

"I know," Heather whispered back. "And I know he went missing, a long time ago."

"Twenty years," Elspeth replied automatically.

Then she raised her hands to her head. She could feel a headache coming on. She was searching, racing through every corner of her brain, looking for a reason why Adam knew anything about Eric and her gaze fell upon the pile of knitting under the armchair. The half-finished scarf or shawl or whatever woollen monstrosity her mother had been working on ... and she got the answer. *Nora*.

"My mother gave Walter to Adam, is that right?" she asked, her eyes still on the pile of grey wool. She could see Heather nodding out of the corner of her eye. "And were you there at the time?"

Heather shook her head.

Elspeth waited – looking at the knitting needles caught in the heart of the scarf, almost buried, bone-white tips showing through the mound of wool, waiting for another person to finish the job.

"But," Elspeth continued softly, her voice still a whisper in the bright sunshine, "do you know what she told Adam about the puppet?"

Elspeth looked up to see the young woman's reaction. The dawning realisation on her face, that of course Nora had told Adam the story of Eric and how Walter had been his toy.

"How could I be so stupid?" she said eventually. "I thought that he was ..."

"Talking to the dead perhaps," Elspeth finished the sentence, shaking her head.

Heather smiled, a tired, wan smile, but one that confirmed it was indeed madness. Who would be so crazy as to think that you could talk to the dead?

"I'd better go check on Adam," she said, standing up, her full coffee cup still in her hand.

Elspeth stood as well. "Yes, I'd better start moving too. There's a lot to sort out and ..." she waved her hand around. "I don't even know where to start, if I'm honest."

"Perhaps you'd like some help?"

They were in the doorway now. Elspeth looked down the hallway towards the darkness and then at the green light coming from the open kitchen door.

She found herself nodding. "Would you be able to? Do you have time? It's just sorting through paperwork, packing boxes, that sort of thing."

"Childcare is a bit scarce at the weekends so I'll have to bring Adam. I've only just moved here and ..."

"That's no problem. Should only be a few days or so. I've got to get back to work myself. Is tomorrow morning OK to start?"

Heather nodded. "Should be fine but I'll take your number in case there's a problem. I don't think I have it anymore."

Elspeth nodded. "I still have yours, so I'll send it on to your phone."

The two women were at the kitchen door now. Adam was still at the table, Walter bouncing on his knee while he moved the puppet's jaw up and down. It looked as though Walter was laughing silently.

"Adam, it's time to go." Heather beckoned to him.

Adam turned and hoisted Walter on his shoulder, as though he were carrying a toddler.

"Can Walter come home with us for a visit, please?" he asked Elspeth.

Elspeth looked at Heather, wondering would she mind. She really didn't care if Walter left home and never returned but it might be a bit much for Heather. But no, Heather didn't seem to care as she gave her a quick nod of agreement.

"Yes, that's fine," Elspeth replied.

"But just for tonight," Heather said quickly. "Because this is where Walter lives. Isn't that right, Elspeth?"

Elspeth looked at the younger woman again and wondered for a moment whether she should agree or not. What would happen if she said, no, please take Walter, he's yours to keep? But she could see the bruises, the lack of sleep plain upon Heather's face.

"I'm sorry, Adam, but Heather is right. Walter will need to come back home. Though I'm sure he'll enjoy his visit."

Adam stood up, cradling the puppet closer, wrapping his wooden arms around his neck.

"And Elspeth needs some help here. So when we call tomorrow we can bring Walter home. That's a good idea, isn't it?" Heather said.

Adam was whispering to Poe now, still in his cage on the table, then he began to nod enthusiastically, Walter's head bobbing against his shoulder.

Elspeth smiled at both of them, her mouth moving automatically, her lips tight against her teeth. She walked with them down the shadowy hall, not really listening as Adam chatted away. Heather was carrying Poe now because Adam's hands were occupied with Walter.

Elspeth pulled the front door open and walked with them out into the sunshine. She smiled again, that same tight sensation, and said goodbye after agreeing a time for the morning. She heard herself saying that she'd get boxes and be ready and then they were gone.

She could hear Adam still talking, his voice thin and high, and Heather agreeing with him as they made their way down the driveway.

Elspeth stood in the doorway, shading her eyes against the sun, watching them, until they were fully gone from sight.

Chapter 26

Elspeth stayed in the doorway – she needed a moment before going back inside. Although she could no longer see them, she could hear them. Adam was singing now, his voice drifting back to the house. It was the same song he'd been humming in the kitchen, the familiar tune.

Then Elspeth realised what it was, and the words came rushing back to her, like a forgotten nursery rhyme.

Poor old Fred,
Lost his head,
Poor old Fred,
Better off dead!

It was Eric's song, a favourite, one their father had made up when they were children. Nora hated it but that made Eric love it more. How many times had he stomped around the house – clapping his hands and marching to the beat, while singing at the top of his voice. He knew Nora hated the song but she wouldn't say anything – she couldn't – it was Frank and Eric's special song so all she could do was smile sourly while Eric sang and danced around the house.

And now Adam was singing the song. But where had he heard it? Not from Nora, who hated it – but who?

Elspeth closed her eyes. It was Eric singing now in her memory and she was fourteen again. They were upstairs in Uncle Harry's room and it was the night when Elspeth had overheard her mother talking to someone in the orchard.

When Nora came in from her walk, the heavy front door slammed shut behind her.

Then she stood in the hall and shouted: *"Elspeth! Eric!"*

Eric jumped immediately. It was her "very angry" voice, the one she usually saved for their worst demeanours and even then she used it rarely.

Elspeth put her hand on Eric's shoulder. She felt a growing sense of unease deep within her. As soon as she'd spotted her mother from the window and realised she been caught "spying" she knew there was going to be trouble.

"Where are you?" Nora shouted again.

Eric's shoulder trembled beneath Elspeth's hand.

"You stay here," she whispered. "It's me she's after, not you. You didn't do anything wrong."

"But what did you do?"

Elspeth shrugged her shoulders.

"I'm coming!" she shouted down the stairs before her mother could find her voice again and come looking for them.

"Stay here," Elspeth said again to Eric and then she quickly ran down the corridor leaving him alone, by the window, in Uncle Harry's room.

Nora was waiting, standing before the tarnished hall mirror, her arms folded across her chest.

"Where's Eric?" Nora demanded as Elspeth came running down the stairs.

"He's getting his pyjamas on. We're having the sleepover tonight, remember?"

The grandfather clock in the front room began to chime. It was eleven o'clock. Nora turned her head towards the sound and waited for the bells to stop, then she looked back at Elspeth.

"Yes, the sleepover. Of course I remember."

"What's wrong?" Elspeth asked.

All the anger seemed to have drained from her mother, her arms now hanging by her sides. She was glancing continuously towards the front door, as though expecting a visitor to call at any moment. She looked at Elspeth again as though she'd only just registered that she was standing there. She thought for a moment, her brow creased.

"You were watching me," she said.

"No, I wasn't."

"I could see you, Elspeth. From the window, looking down."

"No, we were playing hide-and-seek. I was just hiding from Eric. I wasn't watching –"

"Please, Elspeth," Nora interrupted, "I know exactly what you're like, always watching me. Always questioning my judgement. I know precisely what you think of me."

"But I'm not lying, I was just hiding. And then I heard voices and I looked out the window. I thought –" She stopped short. She didn't want to tell her mother that she'd hoped it was her father, come to take them away, come to save them.

"What voices?"

"I heard you talking to someone."

"I wasn't talking to anyone. Who on earth would I be talking to?"

Elspeth said nothing, watching the colour rising in her mother's cheeks – she was getting angry again.

"Well, who is there to talk to? Uncle Harry maybe? Back from the dead perhaps. Just popped by to give me a little gardening advice. Tell me what I should be planting for next spring."

Elspeth said nothing. There was no point in interrupting or arguing with her mother when she was like this, you just had to wait it out. It was like a sudden summer downpour – you just had to stand in the rain and accept that you were going to get wet, no matter what you did.

She was off on a different tangent now – complaining about Harry and how he'd let the house fall into disrepair and squandered all the family money on horses and whiskey. Elspeth stopped listening. None of it really mattered.

And then she heard a noise, a stealthy footstep.

It must be Eric, he hadn't stayed in the room, he'd followed her. Now, not only had he heard the whole sorry saga of Uncle Harry and all the rest of the meaningless accusations but he was obviously trying to sneak away in case Nora heard him. There really would be hell to pay if she caught another child eavesdropping.

Elspeth was standing still, captured within the storm of her mother's anger, wondering how she could escape, when she heard a huge bang upstairs and the sound of breaking glass.

"*Eric!*" her mother shouted and began to run up the stairs with Elspeth following.

Eric was standing at the top of the stairs, his head bowed and both his hands covering his ears. Shards of glass lay around him, glinting and sparkling in the low light.

"What the hell happened?" Nora asked, stopping herself before she stepped on the broken glass.

Eric glanced upwards and Elspeth realised the chandelier had fallen. Nora followed her gaze and they all looked at the heavy chain, still swinging from side to side.

"*But how? But how?*" Nora was saying, shaking her head. "*How did it fall?*"

"Are you all right, Eric?" Elspeth asked.

He nodded in response.

"Maybe if you step over this way, you'll be able to get out," Elspeth said, showing him a path through the shattered crystals.

Nora was still standing open-mouthed, looking at the broken link which once held the chandelier in place.

Eric stepped carefully over the shattered remains and Elspeth held out her hands. Tiny chips of glass shimmered in his hair. Two of the metal arms had fallen to one side and the broken light bulbs were still attached to the circular frame.

"I'd better clean this up," Nora said, not looking at either of them. "The whole bloody place is falling to pieces."

Elspeth and Eric skirted past the debris and went into his room, closing the door behind them. Outside Nora seemed to be sweeping or at least pushing the broken glass around. They could hear the sound of glass scraping against the wooden floor.

"What happened to the chandelier?" Elspeth asked.

Eric shook his head. "I don't know. I was just standing there, and then it began to swing really hard and when it swung back above me it fell ..."

"Why didn't you stay in the room, like I told you?"

Eric shrugged. "I don't know. Why was she shouting so much?"

"Oh, she just lost it. She's fine now," Elspeth replied, trying to make little of the shouting and paranoia.

"Was she really talking to someone outside?"

Elspeth sighed – he'd obviously overheard the entire conversation. "No," she said, shaking her head. "I was mistaken."

"It wasn't Dad then."

"No." Elspeth shook her head again. He must have been hoping the same thing as her. "Look, let's get some sleep. Here, you take these cushions and we'll sleep under the window."

"No," Eric said. "Not there."

"Well, over here then, beside the door," Elspeth shrugged, gathering up the pillows.

"No." Eric shook his head vehemently.

"Why, what's the difference?" Elspeth asked. "Where do you want to sleep?"

"We can't sleep," Eric explained. "We have to stop him."

"Stop who?

"The ghost."

Elspeth sighed and rolled her eyes. "Really, Eric. What did I tell you? There are no such things as ghosts, remember?"

Eric nodded – his face half-hidden behind the pillow he was carrying.

"I was hoping it was Dad," he said softly in a whisper that she had to strain to catch. "But it's not."

"Who?"

"The ghost. I hear him at night, every night. He comes up the stairs and goes next door." Eric turned his head towards Nora's room.

Elspeth could hear Nora on the landing. She was still clearing away the glass. The rhythmic sound of the sweeping and the noise of the broken glass sounded like a waterfall, shushing and tinkling. She thought again of the wet footprints, drying in the sun. Then she looked back at Eric, his pale face.

"Come on," she said to him. "We'll set up camp here, away from the door. Bring your blankets and I'll tell you a story."

"I don't want a scary story."

"No, don't worry – it's something different."

Elspeth could still remember how small he looked, curled up beside her and how she knew her mother had to be stopped. There was no point in pretending they were on holiday anymore. They had to get away from Crowfield and the sooner the better. She knew she had to get in touch with her father but, for now, all she could do was wait for the opportunity.

"OK, are you comfy? I'm going to tell you about the brave knight and the time he met a dragon. It began one winter's day, just after ..."

Chapter 27

Heather let Adam walk on in front of her. Walter kept sliding down his shoulders and Adam was fussing over the puppet, hitching him upwards and arranging his wooden arms around his neck as though he were a toddler and Adam was giving him a piggy-back.

Heather was carrying Poe in one hand and Adam's schoolbag in the other. The picnic lunch was long forgotten.

Adam was singing the daft song and swaying erratically into the road in time with the tune.

"Poor old Fred,
Lost his head,
Poor old Fred,
Better off dead!"

"Be careful," Heather said in a flat voice. She didn't know what to say or think. She was slightly dazed. Nothing had turned out the way she'd hoped and now, for some insane reason, she'd volunteered to give the little bird-lady a hand with packing up the madhouse. She just wanted to stop and sit down among the grasses at the side of the road. She needed to close her eyes, just for a minute, to give her head a chance to catch up with all that had happened that morning.

From the moment she agreed to let Adam visit Crowfield she should have known there would be trouble. She should have stopped him there and then, marched him back down to their house. And, now, look at the mess! Adam had the cursed puppet back in his possession and they had to help Elspeth the next day. Or did they?

She could make up some excuse, cut her ties with the family and that bloody house. She would have to find a way to take Walter back as well. The bird-lady had seemed a little too relieved to see the back of the puppet. Should she believe her though? Had Nora told Adam a story about Eric and Walter? Was it all that simple?

Heather tried to think back to the Saturday when she'd been cleaning the morning room. Nora and Adam had gone down the hall and then she'd heard their footsteps overhead. That was when she gave Walter to Adam. He must have been upstairs, packed away – waiting for his next owner. Of course Nora wasn't to know about Adam and how attached he could become to certain objects. She was now sure the puppet was simply a well-intentioned gift and Nora had only wanted to talk about her missing son.

"Walter wants to know what we're having for dinner this evening? Adam called back to her.

Heather resisted the urge to roll her eyes. She had to play along. She seemed to be getting everything wrong lately. Every decision, every step she took brought more trouble to her life. Why had she tried to use the Tarot cards the night before? Cass was right, she had no gift.

She gritted her teeth and replied. "What's his favourite food?"

Adam pulled the puppet closer to his ear.

Heather had almost drawn level with them at this stage and she could clearly see Walter's arched eyebrows. In a different, more suitable setting, like a puppet show, he might have appeared almost comical but, after all that happened so far, she couldn't help but see him in a more sinister light.

"Peanut butter!" Adam announced

Heather shook her head. She had to draw the line somewhere.

"We are not having peanut butter for dinner, young man."

Chapter 28

Elspeth could hear the crows, fighting and arguing, their sound the one constant at Crowfield. Heather and Adam were long gone. The song he had been singing had brought back another memory, another piece of her past. If only she could remember the night that Eric disappeared, that was the one that really mattered. She needed to trigger that one most of all.

She needed help and there was only one other person left she could talk to. But what would she say? How could she ask for his help? Eric's disappearance was obviously something that Martin O'Neill still thought about. He'd made the effort to come to her mother's funeral and made it his business to give her his contact details.

The card was still in her pocket. She knew there was no point in trying to use her mother's phone. It had been cut off. Nora had forgotten to pay the bill. Elspeth pulled out her mobile and began to wander the courtyard until she got a signal.

Martin answered the call on the second ring. His voice just as calm and reassuring as she remembered, right up to the point where her mother threw him out of Crowfield, while screaming like a banshee.

"I was wondering if you are still around?" Elspeth asked. "Perhaps you'd like to come over to Crowfield?"

Martin said he had no plans and agreed to call over.

Elspeth felt a strange sense of relief after that. He wasn't calling until lunchtime so she had a few hours to wait. She made her way down to the morning room and curled up on the couch again, pulling the quilt around her shoulders.

At exactly five to one, he knocked.

She took a deep breath and threw off the quilt. She hadn't slept although that was all she'd wanted to do. But every time she closed her eyes it seemed as though the house made another, different sound. She could hear strange scraping noises from behind the walls and at one stage she was convinced she heard footsteps, just like before.

Then Martin knocked and the house fell silent.

He was standing in the middle of the courtyard when she opened the door.

"Elspeth!" he said warmly. "It hasn't changed much." He waved towards the outbuildings and the overgrown yard.

Elspeth looked at it all as if through the eyes of a stranger – at the rampant weeds and nettles, Uncle Harry's old car rusting away in one corner.

"Yeah, my mother was a traditionalist – she didn't believe in change," she replied wryly. "Please come in."

Once inside, Martin paused again, looking around him, glancing towards the stairs. Elspeth wondered if he was remembering the morning when Nora threw him out of the house.

She gestured down the hall and began to lead him to the kitchen.

"You called to see me when I came home from the hospital," she said.

"Yes." He nodded. "We never really got to talk though."

"I think you called to the hospital as well, didn't you?"

"I did. But your mother was always there. She was very worried about you."

"Really, I don't remember that. I don't remember very much, to be honest."

"You were very sick, Elspeth. Double-pneumonia. It took quite a while for the infection to respond to treatment."

Elspeth shook her head. "I didn't realise. I knew I had pneumonia but my mother and I never talked. About any of it really."

They were in the kitchen now and Martin pulled out a chair and sat down. He was still looking around him.

"I'm guessing you don't live here anymore."

"No," Elspeth replied. "I moved away after university. Well, even before that. I went to boarding school that September ... after ... you know. My dad arranged it all."

She busied herself with the kettle and turned her head away, thinking of how happy she'd been to leave Crowfield, how she couldn't wait to escape. From the corner of her eye, she could see Martin looking around. He was obviously still invested in what had happened that summer. She wondered if he had any other cases that he was still trying to solve. Perhaps he spent his retirement travelling the country, trying to get people to talk to him, trying to jog their memories.

She turned around and pasted a smile on her face.

"So, where to start?" she said brightly.

The kettle was beginning its familiar noisy battle with the water.

Martin held out his hands. They were empty, like any good magician's.

"At the beginning," he said.

"Mine or yours?" Elspeth asked.

"I think we need both. But do you mind me asking you something before we start?"

"Of course," Elspeth answered, wondering if she had to agree to be interviewed. Perhaps there was some protocol, even with retired detectives that were spending their golden years simply catching up on old faces.

"Why now?" he asked.

Elspeth needed a moment. She knew the answer but it didn't make sense to her so how would it make sense to a stranger? She fussed with mugs and spoons and getting out the milk and coffee jar. The water had finally boiled and the kettle switched itself off.

She made the coffee and finally sat at the kitchen table opposite Martin.

She wrapped her hands around the mug and looked at him. "Why now? You know, I've asked myself the same thing, especially at night. I should probably walk away from here. Go back to my own life. But then I think of Eric. And for so long I tried not to. My mother never wanted to talk about him. I mean, you saw for yourself what she was like and I know my mother had a lot of ... " she paused, searching for the right word, "issues. I suppose that's what you'd call them today. But it wasn't something that was talked about years ago. And it didn't make a whole lot of sense to me as a teenager. I can probably see her perspective a little better now. Back then it was always easier to pretend that nothing had happened. I used to just go along with my mother and say nothing. But now, now that she's gone, I've realised there's no one left. There's only me now. My dad died, maybe six years ago. So that's it, I'm on my own – the last one who cares and I do care, I've always cared about what happened. It was just easier to pretend that I didn't."

Martin moved his coffee mug to one side and, reaching across the table, took Elspeth's hands between his own. "I care as well. I never knew your brother but I always cared. It's the reason I'm here now. I'm not just trying to solve an old case. It's means more than that to me."

She felt tears pricking her eyes. She pulled her hands away and stood up. She wasn't ready for this – it was still too raw.

"There might be biscuits somewhere. I'll have a look," she said awkwardly, turning away to riffle through the cupboards, waiting for her emotions to subside.

When she sat back down at the table, Martin explained that the case was dormant at this stage. Sometimes they revisited high-profile cases, asked the family to make an appeal, because after ten, fifteen, even twenty years things change and people that were previously unwilling to give evidence could finally come forward. In Eric's case, though, it wasn't quite that simple.

"Your mother wanted the case closed," he explained. "As soon as you were out of danger and able to come home from the hospital, she asked me to call. I thought that you'd remembered something and she wanted me to talk to you. But as soon as I came through the door, I realised something was wrong. Your father was here as well. He was waiting in the library and the atmosphere was fairly tense. I can't say if there had been a row between them earlier but there was a coldness. She started shouting at me within the first few minutes. She was accusing me of trying take you away. She kept saying that she wasn't going to lose both children. Your father stayed in the library and I got a sense that the whole scene was engineered for him. So, she was shouting at me but it was really at your father, if that makes sense."

Elspeth nodded. How many times had herself and Eric been caught in the crossfire of their parents' battles?

Martin leaned closer and placed his hands on the table. "I know you understand that we're just two people, having a conversation, Elspeth. But if there is anything at all that you remember, or that your mother said, then perhaps we could look at re-opening the case. I'm not making any promises, because it all depends on so many variables. But would you like to see the case re-opened?"

Elspeth thought for a moment. "I'm afraid that I'm no use, though. I still don't remember anything about that night. If the case was re-opened, would it help? They found nothing the last time, what would be different now? It's been so long – surely there's not much hope of finding anything at this stage?"

"You'd be surprised what might come to light. For instance, what about your mother's papers, letters, notes? Have you looked through any of those yet?"

Elspeth supressed a shudder and tried not to think of her mother's room upstairs. "No, not yet. I don't know if she left anything. Knowing my mother she probably burned anything that might contain information."

"Why?"

"Oh, she was getting a bit paranoid as she got older. She used to burn bank statements and any correspondence with her name on it. I think she may have had the beginnings of dementia."

Martin nodded. "Still, it might not be a bad place to start. Maybe look through any papers, letters, anything that has survived. Then we can meet this evening, at the hotel I mentioned. I'm staying there for the next week or so. Your never know, we might have a breakthrough, get some answers. What do you think?"

"Yes, that would be great. And one more thing ... is there any way at all that I could see the files or the paperwork from when Eric disappeared? I'm hoping it might trigger a memory. Help me remember what happened."

Martin shook his head. "I don't think so. It's in archive storage at this stage and, strictly speaking, it's not publicly available."

She nodded and Martin stood up. He was too tall, too big for the room.

She got up and they walked back down the hallway together, Martin taking his time as though he were trying to absorb some of Crowfield's secrets before he left.

At the front door, he turned and took her hand.

"Thank you for talking to me," he said.

"Martin, there *is* just one more thing."

"Yes?"

"Was I ever a suspect?"

His face creased and she could see how uncomfortable he was. "Well, yes, strictly speaking both you and your mother were suspects. Statistically most missing child cases involve close family members. We can talk about this later though if you like."

Elspeth nodded slowly. "Just one more thing before you go. Was it my fault?"

"No. Why do you think that? Why would it have anything to do with you?"

"My mother," she answered. "She told me it was my fault. Well, she always implied it was my fault and ... it's just I can't remember ..."

"Elspeth, please listen," Martin said, still holding her hand. "You were fourteen. Your mother had left you and your eight-year-old brother alone in the house. If anyone was at fault, it was her."

She felt the tears stinging her eyes again and she pulled her hand away from his.

"Elspeth, don't let my interest pressurise you in any way," he said gently. "Perhaps you should go back to your own life. Let the past stay there. You can't save Eric, it's too late for that. But you can think of yourself."

Elspeth was silent, letting all the words sink in. She'd needed to hear them from someone else, an adult, someone who'd been there that summer. She wasn't at fault. She hadn't let her brother down.

"I'm sorry to rush off," Martin said, glancing at his watch. "I do have to go now but I'll see you later."

Chapter 29

She was alone again, it seemed to be a recurring theme. Martin was gone and he'd left more questions than answers. Elspeth had guessed that she probably wouldn't be allowed to see the files from when Eric disappeared but it was worth asking and now her teenage self was vindicated as well. It wasn't her fault, it was Nora's.

It was Nora who had left them alone, that awful night. The night of the storm, where the power went out and the lightning hit the weather vane outside.

Elspeth closed her eyes. She was the only one left, she had the knowledge within her. But how to unlock the memory?

She looked at the stairs. So far she had only gone upstairs to use the bathroom and, even then, she'd kept her eyes firmly on the ground while walking. All the doors seemed to be closed and she was quite happy about that, all the less to see. She wondered if they were locked again, like when they first came to stay that summer.

She paused for a moment on the first step, then she gripped the banister and continued. The house seemed to have settled down again, no strange noises – if anything it seemed too quiet. If she stayed still and listened all she could hear was the crows, fighting and disagreeing in the woods behind the house.

Upstairs, she looked down the corridor. She was right – all the doors were closed. Which room first, she wondered. Hers – it was probably the safest and she needed to get it set up for tonight. There was no point sleeping on a couch when there was a perfectly good bed waiting up here. She pushed the door and it opened without so much as an ominous creak.

The blinds were drawn and the room in darkness but it was just as Elspeth remembered, the bed on the left-hand side. The same as Eric's room, his was a mirror-image of hers. Trying not to think, she walked across and firmly pulled the curtains. Dust rose instantly, making her cough.

She looked down into the courtyard and watched the falling leaves for a moment, then she went over to the bed. She lifted the pillows and the bedspread – everything seemed to be covered in years of dust – she dragged them off the bed, she could wash them later.

The wardrobe was empty, just a few metal hangers bumping against each other, like nasty wind-chimes, ringing with a dull, ugly note.

She closed the door and opened the chest of drawers, also empty. Some crumpled sheets of faded newspaper lined the bottoms. She took one out, searching through the spotted print for a date: August, 1974.

She slid the sheets back into the drawer and closed it. Where were all her old clothes? Her mother must have cleared the room at some stage and not told her. Maybe she did, maybe she did tell her and she forgot. Anyway, it didn't matter – there was nothing in Crowfield that she'd wanted to keep.

Back in the corridor she found that she couldn't go into Eric's room so she went to her mother's room instead. Outside the door, she stopped for a minute. She hadn't set foot in this room for so many years. She took a deep breath and opened the door. If there were any notes or letters, they would possibly be in here. Where to start though?

She went to the oversized chest of drawers and pulled open the top drawer. Nothing but old stretched tights and bobbled socks. She ran a hand through them, feeling for any papers or boxes perhaps but there was nothing there. The next drawer held nightdresses and underwear, Elspeth ran her hands through the contents, checking for any letters or papers while the heavy, musky scent of her mother's stale perfume rose in the air. She searched the other drawers but it was a futile search. They held nothing but clothes.

She shook her head, thinking. The room felt heavy, the stale air catching in her throat. She went to the window and with a pull managed to get it open. She leaned out, swallowing the clean autumn air. The room still felt heavy, leaden, but she knew it was just anxiety – she'd done well to make it this far.

She made her way to the open door. She could see the stairs and the banisters, the place where the crystal chandelier had fallen. Her mother had never bothered replacing it, there was just a solitary lightbulb hanging there now.

Then she heard a noise downstairs – in the hall. But no-one had knocked, had they? Perhaps it was Martin, perhaps he'd forgotten something? *But you didn't hear his car, did you?* a little voice whispered in her head.

She stood frozen, rooted in fear.

She tried to open her mouth to call out but she couldn't. It was as though she'd been pushed back in time and she was a girl again, in the bathroom – listening to stealthy footsteps as they came up the stairs.

She heard the first tread on the wooden stairs, quiet, a slow, sneaking sound.

She managed to put her hand to her mouth to try to still her breathing. Someone was coming up the stairs. She watched as the outline of a head began to rise through the banisters. It was a man. Although still deep in the shadows, she could see he had a beard and longish hair. He stopped and turned towards the open door of Nora's room, as though he had felt the weight of her gaze upon him.

They locked eyes.

He quickly turned and began to descend the stairs, his racing footsteps loud in her ears.

"*Wait!*" Elspeth shouted. "*Wait!*"

She ran down after him, but he was gone. She could hear his footsteps on the gravel. She ran to the door and she could see him as he ran up the drive, his hair flying out behind him. He didn't look back.

She knew him, knew his face. She had seen him before, but who was he? Was he a friend of her mother's or just some local man from the village?

She made sure the door was locked this time. She checked it twice before going to the kitchen. The strangest thing of all was that she hadn't been afraid. He seemed more afraid of her. Of course he was sneaking around her house, but that didn't explain why he ran away. If he meant no harm, then why did he run?

It made no sense. Instead of finding answers she was uncovering more mysteries.

Chapter 30

Back at the house, Heather forced a smile as Adam propped the puppet on a chair beside the table.

"He's really hungry," he explained as he arranged the wooden hands carefully.

Heather nodded, feeling the smile on her face turn into a grimace.

Adam didn't notice – he was busy trying to arrange Walter's limbs.

"Here's your fork," he said, placing the wooden hand over the handle. "He's so hungry," he told Heather again. "He hasn't had dinner in *so* long."

Heather was trying not to think about Elspeth and the conversation they'd had in the sunshine-filled room at Crowfield. The puppet is not possessed, she told herself. Still, she couldn't bear to look Walter in the eye. There seemed to be a horrible gleam of intelligence in those flat, painted orbs.

Then a sudden and shocking thought came to her. What if Elspeth was the reason her brother was missing? Her mother, Mrs Collins, had seemed scared of her and she'd said something, once, during one of her episodes when she thought Heather was Elspeth. What was it?

Adam was tapping her wrist. "Aren't you listening?" he said.

"Sorry, Adam. I was miles away."

"Walter was saying that the man is back."

"Oh, that's nice."

"Yes. He went to visit Elspeth."

"Did he?"

"Yes. He's at the house."

"OK."

"He's looking for Eric and then he might visit us because Elspeth is going away now."

Heather didn't know what to say. The casual way that Adam talked about Eric, as though he were a school friend or a cousin. She tried to steer the conversation back to normality.

"And where has Elspeth gone? On her holidays perhaps. Or to the beach maybe?" she asked, forcing another smile.

"He doesn't know, dinner maybe. But she needed to go out, didn't she? Walter said she is always in the way."

Adam looked at Heather as though the strange conversation was completely normal. They might as well be discussing homework or talking about going to Patsy's shop.

Heather felt the hairs begin to stand on the back of neck. She tried to continue smiling and nodding but she could feel the corners of her mouth beginning to drop.

"And how does Walter know all this?" she asked.

Adam laughed. "He's a familiar, like Poe. You're so silly, Heather! I've told you this before, remember?"

Heather was quiet for a moment, thinking. "And if Poe is Cass's familiar, then who does Walter belong to?"

"Eric, of course." Adam laughed. "He's really funny and he knows so many rhymes and jokes. Wait – I'll ask him to tell you one."

"No, no, that's fine. Perhaps I'll give Elspeth a quick call. Just to check the time we have to be there tomorrow."

Adam nodded and pretended to feed Walter a strand of spaghetti. It clung to his painted mouth and Adam leaned closer as though Walter was whispering in his ear.

"Walter wants to know if I have to help with the boxes? Or can I play with him?"

"You can play with Walter. The boxes would be much too heavy for you," Heather replied absentmindedly. She was more concerned with finding Elspeth's number on her phone.

"But I have muscles."

Heather nodded. "I know you do."

"But it's better that I can play with Walter. We're going to play hide-and-seek. Eric knows all the best hiding places."

"*Mmmm ...*" She held up a finger – she was still scrolling through her phone.

She got up from the table.

"I'll just be a minute," she said. "Please, finish your dinner."

In the narrow hall, Heather listened to the phone ringing. She was counting now – one, two, three rings. Elspeth wasn't going to answer, was she? Four, that bloody puppet was right. Five. Something strange was happening at Crowfield. Six rings. She would have to go over, wouldn't she? Seven. Eight rings.

"Hello?"

"Oh, hi. It's Heather, I was, *em* ..."

"Hi, Heather. Is everything all right?"

"Yes. About tomorrow, I was – " Heather thought frantically – what excuse could she use? She could hardly say that Walter had implied she was dead. Or had he?

"Yes, sorry, Elspeth. Just checking what time to call tomorrow?"

"Eleven – if that suits?"

"Yes, perfect. We'll see you then."

"Bye, Heather."

"Bye."

Heather looked at the phone in her hand. She was losing her mind, what was she thinking? She stood outside the kitchen door. She heard a wooden thump, Walter's hand banging off the table most likely. Adam laughed.

Chapter 31

Martin was waiting at a table as Elspeth made her way through the busy dining room.

"Sorry I'm a bit late," she said as she sat down.

"Not at all," he said with a smile. "I'm glad you could make it."

"It's good to be out of that house."

"It must be," he said, concern plain upon his face.

She picked up a menu and smiled. "At least I'll have some company tomorrow. Heather – a young woman who did some cleaning for my mother – is coming over."

"Would she remember anything? Perhaps your mother confided in her?"

"No, they weren't friends. In fact, she barely knew her – she'd only just begun to work for her. She offered me a hand, packing some boxes. That way I can cover more ground, go through paperwork, hopefully."

"And how did you get on today? Did you find anything?"

Elspeth half-smiled. "Well, I didn't find any paperwork. But I did find an intruder."

"Oh, like squirrels or mice?" Martin laughed.

"No. A man."

Instantly his demeanour changed. "Elspeth, why didn't you call me?"

"He ran away as soon as he saw me. There was no point worrying you. He was long gone."

"Still, Elspeth, this is serious –"

"I know," she interrupted. "But it's my own fault, I'm an idiot. I left the front door wide open."

"But he must have seen your car."

"I know. Perhaps he thought I left with you. It's very odd. And this is the really strange bit. He seemed afraid of me because as soon as he saw me, he ran away."

"Burglars tend to do that," Martin said, dryly. "But perhaps he came in through the back?"

"How? The back door was locked."

"Very odd." Martin frowned, then shook his head. "So, it was just after I left?"

"Not long after. You might have seen him."

Martin thought for a moment. "Yes, there was a man. He was walking along the village road. I'm afraid I didn't even give him a second glance. Did you get a good look at him?"

"I did and that's the other funny thing. I knew him. I mean, I've seen him before. I can't remember where though. Perhaps from when I was a child. It was his eyes because obviously his face, you know, he's older and he had a beard ..." she trailed off.

"How old?"

"Older than me, in his forties perhaps. Longish hair. Blue eyes."

"Would you recognise him again if you saw him?"

"I think so, yes. But surely it's just some nosy local wandering around? These things happen after someone dies and there's an empty house."

"But the house wasn't empty. You were there. And so was your car."

"I'll be more careful. I'll lock the door tonight, I promise."

"But you think you would recognise him again?"

"Why? Do you know who it might be?"

"Do you remember earlier when you asked if you were a suspect?"

She nodded slowly.

"Well, there was a suspect. A young man."

Elspeth was shocked. She didn't know what to say. Eventually she found her voice.

"Do you think he had something to do with Eric's disappearance?"

"Perhaps, but we never managed to track him down."

"Why did you suspect him?"

"I'm not sure how much I should tell you, Elspeth. I don't want to give you a false story because we got nowhere at the time. The first we heard about him was from an anonymous phone call. A woman rang in to tell us about this man. He was young, late teens, early twenties, so only five maybe ten years older than you were. He'd been living rough in that old cottage not far from Crowfield. Some other people in the village remembered him as well, but they thought he was harmless, just a summer drifter, living in the woods. They assumed he would move on as the weather got colder and they were right. He disappeared. We found bits and pieces up at the cottage, nothing incriminating, but enough for us to see that someone had been living there. By the time we checked it out, he was long gone. We had some sketches made from descriptions and we asked your mother – but she'd never noticed anyone in the woods."

"She used to go walking there all the time."

"Well, the cottage is a bit off the beaten track. It's entirely possible they never met."

"Wait, I remember her talking to someone, one evening, just outside the walled garden. And then she denied it. But there was definitely someone there."

"That's very odd." Martin frowned. "She never mentioned anything like that to us."

"But there was no actual evidence against that man?"

"No. But he was a suspect until we got to talk to him and we never did."

"But if it is the same man, why would he come back? Why now?" Elspeth asked.

"It might be as simple as you said before. Things change when a person dies and a house is empty."

※ ※ ※

After dinner, as she drove back to the house, Elspeth tried to clear her thoughts. When Martin asked her earlier if she was happy to stay alone in Crowfield that night, she'd said yes. And at the time she'd meant it. But they were in a crowded restaurant then, with noise and purpose, other people milling around. Now, as she drove back on the deserted road, fears began to crowd her mind.

She never knew there was a suspect, although it made complete sense now. For so long she'd thought about Eric's disappearance through the lens of her fourteen-year-old self. She'd willingly accepted her mother's refusal to ever talk about what happened and she'd been glad of the memory gaps. It was as though Eric was there one day and gone the next, with no outside interference or anything suspicious. It was just an unfortunate thing that occurred, like a storm or an accidental fire. No one was to blame, except her of course.

And now she couldn't ask Nora any questions. Not that it really mattered – she wouldn't have been truthful anyway, would she? But it was all coming out, the elaborate house of cards her mother had built and spent so long preserving and maintaining. It was beginning to fall apart.

Her headlights picked up the gently moving sign. She was back at Crowfield already. A familiar knot began to build in her stomach as she drove slowly along the driveway to the house. It was in darkness.

Why come back now, she thought. Who was this person and what has changed? Perhaps he was looking for something?

Elspeth got out of the car. She could hear the wind beginning to build in the trees behind the courtyard. A storm was building – she could feel it in the air, a tangible heaviness.

Once inside, she clicked the heavy switch and the lights came on. She thought about running through the entire house and switching on all the lights. That way, there would be no shadows, nowhere to hide.

The door to the library was open and she stepped inside. This was where her mother had died. She'd avoided the room since the first night, even now she tried not to think about Nora's death. Dr Lacy had told her very little – perhaps that was part of her job, to try and spare people the gory details. All she knew was that Nora had been sitting at the desk and then collapsed. And the postman had found her.

Elspeth closed her eyes and then opened them. It was just a room, she told herself, nothing more, just another room. She looked around. The desk surface was covered in books and newspapers. Perhaps she should have begun her search here and not upstairs in her mother's room?

She sat down. This was where the missing keys had been found, long ago. She pulled at the handle on the right but the drawer was locked. Then she began trying the other drawers, but they were locked too.

She left the library, pulling the door closed behind her. She would look for the keys tomorrow and go through the drawers.

She stood for a moment in the bright hall. She could hear something – the wind whistling? It was coming from upstairs. She made her way slowly up the steps, pausing on each tread, listening for the sound. It was coming from her mother's room.

The door was open and the curtains blowing wildly in the rising wind. Elspeth realised she'd forgotten to close the window earlier that day.

She hurried to the window to shut it and, looking down through the rattling leaves of ivy, she wondered if it was possible to climb into the house that way – but it looked too dangerous. She pulled the window shut with a struggle and turned back to face the room.

Now, I must think like Nora, she told herself. Where would I hide something?

In Eric's room.

It was as though she'd known the answer all along but she hadn't wanted to say it out loud, or even think it.

The door to his room was shut, of course. She braced herself and pushed it open. At least that grotesque puppet wasn't sitting on Eric's bed, waiting for a bedtime story – the one about the boy who never came home perhaps.

Inside, the room was perfectly preserved, not a single thing out of place. The bedspread hung in neat, straight lines and the pillows were fat, freshly plumped – waiting for a tired head. An array of items lay across his bedside locker. There was no dust here – each memento shone bright. There was a tiny, silver-coloured pocketknife, a smooth, polished stone, a snowglobe and a tarnished medal on a faded ribbon. There was also a comic book, its corners curled and yellowing.

Elspeth stepped forward, on her tiptoes. It felt like she was looking at a display in a museum case. Soon an automated voice would start talking and explain the relevance of the artefacts before her.

And here we a have a very useful item, a pocketknife with two tiny retractable blades. This was possibly the most-used item in a small boy's arsenal and was frequently employed in carving initials, into tree-bark, mainly.

Despite herself, she smiled at the memory. If she went down through the orchard, she would probably find scarred tree-trunks, his initials forever branded into their bark. Without thinking, she sat on the bed and it made a strange noise, as though she'd sat on wrapping paper. She stood up and pulled back the bedspread and then the sheets and blankets. A great patchwork display of assorted newspapers and clippings lay before her.

She began to take them out and arrange them on the floor. They were all from different newspapers, but they were all from the same time, the summer Eric disappeared. Why had she hidden them here? Had she even read them? Given that Nora had been in such denial about his disappearance, it seemed strange that she'd kept physical evidence of it.

Elspeth looked at the windowsill. There was a tiny pool of wax with a burnt wick sitting there. How long had it been since Nora lit candles in the window at night? How long had it taken her to realise that Eric wasn't coming back?

Chapter 32

Heather woke with a start. She hadn't slept well. She'd been dreaming again – well, it was more a nightmare than a dream. She couldn't remember it all, just snapshots, grainy scenes running together. There was a wood and the sound of water – a roaring, surging noise and then she was in an abandoned cottage with broken wooden laths at the windows. She was trying to leave and she couldn't. Someone was coming, then there was a shadowy figure standing in the doorway.

She sat up. There was the faintest trace of light outside, it would be daybreak soon. Heather rolled over slowly and pulled back the bedclothes. She felt as though she hadn't slept at all and now she had to go to Crowfield and help the little bird-lady pack up boxes. She wanted nothing more than to crawl back under the warm covers and pretend she'd never heard of Crowfield, but she didn't. Instead, she pulled on socks and a hoody, wrapping herself up against the morning chill as best she could.

Yawning loudly, she left her room. She peeped into Adam's room. She could hear his breathing, deep and slow. No nightmares for him, despite the ghoulish creature that had shared his bed all night. Yes, there was Walter, the silver buttons on his jacket glinting in the light, still in the same position that Adam had placed him in the night before, his head on the pillow and his hands nicely tucked beneath the blankets. Adam was curled into a ball, like a puppy.

Heather stifled another yawn in case she woke him and then quietly pulled the door closed behind her.

In the kitchen she waited beside the kettle, not wanting to move around for fear of waking him. She quietly took a mug from the cupboard and made her coffee. At the table she slid the mug to one side, unsure if she even wanted it now. Her thoughts returned to Crowfield House, again and again, and the two women, mother and daughter, so different, as unalike as they could be.

Then she began to think of Cass. Was she like Cass? Certainly not in looks, but possibly in other ways – it was hard when you didn't know a person that well. They'd only managed to live together as a family for six months before Cass got sick and their lives had changed irrevocably. After that Cass was in and out of hospital and then eventually the hospice.

Heather sighed and began to drink her coffee. Everyone tells lies, she decided, even Elspeth, the little bird-lady of Crowfield. She was lying, of that Heather was certain. But it was a funny kind of lying, as though she didn't know the truth. And her mother, Mrs Collins, she'd also been lying but that was possibly because she'd forgotten the truth. But what about the missing boy poor little Eric – nothing left of him but his old toy puppet Walter as evidence of his existence. Who were they trying to save with their lies?

There was a thud from Adam's room. Walter falling out of the bed, no doubt.

She stood up. It was fully bright now, the half-darkness finally gone. She made her way to his room but when she went in Walter was in the same place, propped on the pillow and Adam was still fast asleep.

Heather shook her head. She was certain she'd heard the puppet falling but yet, there he was, still dreaming, his wooden head resting peacefully on the pillow. Heather bent down, staying as far away from Walter as she could.

"Adam, it's time to get up. We have to go to Crowfield today, to help Elspeth, remember?"

And just like that, he was awake. It never ceased to amaze her, his ability to go from sleeping to waking in the blink of an eye.

"*Yay!*" Adam shouted, throwing back the covers and getting out of bed. "We can play all day today," he said to Walter "All day. I promise!"

In the kitchen Heather decided to make fresh coffee and, as she waited by the window watching the steam rise from the kettle, she wondered how she could manage to leave Walter at Crowfield. That was where he rightfully belonged and then there would be no more visits, no more sleepovers, no more cosy chats with Walter. But she knew Adam and she knew it wasn't going to be that simple.

After breakfast they began the slow walk out to Crowfield. This time it was Heather dragging her feet, not Adam. The weather had changed and she had made Adam wrap up with his scarf and hat before leaving. She was also bundled up but the wind was tearing at her face, making her eyes water. Adam was laughing and running on ahead. As the road twisted and curved, Heather lost sight of him. A momentary panic gripped her when she realised he was gone and she called out to him to wait for her. Her footsteps quickened until she turned the corner and there he was – still laughing and singing to himself. Her heart stopped racing and her mind settled again.

"Too much coffee," she muttered to herself. "And not enough sleep."

Finally, they were on the last stretch of road. Heather could see the rusty sign – in fact, she almost thought she could hear it squeaking even though it was too far away. She watched as the wind caught it, rocking it back and forth – *welcome back, welcome back*, it squeaked.

"*Heather!*" Adam called. He had stopped singing and now was looking anxiously back.

"*What's wrong?*" she called but he didn't answer, gripping Walter to his chest in a death-hug. "*Adam?*"

Then she saw a man on the road, coming the other way. He was walking fast with his head down and his long dark hair covering his face. He was right beside Adam now – so close that if he stretched out his arm, just a few inches, he could have touched his face.

"*Adam!*" Heather shouted.

The man looked up at Heather and then he began to run back in the direction he had come. Heather started to run as well, while Adam remained where he was, stock-still, as though he'd been planted there.

Moments later Heather was by his side.

"Are you OK?" she panted.

The man was gone, even the sound of his footsteps had faded away.

"He's looking for Eric."

"What?"

"That man. Walter said that he's trying to find Eric."

Heather stood for a moment, speechless, and then the anger began to build within her.

"I'm sorry, Adam, but I've had enough," she said eventually in a low voice. "I know you're friends with Walter but when we give this puppet back to Elspeth I don't want to hear any more about Eric or Walter, ever again. Do you understand?"

"*No, please, no, we can't! He has no friends, he needs us! We have to help him!*"

"Come on, let's go," Heather said, catching him by the shoulder and propelling him along the rutted driveway to Crowfield. "This madness has to stop, Adam."

"*It's not Walter's fault. He needs me!*"

"Adam, listen to what you're saying! This is crazy talk. You're being weird."

She felt as though she might start crying at any moment. She wanted to kneel down and apologise to Adam, to tell him that he wasn't weird but she couldn't.

"Ask her," Adam said stubbornly.

"Who?"

"Elspeth, the bird-lady."

"What did you say?"

"The bird-lady. That's what you call her, isn't it?"

Heather stared at him, wide-eyed. Yes, that was what she called Elspeth, but she was certain she hadn't said it out loud, and definitely not in front of Adam.

"Never mind what I call her. We need to leave Walter here. This is his home."

"*No,*" Adam said firmly, walking quickly towards the house.

Heather followed, feeling powerless.

Adam had reached the front door. It was open.

"Adam, wait! We have to knock!"

"She won't hear us! She's asleep." He stepped inside, disappearing into the well of blackness.

"*Wait!*" Heather shouted but he was gone.

She stood for a moment at the open door, her hand raised as though to knock, manners so ingrained that they made her pause momentarily though she could hear Adam's runners slapping against the wood, as he ran down the long hall. She cursed under her breath and then, glancing back to make sure that the strange man from the road hadn't followed them, she stepped inside.

She hurried down the hall to the kitchen.

Adam was there, standing by a chair, his hand on Elspeth's shoulder. She was slumped across the table, her arms outstretched and her head resting awkwardly against one of her arms. The entire table was covered in piles and sheets of newspaper. An empty wine bottle stood on the table, an overturned glass beside it.

"*Adam*," Heather began but he raised his hand to silence her.

"*Shhh*, don't wake her!" he whispered.

"Is she ...?"

"Asleep, yes, I think so," he whispered again and then he looked at Walter as though expecting him to have an input into the whole crazy scenario.

Heather shook her head. She'd had enough. She walked across the floor and shook Elspeth quite roughly by the shoulder.

"Elspeth, can you hear me? It's Heather."

Elspeth stirred, her head moving slowly.

"What?" she murmured. "I was just ..."

Red wine had spilled across one of the newspapers, blotting out the photos and the words. Heather realised they were all old – faded and yellowing. A large headline caught her eye, MISSING BOY ...

"It's not her fault," Adam said.

Heather ignored him.

"Elspeth, it's Heather! We came to help you with packing boxes today. Do you remember?"

Elspeth looked around, blinking slowly in the green gloom of the kitchen. She put one hand to her head.

"Yes, I remember ... and I'm really sorry. I don't know what happened. I don't usually do this." She gestured towards the table, the spilt wine, the overturned glass.

Heather was silent. What could she say?

"It's OK," Adam said, lifting Walter as though he was going to pat her arm in a reassuring manner.

Elspeth recoiled at the sight of the puppet.

"Maybe another day then," Heather said. "Come on, Adam. Let's go."

Adam didn't move. He stayed by Elspeth's side, Walter still in his arms, looking at the sheets of newspaper scattered across the table. He was moving the puppet's head from side to side as though he were reading the headlines.

"Please, don't go," Elspeth said weakly. "You're here now. A glass of water, some paracetamol and I'll be fine in a minute. Please!"

Heather was in the doorway now. Looking down the long, dark corridor, she could see the golden patch of sunlight. She looked back. Adam was standing by the table – reluctant to leave. Elspeth was watching her, her eyes smudged and dark, deep purple – another person who couldn't sleep.

Heather shook her head and stepped back into the kitchen.

"Right," she heard herself saying. "So, where do you want to start?"

Adam pulled up a chair at the table and moved one of the sheets of newspaper so Walter could "read" the rest of the article.

"Let's start by tidying these away," Heather said loudly.

Elspeth had her back to her. She was by the sink now – a glass of water in her hand and two small tablets in the other.

"What about hide-and-seek?" Adam said. "You promised."

"Well, I didn't actually. We're here to help with the boxes, remember?"

Heather was busy, folding the old newspapers. They were soft and worn beneath her fingers, like crushed velvet. She was careful, fearful that they might just crumble away to nothing. She caught sight of the date, even though she was trying very hard not to read any of the articles. You don't need to know any of this, she told herself. *Don't look, don't read*, she kept saying over and over.

And there was a picture of Eric. She couldn't look away. She stared at the grainy photograph, at his face, pale and intense, a heavy fringe falling over one eye. She looked away but it was too late – his face was seared into her memory. She folded the rest of the newspaper sheets while trying to look out the window.

Adam was kicking the floor restlessly, his runners banging against the wooden legs of his chair.

"I'll be back in a minute," Elspeth said and left without looking at either of them.

The papers were folded. Now all Heather could see was an ad for washing powder, whiter than white guaranteed. She pulled out a chair and sat across from Adam.

"Adam, tell me – how did you know Elspeth was asleep?"

Adam looked at Walter.

"Give me strength!" Heather muttered under her breath. She was veering between anger and fear but annoyance was definitely the stronger emotion she was experiencing now. "Adam, we need to give this puppet back. He belongs here, in this house. Now what do –"

A shout from above rang out through the air, cutting her off.

Adam jumped to his feet and Walter fell in a clatter of noise to the floor.

It was Elspeth. She was shouting, "*Wait! Wait!*"

They rushed out to the hallway.

"*Is everything all right?*" Heather shouted up the stairs.

The urge to leave was getting stronger by the second.

There was no reply and then Elspeth came running down the stairs, almost slipping on the steps.

"Did you see him?" she asked as she ran past, her eyes wild and haunted.

"Who?"

"The man! He was here yesterday as well!"

Heather and Adam followed her as she ran out into the courtyard. It was empty.

"He's gone now," Adam said in a soft voice.

"Looks like it," Elspeth replied. She was looking down the driveway, shielding her eyes from the low morning sun.

"We saw him earlier," Adam said.

"What are you saying, Adam? This is stupid, we need to leave."

"*We did see him!*" Adam argued. "On the road, earlier, remember? He's looking for Eric."

"Oh my God, this is ridiculous. It's too much. I'm really sorry, Elspeth, but we have to go. Adam, please put that puppet back inside. *Now.*"

Adam stood his ground. There were tears beginning to form in his eyes but Heather didn't back down.

"*Now,* Adam. You heard me."

She motioned towards the open door.

"I'm sorry, I don't understand," Elspeth said. "Where did you see the man? And why are you leaving?"

Heather was watching Adam making his way slowly back into the house, cradling Walter against his shoulder. She turned to Elspeth and sighed.

"There was a man on the road. When we were on our way here. And Adam got this idea that he's searching for Eric. Look, I realise you have a lot to deal with at the moment and I know I said that I'd help, but I can't."

Heather turned back towards the house, to watch for Adam. She didn't want to look at Elspeth anymore.

Elspeth said nothing for a moment and then she spoke in a small voice. "I understand."

Heather nodded back in response but remained silent.

"I'm sorry. I've wasted your time and brought you –"

Heather shook her head, stopping her. "No, no, it's all right. It's been …"

And she didn't finish the sentence, the words just hung there, like tiny wisps of smoke – floating through the air. It was quiet, so quiet and still, no traffic sound or noise from the birds from the rookery, just the occasional sigh of the wind in the trees.

They waited for Adam. Neither woman spoke. It was as though a spell had been cast upon them. They were like two stone ladies, their eyes downcast, saying nothing.

Elspeth heard the noise first. She glanced towards the open door and then upstairs to the third window across. She could see Adam. He was at the window, one hand raised … no, it was Walter, his wooden hand against the glass, tapping.

Elspeth looked at Heather. She hadn't heard anything. She was still waiting – her arms folded and her gaze firmly on the ground.

"Adam is upstairs," Elspeth said.

"What?"

"He's upstairs, in Eric's room."

Heather followed her line of vision and looked towards the blank windows where the sunlight was reflected. It glittered bright against the glass. She couldn't see anything.

"Which one? I can't see him."

But Elspeth was gone – she was at the front door, going back inside.

"Elspeth, wait, I –"

Heather followed her through the open door. Once inside, the darkness was overwhelming, suffocating. She blinked, trying to see. Where had Elspeth gone?

"*Adam!*" she shouted. "*Adam, where are you?*"

She looked down the long hall – the kitchen door was closing. She could see shadows lengthening on the floor. She hurried down the hall.

"*Adam, come on! It's time to go!*"

For some reason, it seemed very important to get Adam and leave. The walls of the house felt as though they were closing in. It felt as though everything was beginning to fold in on itself. That the house was nothing more than an origami piece and it was about to consume itself. A new trick. Instead of the disappearing boy, it was the disappearing house.

"*Adam!*" Heather called again as she reached the closed kitchen door. She turned the handle and went inside.

It was empty, there was nobody there, just the yellow, faded newspapers. She could see the headline again: MISSING BOY.

But she had folded them and turned the headline away in case Adam read it. Elspeth must have moved them. She ran to the back door and tried the handle, it was locked.

"*Adam!*" she shouted again and went back out into the hallway.

It seemed darker than before and she realised that the front door was now closed. She reached for the nearest light switch. The light came on, flaring brightly and then there was an enormous bang and darkness.

Heather swore under her breath, could this house be any stranger?

"*Adam! We have to go!*" she called loudly again. "*Elspeth, where are you?*"

She made her way back up the hall – her feet scrunching on broken glass as she passed where the bulb had blown.

She was back at the front door. She pulled it open and let the morning sunlight fall inside. There was no one in the courtyard. It was empty.

She went back inside and stood at the bottom of the stairs. She put her hand on the banister. Her heart was pounding. She called Adam again and there was still no answer. She gritted her teeth and then she began to climb.

Upstairs the landing was just as dark as downstairs. She began shouting for Adam and Elspeth. Still no answer.

Then she could see Elspeth, standing beside an open doorway at the other end of the corridor.

She hurried forward, wondering why Elspeth never answered her calls. She was just standing there, looking through the doorway into a box room.

Then she saw Adam was there as well, standing just inside the door.

Heather glanced at Elspeth for a moment, expecting an explanation but she said nothing. Heather sighed. She couldn't wait to leave this place. She brushed past Elspeth and stepped into the tiny room. There were burnt-out candles everywhere, tiny pools of melted wax with twisted, blackened wicks.

She picked her steps carefully to the window.

"He's out there," Adam said, pointing towards a small window.

"Who?"

"The man."

Heather looked towards the window but it was too dirty to see anything outside. The square panes of glass were thick with grime. The window was open slightly and she could hear the crows, they were creating an awful racket, screaming and cawing like an unholy choir.

She turned back to Adam.

"Didn't you hear me calling you?"

He nodded.

"Well, it's time to go. Where did you leave Walter?"

"He's here. I had to give him back, remember?"

"Yes, that's right and I'm glad you gave him back. He belongs here, doesn't he? OK, give me your hand and step carefully. There's a lot of things on the floor."

"Bye," Adam said to the empty room and then they were back out in the corridor where Elspeth was still standing, as though she were waiting for an invitation or a summons.

"We're going to leave now," Heather said.

Elspeth didn't look at them. She simply nodded once and remained where she was – staring as though hypnotised into the darkened room.

Downstairs, Heather had to really tug on the front door to get it open. It was as though the wood had become swollen and jammed within the door frame. Eventually she managed to pull it open and recoiled as she saw a man there, waiting – an older man, tall with broad shoulders and a full head of thick, grey hair. His hand was in the air, raised, as though he'd just been about to knock.

"Excuse me," he said politely. "I'm looking for Elspeth."

"She's upstairs. I'm sure she'll be down in a moment."

Heather still had Adam's hand in a death-grip. She was fearful that he would bolt and run back into the crazy house, but he came along willingly as she led him outside.

"Bye!" Adam shouted again towards the house, and they made their way down the drive.

Heather turned back, only once, to look. The man was still at the open door, waiting for Elspeth.

Chapter 33

Elspeth heard the knocking as though it were coming from another land, another place entirely, a dreamscape. It continued, on and on, though she tried to ignore it. *Bang, bang, bang!* With great difficulty she pulled herself out of her reverie and turned away from the upstairs room.

"*I'm coming!*" she called and began to make her way down the stairs, slowly, each step pulling her out of where her mind had brought her. It was like being caught in a dream or on the verge of sleep – on waking she would forget what her mind was trying so hard to tell her.

As she descended she gradually saw Martin O'Neill standing in the doorway, a mountain of a man, backlit by the morning sun.

"Elspeth," he said, stepping inside. "Sorry. I was worried about what you told me last night. I know you weren't as concerned about the intruder as I was but –"

"It's fine, I'm fine." Elspeth was shaking her head as though she were anything but fine.

"There was a young woman and a boy," Martin continued. "They were leaving just now."

"Yes, that's Heather – she came to help and then she ... she was called away suddenly." Elspeth paused. "Martin, could I show you something?"

"Certainly."

"It's upstairs." She motioned for him to follow her.

"I hope that man didn't come back. Did he?" he asked, his step heavy on the wooden floor.

"Yes, he did actually. I didn't get to talk to him but this is something completely different."

By now they were upstairs and Elspeth walked down the corridor to the darkened room.

"This door was locked, always," she explained. "My mother said she'd lost the key or never found it. I can't remember which now ... anyway ..."

Martin looked at her. "You found the key?"

"No, I didn't. It was the little boy, Adam. He just opened the door and ..." Elspeth gestured towards the open doorway.

Martin walked forward, then stopped. He looked inside. "Will I go in? What do you want to show me?"

"I'm not sure," Elspeth said. "Just, please, tell me what you see."

Martin stood in the doorway but he didn't step over the threshold. It was a small room, just a box room really. He took his time looking. The room was dark and the window grimy, thick with years of dirt.

Eventually he spoke. "I see an open window."

Elspeth nodded.

"And candle stubs on the floor."

"Yes. Anything else?"

Martin squinted, trying to see but the room was quite dark. He found the light switch and flicked it on, then off. Nothing happened. The room remained in darkness. His eyes were drawn to the back corner of the room, the darkest space of all. There was something bundled up there, some clothes, a sleeping-bag perhaps?

Martin craned his neck, trying to see a little better but for some reason his feet were frozen, they didn't want to step across the threshold. This was a place for looking only.

Slowly, very slowly his eyes became more accustomed to the shadows and now he could make out a shape, arms, a head, light catching on a shiny button perhaps.

"It's Walter," Elspeth said softly beside him. "His puppet."

Martin squinted again and now he could see it clearly – the wooden puppet, tucked in, nestled between the covers – and a hand, small, with perfect little bones, holding him tight, wrapped up together.

Martin stepped back from the door and looked at Elspeth.

She said nothing.

Chapter 34

Downstairs they sat across from each other, the kitchen table a vast sea of scratched brown wood, the folded newspapers an island between them.

Eventually Martin spoke. He felt he was just a man, not even a retired guard anymore – all his instincts and training had evaporated. He closed his eyes and then cleared his throat.

"How long?"

Elspeth looked up. It was as though she'd forgotten he was there. Slowly she shook her head. "I don't know. I –" She looked down at the table again and then she squared her shoulders. "What happens now?"

Martin tried to regain his composure, to put a professional slant on things. "There will be an autopsy, to identify the remains and determine cause of death. The case will be reopened and it –"

"*Jesus! Why?*" Elspeth raised her hands to her face.

"Well, in case of any uncertainty, or –"

"No! I mean why did she do this? What the fuck was she thinking?"

Martin looked up towards, towards the room upstairs where Eric lay, his puppet tucked in beside him. It was as if he could see through the lath and plaster, the wooden joists. He closed his eyes and, when he forced them open again, he was looking straight at Elspeth.

"I lied to you earlier," he said.

"What? About what? What –"

Martin put a hand up to silence her. "Your mother did blame you. She never said it in so many words but it was implied, quite clearly, that you were meant to be responsible for Eric, and something happened. You nearly drowned that night as well. It was obvious your mother always knew more than she told us. In fact, if she didn't have that other woman to confirm where she was, we would have thought she was to blame. It was as though she was covering up for somebody or something."

Elspeth was silent for a moment. "I always knew she blamed me. She couldn't even bear to look at me. It was as though she wished I died that night, not Eric."

Martin shook his head. "Please, Elspeth!"

He reached out with both hands across the wooden table. "Please don't say that. It must have been very hard for both of you."

Elspeth let him take her hands in his. His were warm and solid. She could barely feel her own, they were trembling. Her whole body was shaking, like a trapped creature, caught in a wire.

"What happens now?" she asked again, blinking hard, trying to keep the tears from falling. "Do we have to do all those things? The autopsy, re-opening the case? It doesn't seem right to disturb him, not now. What difference does any of it make?"

"I'm afraid I have no choice, Elspeth. There's a procedure involved and things must run their course. We need to find out what happened and we need to –"

"*How?* How are we going to find out what happened? It's not as though we have a time machine! We can't go back to that night and watch it all unfold. We'll never know. What if it is my fault? *What if I killed him?*"

"Elspeth, *shhh*, please," Martin held her hands tighter. "Why would you have done such a thing? Of course you didn't do that. Whatever happened must have been an accident, a tragic mishap."

"But why hide him? Why not tell anyone, even me? What the hell was she thinking?"

"His death may have tipped her over the edge. I've seen grief do crazy things to normal rational people. The way they act, the way it changes them. For whatever reason, we have to accept her actions for now. I know we'll probably never fully understand her reasoning but possibly she couldn't let him go. I'm afraid I've seen similar cases before."

Elspeth pulled her hands gently out of Martin's grasp and stood up.

"Can you give me a night?" she asked. "We can do this together, tomorrow morning. We can make the calls then, inform whoever we need to. But can we leave it for tonight, please? I just need a little bit of ..." She paused, searching for the right word. "Time to grieve," she said eventually, although that was wrong phrase.

She needed time all right but time to go back and see what had happened. Time to think about that summer and the conversations with her mother, all the ones where she'd forgotten to tell the truth. All the times where she'd lied and lied and said nothing.

Martin got to his feet. He looked upwards again, as though seeing through the ceiling to the room above. He looked at Elspeth and nodded.

"I'll see you tomorrow. And please make sure all the doors and windows are locked, just in case that man comes back. You know where to find me if you need to."

They walked together down the long corridor, past the broken glass and open doors. Outside the sky was growing darker and heavier, a strong wind had risen, whipping Elspeth's hair from her face as she stood in the doorway.

"*I'll be here at nine!*" Martin called as he started the car. Elspeth nodded and raised her hand.

Chapter 35

Heather had let go of Adam's hand and now he was too far ahead of her. He was bobbing from side to side, skipping one way and then another, the bobble on his hat dancing in time with the movement. She could hear snatches of a new song floating back towards her. Something about a squirrel and peanuts.

"*Adam!*" she called. "*Adam, wait!*"

He wasn't listening. Heather cursed softly under her breath. That bloody house. She was angry, angry with herself, mainly for going back. No more. From now on she was going to listen to her inner voice, that little warning alarm that seemed to ring incessantly anytime they had dealings with Crowfield or its strange inhabitants. Although it was hard to admit it, Patsy had been right all along. She should have listened to her in the very beginning. Crowfield was not a good place for familiars or children.

"*Adam!*" she called again.

He'd rounded the corner of the road ahead of her and was gone from her view once more. She paused for a moment, trying to still her breathing, listening. Could she hear him? No, nothing, no sounds, just her breath steaming the air in front of her and the beating of her heart. She drew in another great breath and began to walk faster towards the bend. A strange fear was gripping her now. This was how it happened, wasn't it? Just a chance turn of events. All it took was a child to leave your sight for a brief moment and then everything could change.

She was running now, without even realising that she was, her breath coming in great noisy rattles. *"Adam! Adam!"* She was calling his name on each exhale but there was still no answer, still no sign of him.

She turned the corner and there he was, even farther down the road than before. He had widened the gap between them considerably but at least she could see him. She stopped running and tried to catch her breath. And then she saw him, the man, the same man, with the long hair from earlier, the one they'd met on their way to Crowfield.

He was walking towards Adam, on a collision course. It seemed as though he was going to walk straight into the child. He had his head to the ground, walking fast, with his shoulders bowed. Perhaps he hadn't even noticed Adam.

Adam started singing again, the bobble on his hat twisting and nodding with every jump. He hadn't noticed the man either. He was daydreaming, completely lost in his own world.

"Adam!" Heather screamed.

At the sound of her voice, they stopped, all three, paralyzed in place: Heather, the unknown man and Adam.

Adam turned his head slowly back towards Heather and then the man began to walk again, moving out around Adam in a wide arc and making his way towards Heather.

"Wait for me! Stay there!" Heather commanded and she began walking fast. She was getting closer to the man. She wanted to look, to smile or nod, to say something trivial about the weather or explain why she'd shouted, but she couldn't. She wanted to see his face, to look and

see what sort of eyes he had. Were they honest? Or ... she couldn't do that either. She was afraid of what she might see there, if she looked.

Adam was waiting, he hadn't moved, at least he'd listened to her. The man was very close to her now. Heather took a chance and looked up but he was staring downwards, looking at the road and walking quickly, as though determined not to be seen.

He passed by without a word or a glance and she skirted by him, aware that she was holding her breath. Then it was safe – and she could look up again.

Adam was dawdling in the long grasses at the side of the road. He was singing again, his hands running through the dead stems and brittle seed-heads.

"Didn't you hear me?" Heather asked as she finally caught up with him.

Adam nodded.

"Why didn't you wait for me?"

Adam shrugged, the bobble on his hat waving, keeping time, like a woollen metronome, *tick, tick*. "He's off to visit Walter. He knows he's back at Crowfield."

"Who? That man there?"

Adam nodded again. "And then he's going to take him away."

"Walter?"

"No silly, Eric! But I don't think Eric wants to go, not anymore," Adam jumped high in the air, before landing in a puddle. "Can we have pancakes when we get home?"

Heather reached out and took Adam's hand. She glanced backwards but the man was gone. "Yes. Course we can. Come on then, let's go."

They continued slowly back to the house. The rising winds had cleared away some of the dark clouds which had threatened rain and for now it was a bright autumn day with small birds flitting through the bare tree branches and Adam scuffling his feet though the fallen leaves.

Heather felt lighter but she couldn't describe the feeling. It was as though she'd come very close to the edge of a cliff and looked at the frothing sea below, fierce and angry, a force beyond her control and now she was walking away, listening to the waves crashing, breaking, but knowing she was out of danger, beyond their reach.

"Thank you, Cass," she whispered, holding Adam's hand a little tighter.

Chapter 36

Elspeth was in the courtyard, listening to Martin's car as he drove away. She closed her eyes and listened to the void of silence it left behind. The crows were still making noise. They were chattering and complaining as they soared over the roofs of the sheds and the house.

She thought for a moment and then she made her way to the side gate. She walked up the little hill to the rookery. She needed to go there, she needed to be away from the house. She knew that if she got in her car, she would leave and never return.

The wind pulled and pushed her, trying to spin her around as she made her way up the winding path. It used to be bare earth, she remembered that, dry and dusty beneath her sandals when it wasn't raining and a veritable mud slide on the wet days.

The crows had seen her coming and they rose as one, a great, black cloud floating above the trees, protesting at her unwanted presence. Now she was in the shadow of the woods, the noise from the birds and the rising wind deafening, exhilarating. She stopped for a moment, trying to get her bearings.

The house was behind her to her left so the pine woods were to her right. The lost woods, that was what she always thought of them as – a place of loss.

She'd never gone back into the woods after that dreadful night, not even during the summer holidays from school. She'd always just stayed in the house. Sometimes she went as far as the walled garden but that was it. The woods of Crowfield were out of bounds, just like her mother decreed all those years before.

Nora had never stopped walking the grounds. She was out at all hours of the day and night. She never told Elspeth when she was going – all she heard was the door closing and the stillness settling in the spaces around her, as though the house knew she had left.

Back then Elspeth always assumed that Nora was still looking for Eric and that was the reason for the long moonlit walks. She remembered that feeling of loneliness and heartache when she heard the door closing – knowing she was still looking, still searching.

But it was all a lie. She knew where Eric was all along and had told no one. Just another secret, but why?

Elspeth made her way through the rookery, rotten branches snapping beneath her feet as she walked. Most of the crows seemed to have flown away, their nests deserted for now. They hovered on the currents in the sky above, waiting impatiently for her to leave.

She came out the other side of the trees. The gate to the pine woods was in front of her, a rusted five-bar gate, with a "**PRIVATE – KEEP OUT**" sign. The gate was broken, of course, hanging slightly off its rusted hinges.

At this point, Elspeth paused. She could hear the pines sighing together in the wind, like a singular creature, so different to the mix of trees in the rookery – the tall Scots pine and the spindly elm, scattered, growing in random, haphazard arrangements. No, here in the lost woods all the trees were machine-planted, sentinels, standing to attention in precise measured rows.

She passed through the gate and walked into the woods, the pine needles thick and carpet-soft beneath her feet.

Who had planted this forest? Which of her long-forgotten relatives had decided to blanket the hills and scrubby fields with these pointed imposters? She was fully inside now, the sweet, pine smell surrounding her, all the noise from the outside world turned down and damped. It had never changed. It was like stepping into the past.

***

She remembered the first time herself and Eric had found their way in. Nora had warned them off from wandering too far from the house. She deemed the walled garden and the orchard, the rookery and the stables as sufficient grounds for them to wander in. So even though the fields and woods belonging to Crowfield spread almost as far as the village, they were not permitted to ramble there.

"It's not safe," she told them. "I'm not even sure where the boundaries are. And I don't want you wandering into a neighbour's field. What if there's a bull or, or ..."

Nora struggled to finish the sentence. Both Elspeth and Eric were watching her with suspicion but saying nothing.

"Anyway, there's no need for you to roam about the place. Please stay away from the woods. There's a very deep, open well there and an old cottage which isn't safe. The roof could collapse at any moment."

"Who lives there?" Eric asked.

"No one. It's just a ruin."

"What if it's a witch's cottage?"

Elspeth fixed Eric with a jaded look. "I'm sure it's just an old cottage, Eric. No witches, no ghosts, no bogeymen," she said.

Nora nodded in agreement.

But, of course, that meant it became an open invitation. What child could resist the lure of a forbidden place? So the next time Nora announced that she was going to the village, Eric happily watched from the courtyard and waved her off. As soon as he was certain that she was gone, he ran back inside looking for Elspeth. She was in the library.

"Let's go to the wood," he announced. "We can go and see the well and the cottage."

"Fine, off you go, I'm busy. And in case you get lost, take some breadcrumbs."

Elspeth was occupied with the old photo albums in the library. She didn't want Nora to know because, whenever she mentioned them, Nora told her that they were too delicate to take out and would probably fall apart at the slightest touch. She had opened one carefully on the leather-bound desk and was marvelling at the hairstyles and old-fashioned outfits.

But Eric wouldn't take no for an answer. She knew, of course, why Eric wanted to go and that he wasn't brave enough to go alone.

"Come on, Elspeth. Look, it isn't even raining – surely that's a sign?"

He was right, it was the first morning in about four days that the skies were blue.

"Fine!" Elspeth sighed, theatrically, closing the album and tucking it back in the right place, so her mother wouldn't notice it had been moved. Perhaps the woods would be more fun on a sunny day.

They set off, knowing they had at least an hour, maybe more, before Nora returned. Up through the little path to the rookery and down the hill to the edge of the wood. The conifer trees were growing over the crumbling stone walls and bent posts, rusted barbed wire showed through the ferns and nettles.

"Where do we get in?" Eric asked, one hand on a rotten fencepost.

"There has to be a gate somewhere," Elspeth replied, looking up and down as far she could. "Come on, let's just keep going to the right. If there's a gate and it's locked, we can just climb over it."

She was right. A gate appeared, with a shiny new lock and a laminated sign, saying: **PRIVATE – KEEP OUT**.

Elspeth rolled her eyes at this. "I think she might have finally lost it."

"*Huh?*"

He didn't care, he was already on top of the gate. He jumped off in one quick fluid movement and hit the ground running.

"*Hang on, wait for me!*" Elspeth shouted.

Once inside, the woods were as dark and cool as a cave. All sounds became distorted, their voices carrying strangely through the branches and muffled by the thick, pine-needle carpet.

"*Eric!*" Elspeth called, her eyes still trying to adjust to the gloom.

She looked back. The gate they had just climbed over was just a square of green light, like an exit-sign glowing bright, the only light thing all around. Just like the house, she thought, just like the green when the kitchen door is open. We could be swimming here, underneath a lake. She heard a branch crack beside her.

"*Eric!*" she shouted. "*That's not funny, you know!*"

And then she began to run, faster and faster through the overgrown path, branches catching her hair, tiny pine-needles worming their way into her shoes and between her toes as she ran. That'll show him, she thought, trying to sneak up and frighten me.

Then she stopped. She had been going downhill for quite a while and the trees were beginning to thin out. They weren't pine trees anymore – now they were thin, spindly ash and sycamore trying hard to reach the blue sky. The ground beneath her feet changed – it became soft and mossy, the pine-needles were gone. But the air didn't feel right. The place felt sick, as though it were gasping for air, a tiny, little island surrounded by the suffocating conifers.

"*Eric!*" she called, expecting to hear him coming thundering down the hill after her.

There was one bird singing, not a rook or a crow but something else. It wasn't a sweet song, it was harsh and broken.

"*Got ya!*"

Elspeth screamed. "*Why, Eric? Why would you do that?*"

"It's funny!" he said, laughing. "Seeing you jump!"

Elspeth pulled a face at his humour and watched as he lifted a rotten stick from the forest floor. Mushrooms grew in fat bunches along its spine, pale white clusters clinging to the branch.

"So, what do you think?" he asked.

"Of the wood? Nothing much really, it's just a wood."

"Where's the well, though?" he asked, looking around him. He had scraped all the mushroom flesh off the stick and a strange rotten odour hung in the air.

Elspeth moved away, holding her nose, Eric seemed oblivious to the stink.

"Eric, you do know there's probably no well? She just likes making stuff up to scare us away from places."

"Why?"

"I don't know! I mean look at the effort she went to, putting up a sign and buying a lock for the gate."

Eric was hunting around, looking for another mushroom stick. He pointed to something farther down the incline.

"Look, there's the cottage! Maybe the well is beside it?"

"Where?" Elspeth squinted, trying to follow his line of vision, trying to see what he was pointing at through the trees.

"There!" he said. "Come on!"

And he was gone, running over the moss-covered ground, weaving in and out through the pale, waving stems of the sickly trees.

Elspeth looked around. She didn't like this place, the thick beards of moss hanging across the branches like green cobwebs. The thick green moss was everywhere, creeping upwards, dragging the narrow tree trunks back down to join the forest floor.

The wood had become deathly silent. Even the bird had stopped making the strange croaking sound.

She couldn't hear Eric running anymore – he must be at the cottage. She looked down the hill. She couldn't see him.

Then she began to run, just enjoying the feel of branches whipping past, the moss catching against her fingertips, her heart thudding.

And then she saw the cottage.

Eric had stopped running and was standing, one hand on a nearby tree trunk, waiting for her.

He was right, it was a cottage once. Maybe someone had lived there before all the trees were planted in measured rows. Possibly there had been a view of a far-off hill or a town with lights glittering in the dark. But now it stood alone – looking as sick and out of place as the rotten saplings in the clearing above – transplanted from the pages of a fairy tale, a ruin placed there to warn people away. The thatch had turned a dirty grey-yellow and in some places had sunk away completely, exposing the wooden rafters of the roof. There was a doorway and two tiny windows at the front. The door was closed but there were great rotten gaps beneath it, big enough for a child to creep under.

Both Elspeth and Eric kept their distance, neither wanting to get closer. It was as though all the natural light had been directed away from the ruin and it sat alone in a pool of darkness. A wide stream ran between them and the cottage while a moss-covered makeshift wooden bridge straddled the banks. The trickling sound of running water was the only pleasant thing about the whole scenario.

Eventually Eric spoke. "Do you think he lives there?"

"Who?"

"The ghost?"

Suddenly Elspeth's teenage will kicked in and she felt angry, not with Eric or even her mother, but with life and how at the moment she was merely a pawn in another person's game. She had no control over anything and she was going to have to wait for another few years, but she couldn't listen to Eric any longer, talking about ghosts and worrying about shadows in the night.

"Eric, we talked about this," she said firmly, horribly aware that she sounded very like her mother. "Do you remember when the chandelier fell? Do you remember what I told you that night?"

Eric nodded, his face mottled green from the dappled sunlight coming through the trees.

"Look at this place! Do you really think anybody lives here?" Elspeth gestured towards it with a wide sweep of her arm. If the truth be told, that was as close as she wanted to get. There was something about the cottage that made her nervous. It was practically derelict but somehow she felt it wasn't abandoned. It just looked closed, temporarily, as though whoever lived there had merely gone away for a short while and would be back soon, very soon indeed.

"Nobody real," Eric replied in a very small voice.

"Do you want me to go into the cottage?" Elspeth asked and she took one step forward. A branch cracked beneath her foot.

"No!" Eric shook his head. "No, Elspeth, please!"

"I have to. It's the only way."

Then a distant voice, sharp and piercing, came drifting high above the canopy of trees.

"*Elspeth! Eric!*"

"She's back," Eric whispered. "She'll kill us!"

And then they ran, both of them, as though their lives depended on it. The actual real threat of their mother's anger more pressing than the cottage in the woods.

***

And what had happened then?

Elspeth stopped walking and tried to remember. It was frustrating how some things were coming back and yet the night that Eric disappeared was still a stubborn blank.

They didn't get in trouble, at least not as far as she could remember. They ran and ran, climbed the heavy gate, skirted back through the rookery and into the walled garden. And when Nora finally came into the garden, still shouting and looking for them, they were sitting by the old, twisted apple tree, trying not to laugh.

"*Didn't you hear me calling?*"

And all that did was make them laugh even more, until they collapsed into pure hysterics – holding on to one another's arms. Nora knew it was pointless trying to quiz them further so she huffed her way back to the house and left them alone, still laughing, still pretending.

Elspeth shook her head, as though she were trying to right the picture, to see more of what happened after that. It was getting awfully close to the night she couldn't remember, the night of the storm. It was only days away at that point and there they were, two children, sitting under the apple tree, laughing among the fallen apples.

She made her way through the clearing where the pine trees had thinned out. It really was as though time had stood still here. The trees had not grown any more from when she was a teenager. They were still sick saplings, completely rotten now with old man beards of moss and lichen covering their trunks. She knew the cottage was just below her – all she had to do was keep walking forward.

She reached out and touched one of the rotten trees, the bark dry and crumbly beneath her fingers. She began to walk, the moss springing up after her, covering her footsteps.

And then she heard the distant voice.

"*Elspeth! Elspeth!*"

It was a man's voice. It must be Martin. She paused, waiting to see if he would call her again.

The house was unlocked, she'd just walked out the door, completely forgetting about Martin's advice. In fact, she probably hadn't even closed the door behind her. Why had he come back so soon? Had he already told someone about Eric? Were they there to take him away?

She turned away from the cottage and began to make her way back to the house.

She was trying not to let her feelings swamp her. It was taking every ounce of strength not to run and panic. It was a strange, suffocating feeling, one that she'd felt before, here in this very wood. Of course it was only a tiny memory, just a fleeting moment but she'd been here before, trying not to panic, trying not to run. Where had Eric been then? Was he already lost at that point? Or was it a different time?

The trees began to thin out and the last light of the fading day broke through the darkness and the feeling was gone and the tiny glimpse of memory went with it also. She was back at the barred gate. This time she decided she would take the most direct route, the one through the walled garden, the path through the rookery would take too long.

"*I'm coming!*" she shouted, her voice lost in the noise of the rising wind.

The metal gate was open, swinging and banging against the stone wall. Elspeth grabbed it and held it for a moment. She took her time closing it again behind her – she was measuring every step now.

The closer she came to the house, and Martin and all the people that he'd probably brought with him, the nearer she was to the end. This was the way it was always going to be. This was always the finality that she'd seen in her dreams and nightmares.

At least her not knowing had kept Eric alive, that tiny flame in the window of his room burning low but still lit.

She came round the corner of the house, braced for the cars and the people, the noise, and all the workings that the end would bring ... but it was silent. The courtyard was empty. Falling leaves from the horse chestnut and oak trees blew in circles through her legs and danced around her feet. The front door of the house was open. She had forgotten to close it. Darkness surrounded her, the only light a thin yellow beam coming from the doorway.

Who had called her name?

Chapter 37

Adam was in his room and Heather was sitting in the kitchen. She was watching the wind in the trees at the back of the house. The weather seemed to be changing by the hour, from the blue skies that morning to grey darkening clouds and now a wind that seemed to be rising by the minute. A storm was coming, that was certain.

She yawned. The sleepless nights were catching up on her and all she really wanted to do was put her head down and close her eyes, just for twenty minutes.

She heard a noise from Adam's room. After the pancakes were eaten, he had gone back to arranging his cars on the farm mat, creating small worlds of wood and metal, a world where all was safe and secure, where the plastic cows never wandered away or got sick.

She only needed a short nap, just to close her eyes, Adam wouldn't even notice. She crossed her arms on the kitchen table and laid her head down. Just five minutes – that was all she needed.

Outside, the wind was busy – stripping the trees of their remaining leaves, whipping them away and throwing them skyward in tight spirals. At Crowfield, the crows rose higher and higher on the wind swells, their rusty calls cut short, lost in the crosswinds and the creaking sound of tree branches.

When Heather finally woke, lifting her head slowly, her right arm felt quite dead beneath her. She tried to move it but the pins and needles made her wince. The house was silent and still. Long evening shadows stretched across the table and floor. Something was wrong. She felt it immediately.

"*Adam!*"

No reply, no sounds coming from his room. She got up awkwardly, her arm a dead weight, and she rushed along the corridor, stumbling and bumping against the walls, her numb arm feeling like a piece of wood, a puppet arm.

The door to the room was open. The little world still set up on the colourful mat, a fire engine and an ambulance parked side by side in a field surrounded by cows. The farmer was standing by the ambulance and a horse had fallen over.

Heather turned on her heel and ran back down the hall. "*Adam, are you hiding?*" she called, her voice cracking. "*It's not funny! Come out!*"

But she knew he wasn't there. She'd known it as soon as she'd woken up. He was gone, he wasn't in the house anymore.

She pulled the front door open. The sky was a dark ominous grey, full of threatening rainclouds. It would be fully dark in two hours, less if the rain started. She began to run. She knew exactly where he was. Crowfield. He had gone back. Back to Walter.

The rain started falling as soon as she left the village. The orange street-lights had come on earlier than usual because of the failing light, casting alternate pools of light and darkness as she ran under them. Darkness into light, into darkness again. Crowfield wasn't far. She knew he would be there, upstairs – cradling that bloody puppet, whispering

283

to him, and where was Poe? She hadn't even checked to see if Poe was still in the house.

Why had she even dared think that things were starting to finally settle down? It had all been too easy. And what was that he had said? Something about Walter being back at Crowfield or the man was going to visit Walter or some nonsense like that.

Heather tried to remember the exact words as she ran but it didn't matter. All she wanted to do was get to Crowfield, find Adam, bring him home and then, then she would worry about that gift he'd inherited from Cass. The one that had thankfully passed her by.

She was getting closer. She could hear the metal sign squealing in the wind. The rain was spitting against the remaining leaves on the surrounding trees, machine-gun noises, the only other sound her runners slapping against the wet tarmac. She ran past the squeaking sign.

The wind was really picking up now, starting to sound like a living creature within the trees. She could see the house ahead. There were no lights on, it was in complete darkness. Then, as if someone heard her thoughts, the house was suddenly ablaze with light, illuminating the courtyard and even the woods beyond.

Chapter 38

When Elspeth stepped inside she had turned on the light switch. She'd half-expected it not to work. On stormy evenings like this the power always seemed to flatline, leaving them with only candles and firelight. But as soon as she'd touched the switch the whole house lit up. She'd jumped back from the switch – this was a new development.

Now she could hear something – outside – footsteps – someone was coming.

Heather came running through the open doorway. She was soaked through.

"*Where – is – he?*" she asked, the words coming out in strangulated bursts, more gasps than anything.

"Who?"

"*Adam!*" She pushed past Elspeth and ran to the stairs. "*He's here, isn't he? I know he is!*"

"Heather, I haven't seen him! I wasn't even here!"

But Elspeth was talking to Heather's receding back, as she ran up the stairs, taking two at a time.

"*Wait!*" Elspeth shouted, realising where she was going. Upstairs to the now unlocked room, the one where Eric was lying, tucked in with Walter. How Heather hadn't noticed earlier she didn't understand. But if she was searching for Adam, she was sure to notice Eric this time, especially with all the lights on.

"*Heather, wait!*" she shouted as she began running after her.

Upstairs, all the lights were on in every single room – blazing, illuminating every dark corner and cobweb that Crowfield had been hiding for years.

Heather had already vanished from view.

She must have gone into the box room already. Elspeth braced herself, waiting for the inevitable scream but it didn't come. She ran down the corridor. The door was open and the lights were working now, nowhere to hide.

"Heather," she said softly and stepped inside.

But the room was empty. No Heather, no Eric. Even Walter had disappeared.

She went back into the corridor, nearly colliding with Heather who was running from room to room, flinging doors open and searching for Adam as she went.

"*Where is he?*" she shouted, pushing past Elspeth, and scanning the now empty room.

Elspeth could see the pain, the tears, the panic in her face.

"*Stop!* Heather, please, slow down and tell me what happened."

"We went home, Adam was in his room, playing. I fell asleep, in the kitchen, and when I woke up, he was gone. I checked his room and it was empty and –"

"So why here? Why do you think he's here?"

"That puppet, that's why. He formed an attachment to it – do you remember me telling you? He was talking to it and dreaming about it and then he left it here earlier. It was all too simple, too easy, I knew it at the time. And that man. Who is he? Why is he here? He has something to do with all of this, I know it. He just keeps turning up everywhere. Adam said he was looking for Eric. Why would he say that?"

Elspeth was trying to keep up, trying to fit all the pieces together in her mind like a puzzle. She knew she was getting close. She just needed one final memory.

"You said before that he was dreaming about Eric?"

"Yes."

"And now Walter is gone." She gestured back towards the empty room. And Eric has disappeared as well, she thought, but she kept that piece of information to herself.

"Do you think something's happened to Adam? The same as Eric? Is it something to do with that man? The one you were talking about before?" Fear had completely gripped her now, her eyes were just two pools of darkness, her face a porcelain mask of white. "We need to call someone, now." Heather began to fumble in her pockets, and pulled out her phone.

"I'm sorry, Heather, but it's a dead spot here. Sometimes I can get a decent signal in the courtyard though. The landline doesn't work, my mother probably forgot to pay the bill."

Heather was crying now and Elspeth put an arm around her shoulder.

"Let's go. I'll check all the buildings outside and you can try and get reception. Here, take my phone as well. How long is it since you last saw Adam?"

Heather glanced at her useless phone, checking the time. "Three hours, maybe more."

Outside the rain was starting to get heavier and within minutes both women were soaked through.

Elspeth left Heather walking around the courtyard trying to get a signal while she pulled open the great wooden doors of the stables.

"Adam!" she called. *"Adam, are you in here?"*

She wasn't expecting an answer. She kicked at an ancient bundle of hay and watched the dry twisted stalks scatter upwards. Adam would surely not have come all the way here in the dark and in such weather. But where had Eric gone? Someone had obviously been in the house when she was in the woods. But who had called her? It was a man's voice. The mystery man, the man with the beard and dark hair, it must be him. He was the last piece of the puzzle. She might not need the missing memory at all.

"Elspeth!" Heather screamed.

Elspeth ran back into the courtyard. Heather had dropped Elspeth's phone. Its illuminated screen light pointed upwards reflecting against the thing in her hand. It was a bobble hat with a white name tape sewn inside. Elspeth felt her heart sink.

"Where did you find it?" she shouted above the sound of the rain.

Heather pointed towards the walled garden gate and the orchard beyond. Elspeth bent to grab her phone and together they ran through the gate. Using the phone as a torch she shone it around the stunted old trees, their shadow branches lengthening and stretching in the flickering light, gnarled fingers creeping against the old stone walls.

"Adam!"

"Adam, where are you?"

Elspeth stopped abruptly, still holding the phone as a torch. She'd noticed something on the ground, a footprint, the size of a child's shoe.

Heather bumped into her,

"Heather, look down here."

The tiny light was picking out the whirls and corrugated lines in the compacted dirt.

"Oh my God! Where is he? Adam!"

"There are other footprints," Elspeth said. "Look!"

There were other tracks, going both ways. It was miracle that Elspeth had managed to see that one print so clearly amongst the others. She looked up to see where the footprints were leading to.

"He's going to the cottage," Elspeth said in a flat voice.

"What cottage?"

"It's in the woods. He's taking Walter ... *home*." Elspeth said the last word in a whisper. There was no point in upsetting Heather more than she needed to. "Heather, you need to go back to the village to call for help. Take my car, the keys are in the ignition. I'll go into the woods and see if I can find him."

The rain was falling in stair-rods around them. The storm had got worse and it was becoming difficult to talk above the noise of the screaming wind.

"*No!* I'm coming with you. I have to."

Elspeth didn't have the energy to argue with her. The whole scenario was starting to feel like the night Eric disappeared. The only thing she had to rely on was her gut instinct which was telling her to get to the cottage in the lost woods.

"Come on then!"

Both women began to run, the ground wet and sodden beneath their feet.

The gate to the lost woods was open. Someone had gone through before them and had opened it completely – pulling the rotten metal pieces away from the briars and overgrown grasses. Though this was new and had only happened a few hours since Elspeth had been in the woods, she said nothing to Heather.

They ran through the gateway and began to make their way up the steep incline.

The light on Elspeth's phone had begun to dim. She knew it would die soon but she didn't want to turn it off. Heather was also using her phone but the light from it was bright and steady.

"Maybe you should turn off your phone," Elspeth called back to Heather.

"Why?"

"We might need it to ..."

She left the sentence unfinished but Heather realised what she meant and turned it off. Now the only light was the dying glow of Elspeth's phone, the sky still completely leaden.

Elspeth reached the clearing at the top of the hill, Heather running behind her, her breath coming in great ragged gasps.

"*He's there, look!*" Elspeth said, pointing.

Adam was making his way cautiously through the thinning trees. He was walking slowly and carefully, carrying Walter in his arms. He was almost at the bottom of the incline. The place where Elspeth had stopped earlier, when she'd heard someone call her name.

Now he was at the little river which had been transformed by the storm. It was no longer a shallow stream – it had become an overflowing, roaring beast. All the water runoff from the hillside seemed to be flooding through its channel.

Then the door of the abandoned cottage opened and a flickering, yellow light spilled out into the darkness.

"*Adam!*" Heather screamed. "*Adam! Wait!*"

But he couldn't hear her – the noise of the swollen river and the torrential rain was too great.

She began to run and Elspeth, who had been standing in silent horror – watching the dreadfully familiar scene unfold – followed her.

Chapter 39

It was all coming back to her, in a mess of jumbled pictures and the familiar dream, the water sound, Eric's hand, her voice calling him on. A floodgate had been opened, much like the roaring river below and the supressed memories finally began to spill out, making no sense at first.

She was in the water, it was dark and there was cold and noise in her ears, a taste, a sour blackness in her mouth. She was going down. She was trying to catch his hand. She touched it briefly, like a little warm fish, alive, brushing against her fingertips and then it was gone, pulled away by the currents. The water was so, so cold, and the roaring noise in her ears, darkness, darkness and then she felt his hand again, electric, a shock. His fingers touching hers, reaching, grabbing, trying to hold on – then someone caught her and pulled her away from Eric. And then empty water, his hand leaving hers, nothing to hold, just water and darkness.

⁂

Elspeth ran down the hillside, tree branches catching her hair and clothes, the memories threatening to consume her. She nearly slipped but then she caught sight of Adam again. He was on the bridge. He wasn't going to make it, he was going to fall in, just like before, just like Eric.

Heather was almost there, just a few feet from the bridge.

Elspeth could hear her shouting, calling his name, pleading, but it was as though he were sleepwalking. He just kept going, not turning around, not giving any indication that he heard her at all. Then suddenly he lurched sideways, one arm wind-milling as he tried to keep his balance. But the rotten planks beneath him gave way. He was there one moment, standing, cradling Walter to his chest with one hand and then he was gone, sinking, down into the swollen river, foam and sticks churning around him.

Elspeth heard Heather scream. A sound that cut through the noise of the storm, it seemed to go on forever. And the yellow square of light disappeared. There was someone in the cottage, a man, in the doorway, blocking out all light. A human eclipse.

"*He's in the water. Help him, help him. I can't swim, please!*" Heather was screaming.

And without a moment's hesitation the man ran forward, pulling off his heavy jacket and boots as he ran before launching himself into the teeming river.

Elspeth had finally reached the bank.

Heather was crawling towards the water. Elspeth knelt down beside her, putting an arm around her, holding her back, keeping her from following the man into the dark swell. They were both gone from sight, man and the boy. There was nothing only darkness and the sound of water.

Then the thunder came and a flash of sheet lighting that illuminated the entire wood and she saw them, first Walter, his painted, grinning smile, and bright red cheeks and then the man. He had found Adam, he was pulling him, trying to make it to the bank. Then the darkness covered everything again.

Elspeth tried to lift Heather up but she couldn't move her, it was no use. Then the lightning flashed again and this time Heather saw them too. The man was at the side, standing in the water, waist-deep, Adam in his arms.

They ran to him, he held Adam out and Heather took him.

Elspeth reached down grasped the man's arms and pulled him to the bank.

Adam was on the ground, heaving, his body jerking convulsively. The man ran forward and placed him in the recovery position. Adam began to vomit and then was still. They waited, tears running down Heather's cheeks.

"He's breathing!" the man said. "He's breathing!"

There was a rumble of thunder, low and ominous, and then one final tiny, burst of lightning. The storm was beginning to pass but in that moment of brightness Elspeth saw the man's face, clearly, for the first time.

She knew him, she knew his face.

Chapter 40

The silence after the rain was absolute. Every sound became magnified tenfold. Heather was wrapping Adam in her coat, the wet crush of material making a rasping noise and her whispered questions, asking him if he was all right, sounded more like a shout than a whisper. Adam nodded weakly in response.

Elspeth was standing by the man.

"You saved me," she said in a low voice. "You pulled me from the water, the night Eric disappeared. Do you remember?"

The man looked at Elspeth as though seeing her for the first time, then he glanced at Adam who was beginning to shake.

"We need to get him back to the house. We need to go, now," he said abruptly. "I'll grab my coat." He made his way over the bridge, keeping to the side where the planks were sound.

When he returned, he took Adam from Heather's arms. He lifted him against his chest, holding him as though he were a baby. They began to make their way up the hill. The two women followed single file as they made their way slowly back through the sodden woods.

Elspeth was last in the line, and as they reached the top of the hill, she wanted to look back at the abandoned cottage, but she was afraid to. She was fearful that there might be a small silhouette in the open doorway –

watching them leave, saying goodbye. She was shaking as well now and every step seemed to take an enormous effort.

She could hear Heather talking to the emergency services on her phone, her voice coming and going in waves. It was as though it were coming from another time, another storm-filled night. It might well be her mother talking, telling them to hurry, a boy needed them, but at least Adam was saved, he wasn't going to be lost forever, not tonight.

At last the sealed box of memories was fully open and she'd finally pieced most of the puzzle together. She'd been trying to help, she remembered that. She'd wanted to prove to Eric that there were no ghosts. She couldn't bear to hear him crying each night, the recurring night-terrors, the fear that someone or something was in the house with them.

⁂

Nora had left that evening in the car, which was most unusual. She didn't like using the car as it was expensive to run and not very reliable. At most they'd only ever travelled to the village on a handful of occasions – Nora cursing softly beneath her breath as she struggled to change gears, the engine whining in protest.

"I'm going out," she announced early that evening and, although Eric seemed surprised, Elspeth wasn't.

She'd known for some time that something was going on. There'd been a lot more trips to the village phone box and Elspeth had a distinct feeling that her mother's small supply of money had finally run dry. Nora had started suggesting they go foraging in the hedges for wild mushrooms and berries most evenings, despite Elspeth's protests.

"Now, I don't want you to leave this house," Nora instructed. "There might be a storm later, one is forecast. It might only be a bit of rain but you're to stay here, in the house. Do you hear me?"

Elspeth and Eric nodded in unison but, as soon as the door closed behind her and the rattling car started in the courtyard, Elspeth revealed her plans to Eric.

"I'm going to go the woods, to that old cottage," she said.

She remembered the small thrill as she watched his eyes widen in fear.

"No, you heard her," he said. "She'll kill us both. It'll be worse than the night the chandelier broke."

Elspeth shrugged. She was beyond caring what her mother thought at this point. "You stay here. Just tell her I went to bed or something if she comes back before me."

"But why are you going? What do you think is there?"

"The ghost, of course. This bloody ghost that you think is coming here every night."

"But, but you said there ..."

Eric had run out words, just as Elspeth knew he would. She felt a little cruel at that point but only for a moment – it was for his own good. All she was going to do was head off into the woods, hang around for a bit and then come back to the house and tell him that the cottage was completely empty. Well, she might spin the story out for a bit, but that should do it, that should make him stop hearing imaginary things at night.

"I'll be back in no time. Stop worrying," she said and then she left.

Once outside she had second thoughts – the wind was rising and it was much darker and colder than she'd expected. Was her mother right about the storm? Or was it just another ruse to keep them safely contained inside? She glanced back at the house and there he was, white-faced at the upstairs window, watching, waiting.

She had no choice but to go into the woods now. Sighing inwardly, she made her way to the walled-garden gate and went into the orchard. She knew he was still upstairs, watching, moving from window to window, room to room, tracking her progress. She could feel his eyes on her as she made her way through the fruit trees. She couldn't look back, she couldn't let him know.

Now she was absorbed in the journey. She might as well make her way to the cottage, go inside, and see what all the fuss was about. There was a reason Nora warned them off the woods. There was no ghost, of that she was certain, but there must be something she was hiding.

As she climbed over the gate and made her way in amongst the green, sighing trees, she let her imagination run wild. Maybe her father had come back, maybe it was all a big surprise. It was getting close to Eric's birthday. Maybe he was staying in the cottage, waiting for the right moment to make an appearance.

A branch broke in the woods behind her. She pretended not to hear it. Would Eric really be that stupid – or brave enough to follow her? She didn't bother to look around, she just kept walking.

It was darker now in among the trees and it was starting to rain. Tucking her hands inside her sleeves, Elspeth thought about going back to the house. Then she heard another branch breaking. This time she ducked off the path and hid herself in among the overgrown firs, hoping he wouldn't see her.

Maybe I should just jump out and frighten him, she thought. Just like he did to me. No, she decided, that would probably be a bit too mean. So she waited. He was coming closer, trying not to step on any branches but doing a poor job. Another stick cracked beneath his feet and she could hear him breathing now.

Then a man appeared on the path, his dark hair falling over his face, covering his eyes. It was him, the same man that she'd seen in the bathroom window upstairs.

She quietly tucked herself further in among the trees and watched him pass by, his long hair flapping in the wind and an old green backpack slung over his shoulder. He was on the same route as she was – he must be going to the cottage. But who was he?

Then she heard more footsteps, a much lighter tread, no branches breaking beneath these feet. She waited and Eric appeared, his face even paler now than when she'd seen him watching from the windows. He was on the same path, following the man. She had to stop him.

"*Eric, Eric!*" she whispered loudly. "*I'm over here!*"

Eric stopped and looked around, trying to see where she was hiding. She beckoned at him and he came over, relief plain upon his face. He knelt down beside her.

"Did you see him?" he said

"Who?" Elspeth asked, wary, wanting to see just how much Eric knew. There was no point in scaring him.

"The man. I was following him."

"Well, yes, I did. But how do you know about him?"

"He was at the house. He came out the back door and into the orchard. I was watching from the window the whole time."

"You mean he was *in the house*?"

"Yes! After you left I went upstairs but I heard a door opening in the front room. So I hid on the landing and that man appeared. He went to the library. I think he must be looking for something. Then I went to the windows to try and signal to you."

Elspeth looked at Eric, shocked.

"There has to be a hidden door in the house," he continued. "Remember how you saw the ghost, the first night we came?"

So now he believed her and knew at last that it wasn't a ghost. "But who is he?"

Eric shrugged. "I don't care but we have to go back. We have to tell her. She'll have to listen to us this time. We can look for the door in the room and block it off. Once she sees that, she'll have to believe us."

"But what if she already knows?" Elspeth said slowly. "Remember the night the chandelier fell. I heard her talking to someone in the orchard. And you've been hearing someone as well, your ghost."

Eric nodded.

"What if he's the real reason she dragged us here?"

"What do you mean?" Eric said, shaking his head.

"Well, I think we deserve the truth. I'm tired of her lying to us. I've had enough of it now."

She stood up. A raw anger was building within her. She knew for certain that if they went to Nora with this, she would just keep lying and lying.

"Come on, Eric. We're going to sort this out and then maybe, maybe we'll go home – to Dad."

"Really?"

"Yeah, I think we have a right to know and Dad does as well."

"Know what?"

Eric was running now, trying to keep up with her, the rain falling faster and heavier but Elspeth hadn't even noticed. She was completely fired up. In fact, the more she thought about it, the more it made sense. This man was the reason she'd dragged them here, away from their father, and he was the reason for all the lies and secrecy.

They'd reached the top of the hill. Elspeth was there first. Down through the trees and sheets of falling rain she could see the cottage. There was a light glowing in the windows, flickering, firelight or candlelight, she wasn't sure which.

"*Eric, come on!*" she shouted, barely pausing to stop and look as he made his way up the incline, slipping and sliding through the fallen leaves.

Elspeth was running down the hill, anger and adrenalin keeping her going. She wasn't going to accept any more lies. This time when she reached the rickety bridge, she didn't hesitate even though the torrential rain had flooded the river and the water was now flowing over the wooden boards of the moss-covered bridge. She gripped one of the rails and ran over. She was at the cottage.

There was light coming from within but she couldn't see anything – the windows were shuttered. She glanced back towards the bridge. She wanted to wait for Eric before she knocked. She'd thought about just opening the door with no warning, but something had stopped her. Fear, perhaps, of what she might discover. Maybe her mother was already there.

She waved at Eric impatiently to come on. He was at the narrow bridge now. She didn't want to shout in case the person inside heard her. She wanted the small element of surprise when she knocked. Eric was still dithering at the far side of the bridge, probably didn't want to get his feet wet. Elspeth pulled a face and mouthed at him to hurry up.

He glanced at her and then he began to run but he didn't hold the side-rail. Elspeth watched as he began to topple over, the fast-flowing water knocking him off balance.

"*Eric!*" she screamed. "*Eric, grab the rail!*" and she began to run.

The door of the cottage opened behind her and a small flickering light cast a useless glow, one that didn't even reach as far as the bridge.

"*Eric!*" she screamed.

"*Elspeth!*" he screamed and then he was gone, underneath the railing and into the churning water. He disappeared beneath the blackness and without stopping to think Elspeth went in after him.

"*Eric!*" she screamed again.

The water was icy-cold and within seconds she could feel her arms and legs beginning to seize up. She bobbed to the surface again, fighting against the cold, her jumper and jeans weighing her down. She kicked towards the last place she'd seen him but a current caught her and spun her around. She was facing back towards the cottage – there was a man on the bank, pulling off his shoes – the current spun her again and she was dragged under. She thought she saw Eric, his face, his eyes open beneath the water, she found his hand, like a little warm fish, then it was gone, and the water was so, so cold, and there was a roaring noise in her ears, and darkness, and then she felt his hand again, then other hands caught her and pulled her away. And then empty water, no hand to hold, just water rushing, flowing, then silence as she passed into darkness.

Chapter 41

Heather could see the blue-and-white flashing lights through the trees. The ambulance had found its way to the house already. She glanced back. Elspeth was behind her. She was walking slowly, her hair soaked through and her mascara had run in two black streaks down her face. She wasn't saying anything. She seemed to have forgotten how to speak.

The man in front was carrying Adam. She could see Adam's face, his blue eyes locked on to hers. Cass's eyes. How would she ever let him out of her sight again? They were right, all of them, she was too young. She was crazy to think that she could be a sister and a mother to him. She hadn't done a good job of either.

They were at the orchard now. There was a paramedic standing in among the trees, the rain beading on his reflective uniform. He took Adam carefully from the man and Heather followed him to the ambulance.

The ambulance stood bright and reassuring in the darkness. It was warm inside and so normal, chrome and plastic everywhere, bright primary colours, no rotten branches or moss. Adam was already on a stretcher, wrapped in blankets. Another paramedic, a woman, was checking him over and the first man began asking questions.

"You're his mother?"

"No, I'm his sister. Our mother is dead. I'm his guardian."

He was wrapping a cuff around her arm, still firing questions.

"*How long was Adam in the water?*"

"*Did he lose consciousness?*"

"*Any vomiting or difficulty speaking?*"

None of this looked good, Heather thought, as she answered the questions mechanically, truthfully – knowing how bad it sounded.

"How long was he missing before you realised?"

"I feel asleep. I don't know."

The woman who was checking Adam over seemed happy but wanted to take him for a more thorough exam in the hospital.

"Better safe –"

"Than sorry," Heather finished the sentence, without thinking. "Can I come?"

"Yes, of course. And we'd like to check you over as well. But give me a minute. I want to confirm the others are all right."

Heather nodded. She'd moved to a seat beside Adam. She reached over and took his hand. It was warm and solid in hers. He smiled at her, a tiny guilty smile.

"I'm sorry," he whispered.

There was just the man left in the back with them, busy checking equipment and noting things on a battered metal clipboard.

"Why, Adam? Why did you run away?" she asked, her voice low.

"I had to help and I knew you wouldn't let me. Eric needed me."

The man looked up from his clipboard. The woman had returned and was busy closing the doors.

"Seatbelts on, please," she said.

Chapter 42

Elspeth and the man stood in the windswept courtyard, watching the flashing lights of the ambulance as it drove away. One quick flare of red from the brake-lights and the darkness enveloped them once more. The rain had stopped and tiny stars were beginning to show among the clouds, pinpricks against the black.

"You'd better come in," Elspeth said and he nodded.

Once inside, she realised just how wet and cold she was and she hadn't been in the river as he had. Her feet were squelching in her boots and she realised, with a shock, that he was actually barefoot.

"Perhaps the morning room," she said as they walked down the hall. "I lit a fire earlier, maybe it's still warm. If you give me five minutes, I'll run the bath for you and get you some dry clothes."

She watched him for a moment, making his way to the morning room, his bare feet leaving puddles of water as he walked. Then she turned and ran upstairs to run the bath and change her own clothes. She could hear him, moving around, putting logs on the fire possibly. In the corridor she looked briefly at the open door to the box room, though she knew there was no point looking in. It was still empty.

The fire was blazing now. Elspeth had found some old clothes from Harry's room and when the man came back down after the bath, he looked different, somehow smaller. The grey pullover, faded shirt and corduroy pants hung loose on him but at least they were dry.

Elspeth had hung his heavy coat over a clotheshorse beside to the fire and now she took the rest of his wet clothes and did the same.

"I'll make some tea," she said, unsure of what to do next. "I'm sure you must be frozen."

She left him staring into the fire while she busied herself in the kitchen. When she returned with a tray, he was sitting in Nora's armchair. He had found her basket of mending beneath the chair and was holding it tightly against his chest, his head low.

"I'm sorry," she said. "I don't want to intrude but ..."

She set the tray down within his reach on the coffee table and sat down on the couch.

The fire was roaring up the chimney – it was almost too hot. She looked at the flames, thinking about her mother. How many evenings had she sat there? Watching that same fireplace, saying nothing, keeping her secrets, waiting.

She pulled her gaze away and looked at the man, the ghost of Crowfield.

"I guess you used to live here?" she said.

"Yes, with my mother. She was an artist."

"She painted horses, did she?" Elspeth asked, thinking of the faded watercolours in the library and along the stairwell, the article in the newspaper and the accompanying grainy photograph – The Lass of Eventide or Promise of a Summer Sun.

He nodded.

"Can we start from the beginning?" Elspeth said. "I seem to have blocked out what happened on the night Eric disappeared, until now that is. Then this evening it was like watching a dreadful memory unfold, so –" She paused and took a deep breath. "So, I'm Elspeth and I'm guessing you knew my mother, and Eric."

"Yes, I'm Ben and I'm so sorry we never talked before. I wasn't able to."

"But why have you come back, why now?"

"She asked me to."

"My mother?"

"Yes, but I was too late."

Elspeth closed her eyes. She didn't want to ask the question but she had to. "Did you love her?"

He nodded and his eyes filled with tears again.

Chapter 43

The ambulance moved steadily onwards, the roads quiet at this late hour. Heather could hear the mechanical sounds of the different machines, a steady *beep, beep* noise and then another machine that sounded as though it were breathing, *whoosh*, in, out, in, out. She closed her eyes and she could be back in the hospice, sitting by Cass's bed, holding her hand, her hand which had changed so much in the space of a few short months. A hand that had become almost skeletal, her skin stretched tight across the knuckles, her nails strange and distorted.

Her hands weren't the only thing that had changed. Cass had seemed to age overnight. Her cornflower-blue eyes had become lighter, opaque, a watered-down version of the vibrant original. Her face was shrunken. She'd joked about finally having cheekbones – that was before the diagnosis. She'd been waiting months for an answer. A barrage of tests and waiting lists for specialists until the disease finally had a name: pulmonary fibrosis. After that, the decline was rapid, inevitable.

"I think I'm losing this battle," she told Heather quietly one evening.

Heather had no idea what to say. Cass had only just come back into her life and now she was leaving, forever.

She shook her head at this statement, murmuring, "No, you don't mean that. You'll get better – they can try different medication."

In response, Cass closed her faded eyes and turned away to face the wall. They both knew the truth but there was no point in saying the words out loud.

"Will you take care of Adam?" Cass asked in a whisper, still looking at the blank wall.

Heather reached across and took her wasted hand in hers. It was bare now, naked, no gleaming, magpie rings, no bangles on her wrists, just tape and wires. She squeezed it gently, trying to hold back the tears.

"Of course I will," she whispered back.

Then Cass turned to face her and it was the first time that Heather had ever seen her cry. Up to then she had been determined, resolute. This was a battle that she would win. She would fight with every ounce of strength. But it was over. The light was fading all around her. Little by little, she was disappearing before Heather's eyes.

She smiled at Heather through the tears and closed her eyes again.

⌇⌇⌇⌇⌇ ⌇⌇⌇⌇⌇

The ambulance jolted suddenly and Heather bumped against the trolley where Adam was lying. They were at the hospital already.

She smiled at Adam. He was watching her, his blue eyes identical to Cass's. And for a moment, just one tiny little second, she felt as though Cass was there with them and then the feeling was gone. Maybe she did believe after all.

She reached her hand for Adam's and squeezed it gently.

He smiled. "Thank you," he whispered.

"For what? Heather asked.

"You know. You kept your promise, to Cass."

They were parked at the hospital now and the paramedic in the back looked up from his notes.

308

"Are we ready?" he asked. "Let's get you checked over, young man. I don't think they'll keep you overnight. It's looking good from this side anyway."

Chapter 44

The logs shifted in the fire, showing bursts of blue and green among the embers. Ben was silent, staring at the changing face of the flames before him. Elspeth didn't want to press him but she had to know.

"But if you loved her then why didn't you come back to her? And why the secrecy about saving me? Why does no one else know what happened that night?"

Ben leaned forward. He put his head in his hands, covering his eyes, and Elspeth knew he was crying again.

"I made her promise," he said eventually in a low voice.

"Promise what?"

Ben sat back again in the chair. After a moment or two he managed to get his emotions under control. The fire was throwing flickering shadows across his face. Elspeth realised that he wasn't a young man anymore, not the man from that summer anyway. His face was lined, his dark hair streaked with grey.

"I was eight when we came to stay at Crowfield," he began slowly. "The same age that Eric was when you came here. This was probably the first home I ever had."

"Did you meet my mother back then?"

Ben shook his head. "No, it was only Harry living here when we came to Crowfield. We were in Cork at a horse fair and she met Harry by chance. She made some arrangement to come and paint some horse of his. That was our life back then. She met people like Harry all the time – 'landed gentry' I suppose you'd call them – by word of mouth or just by chance. Then we'd go to stay with them and my mother would paint and let me be. Most people that we stayed with gave us a cottage in the grounds, but not Harry. No, he brought us in as though we were family, showed us to our rooms and that was it. We moved in. I used to leave the house in the morning with sunrise and come back for lunch. I hardly ever saw my mother – she was outside all the time, painting. She'd already finished the one that Harry asked her to do. He had a funny name the horse, now, what was it – Promise of a –"

"Summer Sun," Elspeth finished.

"Yes, that was it!" Ben smiled at the memory. "She wasn't a very good painter, you know, but people didn't care. Normally as soon as she finished a job, we moved on, but not this time. She was settled, for the first time ever. I think we both fell in love with this place. There's something special here, isn't there?"

Elspeth looked at Ben. "Perhaps," she replied dryly. "I do know my mother and Eric loved it but I seem to have missed out on that particular feeling."

"I'm sorry. I never thought. Of course, after all that's happened here, I can see why."

"I've never heard too much about Harry," Elspeth said. "My mother never wanted to talk about the past. Maybe she was keeping secrets or maybe she didn't know. I've never figured out which."

"Well, he was an old man when we came here. At least I considered him ancient – that wild beard!" Ben smiled to himself. "Have you seen any pictures of him? There are photo albums in the library."

"Yes, I remember looking at them, years ago. There was a woman as well, older than Harry. Do you know who she was?"

"That was Peggy, Harry's mother. She lived to be a very old woman. She dominated Harry completely. I always thought that if there were any ghosts here at Crowfield it would be her. A formidable woman, by all accounts. Harry was terrified of her."

"Oh." Elspeth didn't know what to say. Why had her mother never mentioned any of this to her? Surely she knew something about her past relatives.

Ben was talking again, still remembering.

"Yes, Peggy ran the house and the farm, it was all her way. Harry had no say in anything. She even made him bring her the ledgers and paperwork to her room when her eyesight failed. We moved in only a few months after she died. It was as though Harry had put his life on hold when she was alive. He was an old man when we moved here but in other ways he was like a child. He was useless with money, probably because Peggy never trusted him. I'm not sure why he let Peggy rule his life. He did try to get away when he was younger. I heard him talking about it once. He managed to get a job in England but, when he came home that Christmas, she talked him into staying and that was it – his fate was sealed. He rarely left Crowfield after that."

"How do you know so much? It sounds as though you were really close."

Ben wrapped his arms around his shoulders and leaned in towards the fire. He was silent, thinking. Eventually he began to speak.

"This house has a lot of secrets. I'm sure you've realised that by now. I found the hidden cellar only a few weeks after we came here. I think Harry knew about it but he didn't care that I knew, he just left me to it. It's very damp, more like a cavern. I think it was part of the original house and then it was closed off, forgotten about."

Ben paused again, as though he were weighing up his thoughts and wondering just how much to say.

Elspeth remained quiet, watching the fire.

"Then my mother got a telegram," he continued. "Her father was dying in England. And Harry knew if she left she'd never come back. He didn't want us to go, so he told her that he was going to leave Crowfield to me. And he asked her if she wanted to get married. I think that was the bit that scared her most, getting married, being tied down. We were at Crowfield for nearly two years at that stage, the longest we'd ever stayed anywhere. Harry got a solicitor in, drew up a will, showed it to her as proof of his intentions. Sometimes I think if he hadn't mentioned marriage, she would have come back. But we didn't. We packed that night and got the boat. I never even got to say goodbye to Harry. And once we were in England, we went back to moving around. Then, when I was sixteen or so, I told her I'd had enough. I tried to get along by myself without her. Didn't manage too well. And soon I was moving too, just like her. I couldn't settle. It seemed like I was cursed as well. Then I got a bit of money together, got the ferry and came back to Ireland. And when I got off the boat there was only one place I could think of – Crowfield – and Harry. So I decided to come back. It was closest thing to a home that I'd ever had. But when I got here, I discovered Harry was dead and the house was empty. I didn't think it would be any harm if I moved in. And then –"

"We arrived," Elspeth said flatly.

Ben turned his head towards the corner of the room and nodded in its direction. "That's where the hidden entrance to the cellar is, behind that bookcase. For what purpose it was put there originally, I don't know."

"*Ah!*"

"Yes – you gave me a fair fright that first night. Don't know who was more scared, me or you. Thought you were going to scream the place down."

"So that was you in the corner?"

He nodded. "I wasn't trying to scare you, you know."

"So why didn't you just come out and talk to us."

"How could I? I was little more than a vagabond. What was I going to say? Hello, I've been living here for the last few weeks, so if you don't mind I'm going to hang around here for a while? I didn't know if you had rented the house or bought it. I had no idea what to do."

"So, you decided to stay?"

"I did. I was hoping you might leave. I collected my things that night and moved into the cottage in the woods. I knew nobody ever came that way. I was just buying time, hoping for a solution and then ..." He paused, tears in his eyes again. "Then I met Nora. She was walking one evening – it was almost fully dark. I heard her before I saw her. She was crying, as quietly as possible. And even though she was in a wood in the middle of nowhere she was trying to hold it together. And I saw her as a person just as lost as me, just as lonely, and that's how it began."

Elspeth didn't know what to say. She stood up and reached for another log and threw it on the fire. Tiny sparks exploded and the fire began to crackle and spit. She sat back down and looked at Ben. She didn't want to keep pushing but she had to.

"Ben, I need to know what happened. The night you pulled me from the river and ..."

The words hung in the air, and Elspeth couldn't look away.

Ben shifted slightly in his chair, then cleared his throat. "We had a row," he began, then stopped. He looked down at the knitting, her knitting, which she had looped together, sitting alone in front of the fire. "She wanted to tell you and Eric about me. She'd had enough, enough of the secrecy and the lies. No more sneaking around, that's what she said. She reckoned she was too old for all that and she wanted me to move into the house, make things official. Sure, there was a bit of an age gap between us but we didn't care. But I couldn't do it."

"Why not? You said you loved her."

"I did. But there was another reason I'd come back to Crowfield. It wasn't just because I was homeless. I knew that Harry had made the will so I knew there was a piece of paper here, stashed away safely. I knew that Crowfield was really mine ... so I was ..."

"Searching for the paperwork and then we showed up."

Ben nodded.

"Did you find it?"

"No, your mother did."

"Oh."

"But she didn't realise what it was or what significance it had. She just read it and put it to one side, thinking that Harry must have changed his will again at some stage. That it was just an earlier one. But Harry never made any other will. They thought he died intestate. That was why it took so long for your mother to find out. She was the nearest relative they could find. I never told her that I used to live at Crowfield. I just told her that I'd lived in the village when I was younger. I didn't think it was a problem. It was just a little thing to change. I never thought it would matter. And then she found the letters."

"What letters?"

"The letters that Harry had written to my mother, after we left. Of course they'd all come back to him. She'd lied and given him the wrong address. My mother didn't want to be found."

"What was in the letters?"

Ben looked up from Nora's knitting.

Elspeth could see he was struggling. His hands were twisting a loop of wool over and over between his fingers.

"Harry was actually my father. They first met when Harry was working in England and then by chance in Cork at the horse fair. Harry was no fool – he put the dates together when he found out about me and realised what had happened. He broke her heart, I think, when he went back to Ireland that Christmas and never returned. Course he didn't realise that she was pregnant at the time. So he decided to play the long game. Get her to move here, take it slow, but she could never stay in one place. It just wasn't in her nature."

Ben sighed, his hands were still now, limp. He put down the piece of knitting.

Elspeth was looking at him, confused. "Well, I can understand why he wanted you to have Crowfield then. But why would my mother care? Uncle Harry wasn't even really her uncle. He was just her cousin, some sort of distant relation, maybe a –"

"No. No, he wasn't just her cousin, that was the problem. He was her father as well and that meant we were ..." Ben didn't finish the sentence.

Elspeth opened her mouth several times but no words came out. Eventually she managed to speak. "But – but how? How did you find this out? How the hell did my mother not know this?"

Ben shook his head. "This house is full of secrets. Harry was forever stashing papers away, hiding things. He had secret places everywhere.

There's even one in the bathroom, you know, a loose board under the bath. I think he forgot what he was doing half the time."

"Like my mother," Elspeth muttered quietly to herself.

"When I was looking for the will, I found out about your mother. At first, I didn't realise what it meant. Your grandmother was sent here to stay during the war. She was some sort of poor relative and she was only seventeen at the time. She was meant to be coming to help Peggy in the house. When they found out that she was pregnant it was all hushed up and the loose ends tidied away. Everyone assumed the father was Tom, her boyfriend. He had come to visit her a few times and they arranged a wedding for when he was on leave and then he went back to the army and –"

"Never returned," Elspeth finished. "I remember the story. My mother was always talking about moving from house to house when she was a child. Christmas with one set of relatives, summer with another. How she never really had a home."

Ben nodded. "She wrote a letter to Harry telling him about the baby. I found it hidden away. I do think they loved each other. But your mother wasn't a suitable match in Peggy's eyes. And Harry didn't fight for her. He allowed his mother to dictate what should happen and he let her walk away."

"So many lies," Elspeth said. "Why?"

"It's probably easier. You start with one small lie and then one more to cover the first and then ..."

"You end up like my mother," Elspeth said. "Sitting here, losing your mind, alone. With my dead brother hidden away, in a locked room."

Ben looked as though she'd slapped him.

"No, Elspeth, no. It wasn't like that, that wasn't how it was."

"Then tell me! Tell me how it was! What the hell happened that night?" Elspeth was shouting now and she didn't really care anymore.

"We had a row. She didn't care about the will, like I said. But I didn't want her to ever find out that we were related. I knew I had to leave. I didn't want to. I loved your mother, Elspeth. I would have fought for her, even though it was wrong. We were both so similar, so broken, but in the same way." He looked at Elspeth, his eyes full of pain. "That night – do you remember she left – in the car?"

Elspeth nodded. In her memory, she could still hear the sound of the engine, turning over, failing, wheezing, and turning over again. Eric was in the hall, waiting, the winds just beginning to pick up.

"I had asked her to go and see a friend of mine in the next village. It was about a job in the hotel – she was trying to find work. Your father hadn't sent her any money and Harry's money had run out. But it was only to get her out of the way, there was no job. I wanted to destroy the letters. It was only a matter of time before she put it all together. I didn't want her to find out about us that way. I didn't want her to ever know that Harry was her father. It would have destroyed her. She was eaten up with guilt anyway. Then I was going to pack my things and go. It seemed the only option, the safest thing to do. I was going to get a boat the next morning and go back to England. But I had to wait for you and Eric to go upstairs. I needed to get into the library. I knew where the hidden letters were. As soon as I heard someone walking, upstairs, I ran to the library and got them. Then I went back through the orchard and into the woods. I didn't realise you were into the woods too. I was in the cottage burning the letters when I heard you screaming. I didn't know that Eric was in the river. All I saw was you, jumping in. I thought you'd lost your mind."

"Did you not see Eric at all?"

"No." Ben shook his head. "I remember the flashes, the lightning, one minute it was daylight, brightness blazing, then pitch-black. It was a miracle I managed to get you. I had pulled you to the bank just before Nora arrived. She'd returned to find you missing and the house empty and had come to me for help. Then we realised that Eric was gone. I went to dive in again but she stopped me. You were in bad shape. 'We have to get Elspeth to the house, or I'll lose them both,' she said. She was right of course – you nearly died, you'd taken in so much water." He paused, closing his eyes. "At the house I made her promise that she wouldn't tell anyone about me. I made her swear and then I left just as the ambulance was coming down the drive."

"But you never explained why?"

"No." Ben shook his head. "And she kept her promise. She never told anyone about me."

"But what about Eric? What happened after that? Why was he upstairs?"

Ben reached inside his coat which still hung on the clotheshorse and took out a blue envelope. "I wrote to her once, gave her my address when I finally got settled. But I never heard anything, not until a few weeks ago."

He opened the worn envelope and took out some pages of notepaper which he handed to Elspeth.

She began to read. She recognised her mother's slanting handwriting immediately.

Dearest Ben,

I've thought about writing to you for so many years. I've written countless letters in my head that made sense but when the time came to commit to paper, the words wouldn't come. I have to try now because I'm running out of time and I need your help. So I'm sorry if this doesn't come out right but I'm doing my best, please understand that.

I know now why you made me promise all those years ago. This house is full of secrets and letters and I've spent my time here putting them together, trying to solve the puzzle. I'm going to guess that you didn't know the full truth either at the beginning and when you realised you decided that you had to leave. I know now that Harry was my father and you were trying to protect me. I've told myself, again and again, that it was for the best.

I've never broken the promise we made that night at the river, not even to Elspeth. I don't want her to be punished with any of this and that is how I feel, punished. I didn't know it was wrong at the time. I've spent my remaining years trying to atone for what happened and I feel as though Eric paid the price and we were spared.

At least Elspeth remembers nothing and I pray she never will. If only she hadn't left the house that night, if only we had never come to Ireland – but there are too many variables, too many what-if's.

I have used my time here as best I could, burning papers, destroying evidence. I want to leave a clean slate for her, but there is one thing that I cannot fix by myself alone.

For I have to admit to another terrible crime. It was a moment of madness and then it brought me comfort. It gave my heart peace and then I could hear him, whispering to me at night, and I knew I could never let him go for he's here with me, all the time. I am never alone.

And now this is the hardest part, Ben.

Elspeth paused and closed her eyes. Her hands were shaking and she was afraid now, afraid of what she was going to read and she wanted to put down the paper and not know – but she couldn't. She held the paper tighter in her trembling hand.

I'm going to try to explain something. Please try to understand. I was broken with grief and not thinking straight. I found Eric. It was only two days after and I was walking through the woods. It was still dark and he was by the river. He looked as though he were sleeping, like when he was a baby. I tiptoed carefully, trying not to wake him, and then I couldn't leave him, not there, alone.

So I brought him home. I just wanted a day or two, I was trying to make sense of everything. There were people everywhere, asking questions, paining my head, and it brought me peace to know that he was home and safe at last.

I set up a little space down in the cellar and lit candles and brought flowers, and then I couldn't let go. I didn't want to share him with anyone. I knew he was safe, safer with me than anywhere else. He never liked the dark so I always kept the candles burning – it was the smallest thing I could do. I had failed him.

But I have to let him go now, I'm getting old and my time is running out. I can't ask anyone else for help. You're all that I have left.

Will you help me, please? There is a family plot in the graveyard. I have already placed a little headstone there but I can't do this alone.

Please

Nora

Elspeth folded the pages carefully and handed them back to Ben.

"Where is Eric now?" she asked, her voice small and broken.

"In the cottage. The graveyard is actually pretty close to the woods."

"It won't work," Elspeth said, blinking away her unshed tears.

"Why not?"

"I already showed Martin O'Neill the box room. He was the detective in charge of the case back then. He's retired now but he knows about Eric."

Ben looked shocked. "Why? Why would you do that?"

"I don't know. Perhaps that's the normal response to finding a body! Not hiding them away in a cellar and then in a box room!" Elspeth tried to rein in her emotions – she knew this wasn't Ben's fault. "OK." She thought for a moment. "I asked Martin to give me some time. He's coming back in the morning and then we're going to notify whoever, the authorities, the gardaí I suppose. I'm sure he'll know who to contact."

"But what can we do now?"

"Show me that letter again," she said. "I have an idea that might work."

<hr>

Dawn was beginning to break and a lone sentinel crow began to call, as the weak morning light pushed its way through the windows of Crowfield House.

Elspeth came downstairs and made her way quietly into the kitchen. She didn't want to wake Ben, not yet, she knew he was still asleep in front of the dying fire. She sat at the table, Nora's letter lying before her. She could hear the kitchen clock, ticking softly behind her, each sound a warning bell, a marker. Now there was only one job left to do and time was running short.

She didn't have to wake him – he appeared in the doorway, shrugging on his heavy coat, waiting for her.

"Are you ready?" he asked and Elspeth nodded, folding one of the sheets of paper and tucking it into her pocket. She slid the other one into an envelope and left it on the table.

They went through the orchard. The world around them seemed freshly washed, water dripping from the remaining leaves, the ground sodden and rain-choked beneath their feet. In the lost woods it was even quieter. The wind had dropped completely. It was as though the trees were trying to sleep. Neither spoke, what more was there to say?

As they crossed the bridge, holding tight to the handrails, Elspeth could see that the waters had subsided. There were still traces of the night's storm, dirty, yellow foam-islands had gathered in corners and she could see branches and leaves from where the water had risen to the night before.

And then she saw him, a wooden hand caught in a branch as though he were waving.

Help, help. I'm over here!

She nudged Ben and pointed to where Walter lay, waterlogged and helpless. Ben pulled him from the water. There wasn't a mark on him. He was still intact, silver buttons and all.

They walked the short distance to the cottage. She'd never been inside before. It was tiny, a three-roomed affair with an ancient rusting stove in the middle room. Two rocking chairs stood either side of the stove and for a moment she could see them both, her mother and Ben, rocking and laughing, just two people sitting by a fire. Then she blinked and shook the image away. It was just a room, with water dripping through the thatch and mould creeping upwards along the walls.

"He's in here," Ben said and went into the room on the left.

There was a narrow cot-bed with rusted iron railings, pushed against the wall. Elspeth could see Eric, just a small mound beneath the blankets, wrapped up in the quilt from the upstairs room. He looked as though he were sleeping.

Chapter 45

Adam was tucked beneath a thin blanket, looking smaller than he should. Heather had found a hard plastic chair and positioned herself beside the bed. He was asleep, his breathing deep and steady, no machines needed, no beeping sounds.

"Just for observation," the doctor had said. "I'm sure you'll be going home tomorrow."

The ward was quiet, only one other empty bed and the sounds of footsteps on the corridor. Heather felt her eyes closing. She was leaning against the wall, trying hard to stay awake. She needed to watch Adam, to keep an eye on him, she had made a promise.

Her eyes closed.

It was night-time and Cass was lighting candles. Heather could hear her fingers in the box, selecting a match, and then the soft rasp of the match-head against the side of the box. The sharp *pfttt* sound of the match catching light, followed by the bitter smell of sulphur.

One by one the candles began to illuminate the room. There were mirrors on the walls, throwing shadows, and candlelight glowing in the centre of the room.

Heather looked down. She could see her own hands, palms down, and she could feel warm wood beneath her fingers. She looked up. Cass was sitting on the other side of the table. All the candles were lit and it felt as though she were in a hall of mirrors. But there was no music, no smell of burning sugar or popcorn. The room was completely silent and still.

"Can you see me?" Cass asked, her voice low, just a whisper.

Heather nodded.

A shadow flitted across her face, pain or relief – it was hard to tell. Otherwise, Cass looked much the same as when Heather had seen her last. Her dark curls were lined with grey but her blue eyes seemed brighter – they had regained some of their spark.

Heather waited. It seemed to take Cass an immense effort to speak.

"You are all that Adam needs. Never doubt yourself," she said, her voice even lower than before.

The candles were beginning to expire. The one closest to Cass died first, sending a thin grey spiral into the air. It threw her partly into shadow, then another candle went out. Heather felt panic engulf her. No, she mustn't let the candles die – this was like losing Cass all over again.

She looked around. Where was the box of matches? But they were nowhere to be seen. Another candle flickered, once, twice, gone. And now she could barely see Cass, but her hands were frozen, she couldn't move them from the table top.

"I love you," Cass whispered.

And the last candle died – leaving only darkness and the cloying smell of smoke.

Heather woke, almost jumping out of the plastic chair.

"Adam!" she said, but he was still asleep.

Only now he had a smile on his face and, as she watched, he raised a hand to wave goodbye and Heather felt the tears begin to come and she didn't mind, she let them fall.

"Goodbye, Cass," she whispered and closed her eyes.

They had to call a taxi to take them home the next day. The doctor checked Adam one final time before telling them they were able to leave.

"You're a lucky young man," she said. "You must have someone watching over you."

Both Heather and Adam smiled at each other but said nothing. As they walked out through the glass doors into the bright sunshine, Heather felt as though she could fly. Her feet were barely touching the concrete. Adam was the same, he was practically bouncing beside her.

In the back seat of the taxi Heather reached for Adam and closed her fingers around his small hand.

"I dreamt about Cass last night," she whispered.

"I know," he said. "I had the same dream. She lit the candles so you could see her. She came to say goodbye."

Heather felt goose-bumps all the way along her arms but she wasn't frightened. Was this what it meant to believe, she wondered.

"Will I dream about her again?" she asked.

"That's up to you. Do you need her?"

"No, I think it might be time we let her sleep. We have each other, don't we?"

Adam nodded and squeezed her hand tighter. They were nearly back home.

Chapter 46

Martin O'Neill arrived a little after nine. Elspeth heard his car pull up in the courtyard and placed her coffee cup on the table.

What was it Ben had said about lies? You start with just a little one and then it goes from there, one lie to cover another and then another. She could hear him knocking.

As she passed down the sunlit hall, it seemed brighter, not quite as dark and gloomy as before. The whole house seemed to be waking from a very long sleep. The morning sun seemed fiercer in its determination to reach through the grimy unwashed windows and shine a bright light into the darkest corners.

Elspeth opened the door.

"Martin," she said.

"Elspeth, how are you? I heard there was accident last night, near here I believe."

Elspeth sighed inwardly – bad news always travelled fast.

"Yes, just across from the house, in the woods. Over that way," and she stepped past him into the courtyard to point towards the towering green monsters that were in danger of obliterating the hillside.

"Just like before," he said.

Elspeth nodded and looked up towards Eric's room. The window was a square of golden sunlight, blank, fiery.

"But with a happier ending," she said, nodding.

"Yes, I heard the young boy was in hospital but nothing serious."

"Thankfully. Please come in. Perhaps a coffee, before we …"

There was no rush. Elspeth had known he would come back. He wouldn't let it go and he certainly wouldn't forget. All the loose ends would have to be tied together in a neat bow before Martin O'Neill would close the covers on this particular file.

They sat quietly in the kitchen and Elspeth was glad of the steaming hot coffee. She hadn't slept in so long. She managed to turn her head and stifle a yawn, but he noticed all the same.

"Late night," he asked, one eyebrow raised.

"Yes, you know, with the boy and the ambulance."

"Oh, I didn't realise they were here, at your house."

"Yes, his mother, Heather, she came here looking for him. She thought he might be here, playing hide-and-seek or something."

Elspeth thought of Walter, his clothes dry by now and his wooden face wiped clean of any mud from the river.

"Why would he come here to play?"

"Heather used to clean for Nora and she brought Adam here, maybe once or twice. He was very taken with the suit of armour."

"Oh yes, I met them the other day." Martin placed his cup on the table. "Shall we? I haven't phoned anyone yet. I wanted to let you say goodbye first. I know it must be hard, Elspeth."

She stood up. There was no reason to wait any longer.

The sun was shining in great slanted beams as they went upstairs. It came through the open doors and lay as though it were a solid thing across their path. They passed by Eric's room and then Elspeth's. She could feel the sunshine on her hair, like fire. The box-room door was still open but there was no light there – the sun only came to that part of the house in the late evening.

Elspeth gestured towards the open door.

"I said goodbye last night," she told him.

Martin nodded briefly. She knew that he wanted to check and double-check before he made the call. She didn't think it was because he didn't trust her – it was more that he didn't trust himself.

She waited outside. She knew he was carefully turning the quilt back now and he would see Walter, his eyes closed and Eric, just a shadow now, and there – what was that in Walter's hand? An envelope, a blue envelope, slightly crumpled.

Would he take it from Walter's grasp? It was addressed to Elspeth, in her mother's slanted writing. Her last birthday present, given to her weeks before in the hotel dining room.

Martin came to the open door. He held the envelope in his right hand.

"Did you see this last night?" he asked, his voice low and serious.

Elspeth shook her head. "No. Where did you find it?"

"With the puppet."

"I only went to the door to say goodbye last night. And then Heather came knocking, looking for Adam and things were a little crazy after that."

He held it out towards Elspeth. "Strictly speaking, I shouldn't have touched this," he said. "But perhaps you should read it first."

Elspeth took it carefully from his fingertips. There was no date on the single sheet of blue paper, but it was unmistakably her mother's writing, thin and spiderlike.

I'm going to try to explain something. Please try to understand. I was broken with grief and not thinking straight. I found Eric. It was only two days after and I was walking through the woods. It was still dark and he was by the river. He looked as though he were sleeping, like when he was a baby. I tiptoed carefully, trying not to wake him, and then I couldn't leave him, not there, alone.

So I brought him home. I just wanted a day or two. I was trying to make sense of everything. There were people everywhere, asking questions, paining my head, and it brought me peace to know that he was home and safe at last.

I set up a little space, down in the cellar, and lit candles and brought flowers, and then I couldn't let go. I didn't want to share him with anyone. I knew he was safe, safer with me than anywhere else. He never liked the dark so I always kept the candles burning. It was the smallest thing I could do. I had failed him.

But I have to let him go now. I'm getting old and my time is running out. I can't ask anyone else for help. You're all that I have left.

Will you help me, please? There is a family plot in the graveyard. I have already placed a little headstone there but I can't do this alone.

Please

Nora

Elspeth read the note mechanically, already knowing what it contained. The first part of the letter to Ben was still folded and tucked away, hidden inside her back pocket.

She handed it to Martin who read it once and said nothing. Would he believe the note was really for her? She looked at him. She knew the earlier shock was still in her face – she didn't need to pretend to hard.

"I'm so sorry, Elspeth," he said quietly.

She nodded. She was crying now, but who was she crying for? Eric, her mother, Ben, Harry, all of them. All the secrets and all the lies, all the broken lives.

Martin went outside to make the necessary calls and Elspeth stayed upstairs to wait. There was a heavy stillness in the air. She could hear Martin, his voice coming in brief intervals.

"A boy, yes ... Skeletal remains ... An autopsy, I know ... I'll wait here."

In her mother's room she found a candle, small and dusty. She brought it to Eric's window and pulled back the curtains. Then she lit the candle. Ben would be gone by now. He wouldn't see the tiny flame. He would be on the ferry at this stage, watching the churning grey sea, hearing seagulls calling overhead instead of crows. He was going back to his life there. His home where he had finally settled.

<hr />

His mother was dead, he had told her the night before. When he first returned to England, he had tried to trace her steps. Sometimes the trail went cold for years and even though he left his contact details in every place, she never got in touch.

He was always two steps behind, arriving at a place to discover she had moved on a year before, until finally he came to a dead end, a country house where she never got to finish her last painting. She'd gone to a care home after suffering a stroke but had only lasted weeks, the staff told him.

"I wasn't surprised," Ben shook his head. "She hated being shut away. It would have been better if she laid down before her easel in a wood somewhere, listening to birdsong, soft wind in the trees. That was the ending she would have wanted, not a sterile room with machines keeping her alive. I decided to settle there, it was as good a place as any, I had no reason to keep moving anymore. I got a job with an animal shelter and I wrote to Nora at that time, telling her where I was, that I finally had a home. But she never wrote back. I often thought of her, here, walking the woods and I hoped she was happy. That was all I ever wished for."

⁕⁕⁕⁕⁕ ⁕⁕⁕⁕⁕

Elspeth looked at the tiny flame in the window. Had she been happy? Who was she lighting the candles for? Ben, Eric, herself?

Now there was only one more thing left to do, in order to honour her wishes, her last wishes, the ones she'd never voiced. She would have to wait until later though. She would wait until Eric was gone. Her mother's ashes were ready to be collected. A quiet impersonal voice from the undertaker's had left a message on her phone the day before.

She could hear Martin calling her, his heavy step upon the stairs. He must have finished his phone calls. She stood in the open door of Eric's room and watched him stepping through the pools of light, moving from darkness into light.

"*I'm in here!*" she called to him.

Martin came and stood in the doorway, looking over her shoulder into Eric's room. For some reason she wanted to close the door, she didn't want him looking. This was his room, still a sanctuary, untouched, just as he'd left it. A little boy's room with posters on the walls and comic books beside his bed. She stepped out into the corridor.

"I spoke to the local headquarters and reported it. They're sending a team to collect the remains and you'll have to give a statement. There will be an autopsy as well."

"Is there any way that this can be done quietly?" she asked. "Can we save my mother from all this drama? Will it be in the papers, for instance? I don't think I want that."

"It's a crime to conceal a body. Now, I know she wasn't concealing a murder which would be a different matter altogether. We know it was a tragic accident but she should have come forward as soon as she found Eric. The only person she hurt was you and ultimately herself."

"And my father. He never came back, you know, it destroyed him completely."

"The letter does help," Martin said.

"How?"

"She admitted what she'd done and that there was no one else involved. I wonder when she wrote the letter – there's no date. She never mentioned any of this to you? I know you said that she possibly had dementia at the end."

"No, she never said anything to me. I didn't even realise about the headstone. There were so many things she never told me. I feel like I didn't know her at all, keeping secrets. I don't know why."

"We can wait downstairs, if you like," Martin said. "They won't be long."

Elspeth glanced back into Eric's room. The tiny candle in the window was caught in a draught, it guttered and faded. There was no boy watching for its light anymore.

Chapter 47

It was a small gathering, even smaller than Nora's funeral. They sat, huddled together in the front row, Elspeth, Heather, Adam and Ben back to fulfill his promise to Nora.

There were no outsiders from the village and Elspeth had asked Martin O'Neill not to come. He understood, of course, and made all the right noises throughout the phone call. If he thought it odd, he didn't say. Instead he told Elspeth that he was always there if she needed him.

Elspeth had smiled inwardly at the time and thanked him. There had only been one small article in the local paper about a body discovered at a "semi-derelict" property and how it was not suspicious, no crime had been committed, and they were not looking for anyone in relation to the matter.

To anyone reading it, the suggestion was that a person had died at home and not been found for some time. Tragic, yes, but otherwise a sad but unremarkable occurrence. Thankfully no other papers had picked up on the story and, if anyone in the village noticed and realised what it was about, then they kept it to themselves. Perhaps they too, like Elspeth, just wanted to move on and let the ghosts of the past sleep in peace.

Elspeth sat at the very edge of the seat, next to Ben. She couldn't help but think back to the day her mother had been buried. Ben had only just arrived in the village the day of the funeral, a full week too late. What would have happened if he'd arrived in time?

He would have agreed to help Nora and where would Eric be now? He would be in a plot with a headstone over his head. He would have been lost forever, an unsolved mystery.

She bowed her head. She wasn't one for praying but she prayed now – hoping that all her lies would remain tied together, hoping that in the darkness of night when Martin O'Neill couldn't sleep, his mind wouldn't go back over the story, looking for holes or bits that didn't quite fit.

The priest began the funeral mass, his voice solemn.

Outside in the November graveyard, the wind blew ceaselessly through the bare branched trees and shook the green boughs of the palm trees, sending stray needles spinning to the ground.

Elspeth looked at the open grave where her mother's ashes had been interred the week before, then she looked at Ben, standing by her side. He was trying not to cry. They had met earlier that day in Glenfeale and she'd asked him if he wanted the house.

"It's yours, Ben," she said. "If you want it? You have happy memories from your time at Crowfield."

Ben shook his head, "No, I couldn't live there, not now. I have a home, at the animal sanctuary, my life is there. But perhaps one thing ..."

"What is it?"

"That painting my mother did for Harry. The one of the horse – could I have that, please?"

"*Promise of a Summer Sun.*" Elspeth smiled.

"That's it. I wish things had been different, Elspeth. That we had known each other in happier times. I'm sure we would have been friends but there's too many memories now for me at Crowfield, too much sadness and loss."

✼✼✼✼✼ ✼✼✼✼✼

Elspeth closed her eyes – listening to the prayers and trying to concentrate. What Ben had said was true. There were too many memories at Crowfield. She could feel it each time she returned, the weight of the past, the box room upstairs, Walter back in his rightful place on Eric's bed, all the other secrets the house contained.

She felt as though eyes were watching her every move and when she was in the library earlier that day taking down the picture for Ben, she thought she heard footsteps upstairs. Another echo from the past. Was that why her mother stayed? Did she really believe that Eric was still there?

She looked at the tiny coffin and the priest began to pray the prayer of the dead. It was time to reunite them. Elspeth thought of that other box, the one in her mind where she'd kept Eric hidden for all those years, not realising that her mother had actually done the same and now, finally, they were together at last.

She could never fully free Eric from that box but she would make sure to never forget him again.

After the funeral, they stood together in a little knot beside the grave. Adam had Poe cradled in his arms.

"Thank you for letting us say goodbye," Heather said.

"He's happy now," Adam nodded, looking at Elspeth.

"I hope so," she replied.

"But you can always visit him at the house and talk to him if you want," he continued.

Heather put her hand gently on Adam's shoulder as though to silence him.

The two women looked at each other for a long moment but neither of them said a word. Finally Heather broke the silence.

"We'd better go. It's getting late but thank you for letting us come, Elspeth. It meant a lot."

She nodded and watched them walk away down the gravel path. Adam talking to Heather non-stop and gesturing towards the bird in the cage.

Ben was still standing by the open grave, while the gravedigger, hidden in the evening shadows, waited patiently for him to leave. What a strange job, she thought. How many people has he buried? Ben slowly made his way over to her.

"Are you sure about the house?" she asked again.

"Yes. I know it's well intentioned and possibly in another life I could have been happy there. But not now, not after everything that's happened."

"Did you hear what Adam said?"

"No."

"He told me that I could visit Eric anytime. That he's still in Crowfield."

Ben was silent for a moment. "Elspeth, I think maybe you need to walk away from Crowfield. That house has brought nothing but unhappiness into your life."

"I know, I hate the place, I always have. But what if he's right, what if Eric is still there? He knew so much, Ben. How did Adam know all those things, if he couldn't talk to Eric?"

Ben took Elspeth's hand as the gravedigger stepped from the shadows and made his way to the open grave.

"I can't explain it, Elspeth, and perhaps we shouldn't even try. Did it bring Nora any peace?"

"No, but that was why she stayed. She thought Eric was still there. She could hear him. She said as much in the letter."

"I think she possibly had a breakdown, Elspeth. And I'm not sure what happened afterwards but it didn't bring her any happiness. You said she could never bear to be away from the house. It became a prison."

Ben looked back towards the graveyard, at the gravedigger – working, busy now amongst the dark clay.

"So we walk away, both of us," he said. "Didn't you tell me you were going to New York, to visit your friend, Róisín?"

Elspeth nodded and they left the graveyard, together.

Epilogue

She could see the sign swaying in the wind and in her mind she could hear the chain squeaking against the branches, a small eerie noise, repetitive, ominous. She wondered again who had made that sign? Which of her long-forgotten relatives had painted it, announcing to the world that this was Crowfield House, a home.

As she made her way slowly up the drive, she promised this would be the last time. She'd only come to say goodbye. The courtyard was in darkness, the deep, velvet sky above scattered with a million stars, tiny pin-pricks of far-away light.

She got out of the car and closed her eyes. She let the cool night air wash over her skin and she swallowed the blackness, letting it fill her lungs. She wasn't afraid.

The house was in darkness, no flickering candles in any of the windows. The stillness was immense and she knew it was time. The door opened without a sound, as though the house was waiting and had accepted its fate.

There was nothing more that Elspeth needed to say or do. No part of Crowfield needed saving. It was time to let the secrets go forever.

"I love you, I forgive you, I miss you," she said softly into the darkness.

She could go no further into the house and she doubted she ever would. It would remain what it truly was, a mausoleum.

She was at the open door now, ready to leave. She turned back, one last time.

"Goodbye," she whispered.

Upstairs, a door clicked open.

The End.